DISCOVERING *THE NET EFFECT*

THE
COFFEE
SHOP
THAT CHANGED A CHURCH

STEVE PARR

Deep River
B O O K S

THE COFFEE SHOP THAT CHANGED A CHURCH
© 2014 Steve R. Parr

Published by
Deep River Books
Sisters, Oregon
www.deepriverbooks.com

ISBN – 13: 9781940269078
ISBN – 10: 1940269075

Library of Congress: 2013952443

Printed in the USA

Cover design by Joe Bailen, Contajus Design

This book is dedicated to the pastors and staff that I have sat under, served under, and served alongside, including:

Bobby Boswell
Ron Brent
Larry Burgess
Judy Clay
Bob Crowe
Alan Folsom
Thomas Hammond
Ed Holcombe
Carey Hudson
Marc Merritt
Randy Mullinax
Sue Landrum Rother
David Sharpton
Tim Smith
Joel Southerland
Patrick Thompson
J. Robert White
Mike Williams
Georgia Baptist Convention Staff
Hebron Baptist Church Staff

Nain Brady
Billy Britt
Steve Cohoon
Frank Cox
Marty Duren
Steve Foster
David Harrill
Toby Howell
Hugh Johnson
Kevin Miller
Thom Rainer
Lamoyne Sharpe
Kevin Smith
Mike Soop
Derek Spain
Jerry Vines
John Williams
Larry Wynn

CONTENTS

Introduction 13

Prologue: October Surprise 15

1. Serenity Now 17

2. Run, Forrest, Run 23

3. Squeaky Wheels 27

4. Two Rails of Leadership 33

5. Not a Fan 39

6. Iron Men 43

7. Intentional 47

8. Family 53

9. Begin in Me 59

10. Grounded 63

11. The Doghouse 67

12. New Focus 73

13. Across the Street 79

14. Gutter-Cleaning 85

15. The Hot Seat 89

16. Maximization 93

17. Lost Sheep 99

18. Getting Desperate 103

19. The More I Try 107

20. Business Meeting 111

21. Ready and Waiting 117

22. Sowing Bountifully 121

23. A Slice of Pie 125

24. Equip 131

25. Reverse Mentoring 137

26. Stacking the Deck 141

27. Servant Evangelism 145

28. Converts or Disciples? 149

29. Fashion Statement 153

30. Almost Persuaded 157

31. Home Run Hitters 163

32   Ode to Tammy 169

33. Into the Lion's Den 175

34. Accused 179

35. A Swing and a Miss 185

36. Law and Order 191

37. Doctors and Nurses 199

38. The Eye of the Needle 205

39. Answered Prayer 211

40. Now or Never 217

41. Homecoming 223

42. Awakenings 227

     Epilogue 231

I have never had as much enjoyment in writing as I did in crafting the story for this book. It is much different from anything I have ever done before and I found it both challenging and refreshing to do. I love this story and pray that it will touch many lives.

My life and ministry are the result of many influences throughout my lifetime. I will refer you to the dedication page to see the list of pastors and ministers that I have sat under, served under, and served alongside in my ministry. Some of those on the list were my pastors, some served alongside me, and yet others are dear because of a close relationship that we share. They represent only the tip of the iceberg as I have been so blessed to connect with hundreds of leaders over the past thirty years of ministry.

I want to express special appreciation to those who read this manuscript in its rough draft form and kindly gave me encouragement and feedback. My wife Carolyn heard the roughest cut, as I literally read her each chapter as I completed it. My good friend Danny Rowe was not far behind, along with Lori Palmer who also provided me with editorial help in the earliest stages. Others who read and responded with observations include Dwight Moss, Brad Butler, J.R. Watson, Michelle Watson, Fran Fields, Melanie Williams, Randy Mullinax, Jim Coldiron, and David Mills. I want to thank Marc Merritt and Joel Southerland for their input as we served on staff together leading evangelism efforts in Georgia. My assistant, Kris Hall, read and encouraged as she always so graciously does. I want to thank my former pastor, Larry Wynn, my pastor Kevin Miller and the members of Hebron Baptist Church for their inspiration and affirmation. Thanks again to Dr. J. Robert White and the staff of the Georgia Baptist Convention for their partnership in ministry.

I am thankful for the excellent staff at Deep River Publishing. They have been a blessing to me and I know that God is using their staff to touch many lives through publishing excellent Christian books and resources. You are a blessing to leaders like me that desire to maximize their influence for the cause of Christ. A special thanks goes out to Kathryn Deering for guiding me in the editorial process and making the book the best it could be.

Thanks to my wife, Carolyn; my children, Leah and Greg Manning, Lauren and Tyler Martin, Larissa Parr; my mom, Betty Parr; and my sister and brother-in-law,

Michelle and J.R. Watson for their love and support.

Most of all, I am thankful to God for His blessings and provision. It is only by His grace and power that I can accomplish anything at all. It is ultimately to His glory that I present this book and myself.

During the course of my seminary experience many years ago, I was compelled to read dozens of books and thousands of pages. The same held true for my doctoral studies. I am an avid reader, which likely comes as a shock to my mother, given her trials in seeking to motivate me to perform my academic duties during my childhood and teenage years.

One book that particularly stood out to me during my Master of Divinity studies was a book on preaching. It was written by Bruce Mawhinney and was entitled *Preaching with Freshness*. The book was written in narrative form. As I learned about preaching, I enjoyed a great story and read it with ease.

Likewise, a couple of years ago I read a book entitled *The Five Dysfunctions of a Team,* by Patrick Lencioni. Once again I learned in the most enjoyable way as the author took the reader in story form through the principles of leadership that he desired to communicate. I have now been blessed to author five different books. One of the more recent was a research project called *Evangelistic Effectiveness: Difference Makers in Mindsets and Methods*. It is published by Baxter Press and is available in traditional and electronic formats. It is an academic document much like each of my prior works, and from it you can glean data, research, conclusions, and applications.

I had several ideas for books in my mind but sought to defer to my good friend and mentor Dr. J. Robert White for the subject of my next one. He has been gracious in granting me liberty for writing my previous works, including encouragement to promote them once they are published. (I have been most appreciative of this encouragement because my work would be of little value if I did not have opportunity to get it into as many hands as possible.) I serve as a state missionary under his leadership and felt an obligation to get his input for my next project given that I had sabbatical time available. "What subject would you like for me to tackle?" I asked.

"I want you to write a book about evangelism," he replied.

I have learned a great deal about parenting, but would not begin to suppose I have expertise, even after raising three daughters. Instead of telling you how to parent, I would be more inclined to share a few things that may or may not work. As I began to outline what I wanted to communicate about evangelism, I felt somewhat the same way. I recognized that I do know one of the keys to evangelistic effectiveness, because I have experienced it, studied it, and observed it in many congregations over many years. When and if this key is applied, I have discovered that the *net effect* results in more people coming to faith in Jesus.

As I prepared to write, I was reminded of the books I had read that were written in narrative form. I had learned much and enjoyed them immensely. I wondered if I might take that approach for this book.

From that point, I began forming a story in my mind and building a narrative around what I wanted to communicate. Much as was done in *Preaching with Freshness,* I based the story on a relationship between a young pastor and his mentor. That is where the similarities between the plots end as God has given me a unique story to share here. You will find drama, humor, and instruction all woven together around the subjects of evangelistic effectiveness, tools to be more effective in leadership, and the importance of relationships. The characters are fictional although I drew on qualities and circumstances from many people that I have known through the years. The majority of the witnessing encounters are based on my personal experiences. The net effect reflects the approach I have applied in local church evangelism strategy for almost thirty years.

I want you to read this book to learn and to grow in your leadership, but I want you to enjoy a good story as you take the journey. I hope you enjoy it so much that you will recommend it to others. Ultimately, I pray that more people will come to faith in the Lord Jesus Christ because of the application of what is read here.

Get ready to meet Mitch Walker. He is a twenty-nine-year-old pastor serving his first congregation. The book follows his journey during his third year of service at the Stanton Community Church. I chose a small church as the setting because over 70 percent of churches average less than one hundred in worship. However, the principles that you will learn can be applied to a church of any size, any style, and any geographical location. I challenge you to learn them and apply them. You may already be applying some or several, but I trust you will get additional ideas as you read along.

This book is not just for pastors, but also for deacons, Bible study leaders, staff members, and church members who hold any leadership role in the church. I really do hope you will not only read it, but also apply it, recommend it, review it, and let me know how it ministered to you. I hope you enjoy reading it as much I enjoyed writing it.

One final word: Don't be Lester McDonald. Keep reading. You'll see!

October Surprise

"You're fired." Donald Trump made those words famous. Yet, hearing them while watching a prime-time television show did not carry the same weight as the prospect of hearing them personally. *At least they get to go to a five-star hotel when Trump gets done with them,* Mitch Walker was thinking. You don't expect to hear those words at only twenty-nine years of age. You don't expect to get fired from the first church where you are called to serve as the pastor. Mitch had done nothing immoral. Nothing unethical. Nothing that he ever imagined could put him on the hot seat.

Mitch was growing anxious and a little angry at what he was hearing. He had inherited his father's height, standing just over six feet tall, as well as a long fuse with a cool demeanor. His athletic build was mildly eroding thanks to his wife's good cooking and the transition that seems to overtake most men moving from young adult to mid-life stature. His hair was never out of place, and he always dressed neatly, although he preferred to stay away from formal attire. Tonight he was sweating. The October weather was cooling, but his temperature was starting to rise.

"I make a motion that we call the church together for a vote of confidence." That was Deacon Bruce Rollins. He long seemed to have had a vendetta against Mitch. He was a lifelong member of the congregation and took joy in running things, including the church finances. His brother was a banker, and his family always had a knack for managing money. He was well-dressed at all times and may have been a handsome man, but his very countenance seemed strained by a bitterness that Mitch could never seem to get to the root of.

Deacon John Dollar seconded the motion. He had an opinion about everything, and he was always right. No one could tell him otherwise. He was the type of person who would ask a question even if he didn't have one. He was never at a loss for words and apparently felt that biblical interpretation and debate were his spiritual gifts. Everything was a debate to John: theology, politics, sports, philosophy, science, history, child rearing, or the current temperature.. He was no more than five-foot-six inches and used his self-perceived intellectual prowess as a way to compensate for his disadvantaged stature.

The deacons' meeting was going much worse than Mitch had anticipated. A vote of confidence would mean that the entire church would be called upon to vote on whether or not they supported his leadership as pastor. It could lead to his dismissal if the vote went against him.

"Any discussion?" Thomas McDonald asked, following the motion. Thomas was the son of the church patriarch and puppet master, Lester McDonald. No, he did not lead the puppet ministry for the children. He pulled the strings and no significant church business took place without his consent. He perfected the "lead from behind" strategy long before any politician suggested its merit. His son, Thomas, served as chairman of the deacon board at Stanton Community Church. Thomas was only a few years older than Mitch and possessed a much more congenial personality than his father. He was a blue-collar construction manager for his dad's company and had a no-nonsense, yet amiable, way about him. Mitch had never had any particular problems with Thomas, but could only assume that his sentiments lay with his father.

The other two deacons were James Flynn and Tim Minor. Mitch knew he could count on them for support. Both were like father figures to Mitch. James was in his mid-fifties, and his gray hair served to make him look wise and trust-worthy. He always had a smile and carried a gentle way about him. His former service in the infantry included live combat. He had tasted real battle and was anything but a pushover.

Tim Minor was somewhere in his sixties. He had the build of a sumo wrestler and was imposing in stature. He was a teddy bear, however, and was well-loved by everyone.

"Shouldn't the pastor step out of the room?" Bruce Rollins asked.

"If you have something to say, then I think you should be willing to say it to his face," Tim responded.

Thomas turned to Mitch. "Do you want to hear this, or do you want to step out?"

Mitch sighed and looked down at the floor, knowing the numbers were not on his side if a vote was about to take place. He could never have imagined that a couple of meetings in a coffee shop would lead to this. "I'll stay. I want to hear what these men have to say."

Chapter One

SERENITY NOW

Tuesday, August 13th

"I'll be there as soon as I can." How many times had Mitch Walker said that since coming to Stanton Community Church almost two years ago? His desk was a bit cluttered at the moment with a notepad, two commentaries, a reference book, and a half-eaten Snickers bar. These were arrayed around his pride and joy, a fresh-out-of-the-box Apple computer that his parents had given him for his birthday just two weeks ago. He had come in to his first pastorate bright-eyed, confident, and enthusiastic. The bookshelves in his office were lined with his own personal library from seminary studies and regular trips to the local Christian bookstore. *Why do I feel compelled to buy at least two books every time I go by there?* He had yet to read half of what he already purchased.

He had never imagined the amount of time he would spend serving as a twenty-four-hour "on call chaplain" to a congregation that was needier than he ever imagined would be possible. He learned early on in this first pastorate that firemen are not the only ones who can be called out at any minute of any time of day or night. If he did not go to Mrs. Hudson's house by tomorrow and eat some pie, he would never hear the end of it. It was not that he was opposed to a good slice of pie, but he knew that as wonderful as that slice would taste, it would require him to spend two hours listening to stories about Mrs. Hudson's beloved grandson. *That's what she thinks,* Mitch reflected. *The little brat bit me last Sunday, and I just smiled. No, he's not possessed, but he is a brat. Suffer the little children to come unto me. I was the one that suffered when he clamped down on my arm. Serenity now. Serenity now. Have I grown so discouraged that I am now taking advice from Frank Costanza from an episode of **Seinfeld**? I'll be celebrating Festivus if I don't snap out of it.*

The day had begun with good intentions as Mitch planned to spend serious time in sermon preparation and planning, only to be interrupted within the first thirty minutes. Several church members enjoyed dropping by unannounced to chat about anything and everything from the weather to politics to the newest feats of their grandchildren. John Dollar loved nothing more than to debate some finer theological point. It seemed not to matter that Mitch had no point of dis-agreement. Mr. Dollar just had a gift for being disagreeable. *Is that really a gift? Ninety minutes down the drain, and we're both still premillennial.* Mitch was praying for the rapture within the first thirty minutes, just to be done with the discussion. When Dollar left, they both were still in possession of their earthly bodies.

The members did engage in meaningful spiritual discussions from time to time, but that was not ordinarily the context of the interruptions. Mitch usually enjoyed the interaction on a personal level, but there were times when the spon-taneous gatherings would take a toll on his personal time with the Lord, with his family, and with his responsibility to prepare three sermons and a Bible study each week. He had planned to spend at least four hours studying today. Now it was mid-afternoon, and he had barely spent an hour as he intended. He was en route to an emergency room at Rock Springs Regional Hospital on the other side of the county, almost forty miles away. *Is the speed limit 45 or 55 mph?* He wisely backed it down just in time to smile at the officer with the radar gun sitting next to the Dunkin Donuts. *That location cannot be a coincidence*, he thought. *No disre-spect intended.* Mitch had great admiration for law enforcement, and his dad was actually a retired state trooper.

Where did the morning go? In addition to responding to e-mails from the pre-vious evening, the part-time secretary had him proofread the monthly newsletter so that she could take it to the printer before lunch. He also had three phone calls, and none turned out to be quick conversations. Add all of that to the text message received from Deacon Rollins that was distracting enough to ruin his day in and of itself. *Surely he's not still upset that I did not make it to his daughter's graduation party?* Mitch was thinking. That was almost three months ago, and he could not believe the tension that had been created by the decision to take his family for an overnight getaway instead. It had been just one night into the city with his wife and little girl, but it was like going to an oasis in the middle of the desert. *We've got to do that again soon*, he thought.

No day was typical for Mitch in his pastorate. His week could best be sum-marized as a blend of sermon study, church administrative responsibilities, min-istry to church members, and family time. Other than the part-time secretary, he served every staff role and found himself an ad hoc member of every committee the church had. The secretary, Jerri Minor, was a great help and Mitch did not know how the church would function without her devoted efforts. She was old enough to be Mitch's mom, but already she and her husband, Tim, who served as the Sunday morning Bible study director, could not be more supportive. Even with their help, it seemed that Mitch had more to do than time to do it. *If only we were large enough to afford more staff*, Mitch often thought. He supposed the load could be lightened, and he could spend the time he needed in sermon preparation much less conducting outreach. To make matters worse, offerings were declining instead of increasing.

No one had joined the church in months, although he was elated when the eleven-year-old daughter of one of the members recently trusted Jesus as her Savior and was baptized. However, she would represent the whole of their additions for almost a year. He could not be more grateful for her decision to follow Christ, but the eroding resources and attendance were a growing concern.

Why does every light seem to turn red when you're in a hurry? Mitch lamented as the trip to the emergency room took almost an hour. *It's time to focus. This family needs me.* Mitch had not known all of the details when he left the church, only that the brother-in-law of a devoted church member had sustained a serious injury in an auto accident and had been taken to the trauma center at the Rock Springs Hospital.

Mitch arrived at last, and he found the family understandably anxious when he located them. Barely ten minutes had passed since Mitch's arrival when the doctor came out with the encouraging news that, although serious, the injury was not immediately life-threatening. The transition from grief to elation was immediate.

The next hour of interaction, prayer, and empathy served to give the family a deeper appreciation for their pastor, and their burden was lightened by his presence and ministry. Mitch's day had not gone as he planned, but he felt valued by the response of this family to his ministry and was glad he could be there when they needed him. At least he would be home for dinner with his family tonight. Even as he thought of it, he could almost smell the mouth-watering meatloaf his wife was making for dinner. He still had time to work on his sermons tomorrow, but if he had the same interruptions again, he would be winging it tomorrow night.

A couple of family members invited Mitch to grab a cup of coffee with them before he headed back. The break room on the ground floor was like a small cafeteria with tables, vending machines, and a small window for ordering sandwiches. The room was painted Caribbean blue with palm trees here and there, although the sandwiches were strictly American fare. No sooner had Mitch taken in the surroundings when he spotted a familiar face. *Is that Pastor Benton?* he wondered. Within moments, one of the family members he was with called out Pastor Benton's name. "Come and meet my pastor!" his host exclaimed after greeting the other pastor like an old friend. "Pastor Benton, let me introduce you to Mitch Walker, who pastors our church over in Stanton."

"I know who you are," Mitch said. "You're the pastor of Tabernacle Church here in Rock Springs. Isn't that right?"

"That's right. I'm pleased to meet you. It's always a pleasure to connect with new pastors in the area."

Pastor Benton's Tabernacle Church was known far and wide for having a thriving congregation that had grown incredibly over the past five years. Mitch had heard that the attendance had more than tripled what it was a decade before. Tabernacle had a reputation for reaching out to the community, and they had seen many come to faith in Jesus under Pastor Benton's leadership.

Mitch honestly had a preconceived notion that a leader like Pastor Benton would not take the time of day to interact with a young, small-town pastor. Unfortunately, he had been brushed off by more than one pastor of a larger congregation who did not seem to have the time for someone unknown like he was. When he attended his denomination's annual convention, he was amazed, and yet troubled, at how some pastors could be shaking his hand while looking around to see who else was present. Mitch had learned from his father to always look the person he was speaking to directly in the eye and to engage them in a personal way. *Were those pastors arrogant, or was it poor upbringing?*

Although Pastor Benton was much older, he felt like an old friend within the first few minutes. It wasn't long before they found themselves sitting at a table in the break area, as his hosts went to rejoin their family members in the waiting room. With satisfied nods, both of them added packets of sugar to their coffee and stirred. The white-haired older man looked fit in a navy sport coat and open-collared shirt.

Mitch always felt more at ease without a tie although he appreciated that many of the preceding generation still had an affinity for them. He thought that ties felt too much like a noose. He did wear a coat and tie to Sunday morning services in keeping with the long-held tradition of his congregation, and when he showed up one Sunday last summer without a tie, he had caused quite a controversy. Some of the sweetest little ladies in the church suddenly started acting like rabid animal rights activists surrounding the local butcher. The next morning he was told in no uncertain terms by Lester McDonald that the pastors of Stanton Community Church always have and always will wear ties on Sunday mornings. The thought of that conversation still pained Mitch, and he did not feel that he had handled it well. He pretty much sat there and took it, not knowing how to respond. *I got dressed down over not dressing up.*

Pastor Benton dropped his plastic spoon; Mitch bent down to retrieve it. *Sugar in his coffee, no tie, looks me in the eye, and a friendly disposition? May his tribe increase!*

Chapter Two

Run, Forrest, Run

Two months earlier, on Thursday, June 13th

Today will be a quiet day, Mitch was thinking as he got up from the breakfast room table and placed his bowl and spoon in the sink to rinse them before placing them in the dishwasher. *Why does Melinda always want me to wash dishes before placing them in the dishwasher?* He had learned long ago not to question the logic of his high school sweetheart. They had started dating during the autumn months of their junior year and were inseparable from that point forward. They went to the same college and got married halfway through. Their parents weren't real excited, but Mitch and Melinda had been dating for four years, so it was not really a big surprise when they announced their Christmas break plans. At the time, neither of them envisioned that Mitch would one day be the pastor of a church in Stanton.

Stanton was a small town with only a couple of gas stations, a hardware store, a barber shop, a pharmacy, a sandwich shop, and a small number of other stores that rotated between vacancies and short-lived business ventures. Mitch and Miss Jerri had put together a list of supplies needed at the church, and that meant a trip to Rock Springs where the restaurants, the mall, the movie theatres, and the big-name stores were. He could have gone to one of several towns that were in closer proximity, but Rock Springs was the place to go for the greatest variety of selection, along with an opportunity to treat himself to lunch while he was in the area.

After seeing Melinda and his daughter Haley off, spending some time in prayer, reading the Bible, and eating a bowl of cereal, he needed only to grab his shopping list off the nightstand before heading out the door. Just as he closed the dishwasher, the phone rang.

"Hello."

Instead of the expected polite greeting in return, he heard a deafening scream in his ear. "O, Lord Jesus. Help, Pastor. Pastor, you have to help me!"

"Who is this?" Mitch asked, having no idea who it was or what was going on. The female voice on the other end was gasping for breath and obviously in a state of panic.

"Pastor, it's awful, and you have to get over here right now! Please get over. Help me. O Lord Jesus."

"Ma'am, who is this?"

"It's Jean Hudson, and I need you here—now. Please help me."

Mrs. Hudson was known for her exceptional baking skills, and on many occasions she had graced the Walker family with a delicious apple pie that was specially made to take home. Mitch had never heard her like this, and he was hoping that she was not having some medical emergency.

"Miss Jean, what's wrong? Are you OK?" He sometimes called her by Miss Jean as well as by Mrs. Hudson.

She continued to scream. "Pastor, it's terrible. Please get over here!" The line went dead.

Mitch's mind was racing, considering all of the possibilities. Was someone trying to break into her house? Should he call the police? Or is she having a medical emergency? Should he call 911? Mrs. Hudson only lived about three-quarters of a mile south of Mitch's neighborhood on Folsom Road. With no time to waste and unsure of who else should be called, he bolted through the door, which locked behind him, and ran for the car that was sitting in the driveway. *My keys! Where are my keys?* Mitch frantically fished in every pocket, and then it hit him like a brick. He recalled that the keys were lying next to the shopping list on his nightstand in the bedroom. He had laid them there so he would not forget the shopping list. He reached down for his cell phone. *You are kidding me!* He had not yet clipped it to his belt. He sprinted back to the front door, almost tripping as he hit the second step leading up to the front porch. Locked! *Oh man. I cannot believe this.*

Maybe playing backyard basketball with his neighbor's son was about to pay off. Mitch ran down the driveway figuring there was no time to waste, realizing he would have to run the three quarters of a mile to get to Mrs. Hudson. It was already eighty degrees, and the humidity was always high at this time of year. He was dripping with sweat within minutes and his heart was beating a hundred miles an hour. He ignored a car that honked its horn as it traveled in the northbound lane. *Was that one of my members? I must look like an idiot jogging in slacks and a collared shirt.* He suddenly realized two neighborhood dogs were running right behind him as if he had come to play. Another car passed and a teenager taunted him shouting, "Run, Forrest, Run!" He shook off any embarrassment he should have felt and stayed focused on Mrs. Hudson's plight.

Before he was halfway there, he realized that he was not in peak physical condition at all. But he pressed on despite the fact that he was running out of breath. *What am I going to do if someone has broken into her house?* As soon as he entered Mrs. Hudson's yard, he saw a pretty good-sized rock lying on the ground and grabbed it for at least some form of self-defense if he encountered someone with bad intentions. He arrived and banged on the door. Placing his left hand on his knee, he held the rock in his right as he tried desperately to catch his breath. "Miss Jean. Miss Jean!" he shouted.

Mrs. Hudson opened the door with a panicked look on her face. She seemed impervious to Mitch's condition as she grabbed her pastor by the neck, sobbing as if she had lost her best friend.

"Miss Jean, are you OK?" Mitch asked, trying to catch his breath. "What's wrong?"

"It's back here, Pastor. You've got to help me. I can't stand it. Please help me!"

Mitch, puzzled, followed Mrs. Hudson through the house and to the back door, gripping the rock tightly, ready for combat if necessary. The back door opened to a screened-in porch where Mitch had often eaten warm slices of pie as she regaled him with stories about her grandchildren. As she peered through the window, she began to whimper, "O my goodness, there it is. I can't believe this is happening."

Mitch wondered if perhaps someone had died on her porch. He looked over her shoulder and through the window. He saw the plastic patio furniture and the metal table with four chairs under a ceiling fan that always made for a pleasant place to sit and visit. "Do you see it?" she asked as she continued to weep softly. Mitch didn't see anything out of place.

"What is it, Miss Jean? I don't see anything."

"Over there under that chair. Do you see it? There's a snake on my porch."

Mitch did not know whether to laugh or cry. Here Mrs. Hudson was safely locked behind this door, and he had just run almost a mile in steaming hot weather because she had a snake on the back porch. "Go and get me a broom, Miss Jean." She quickly went and grabbed a broom, sobbing softly. Mitch took the broom from her and handed her the rock. He slowly made his way onto the porch to do battle with the menacing reptile. Mitch was no herpetologist, but it was evident to him that this eight-inch creature was not a major threat. The snake could have barely overpowered a cricket and was no threat at all to the human species.

"Kill it, Pastor! Kill it!" Mrs. Hudson began screaming. She was in an absolute panic. Mitch took the broom and swept the small creature toward the door. Suddenly, the rock flew past Mitch's left elbow as Mrs. Hudson hurled it at the snake. *She's got a pretty good arm for an older gal*, Mitch thought.

"It's OK," Mitch turned and said. "I've got it." He brushed the snake out the door and turned to his frightened parishioner. "Just calm down now. It's gone."

"Oh, thank you, Lord. Thank you, Pastor. I thought I was going to die."

As Mitch made the trek back home, he tried to figure out how he was going to gain entry into the house to retrieve his keys and his phone. He would also need to shower again before heading to Rock Springs. *Is this what my job is? I guess I can add animal control to the list of my duties as pastor of Stanton Community!* He realized that he might not even get to Rock Springs before lunch and that he would now likely have to eat fast food instead of treating himself at a quaint café or restaurant. But that was not his greatest concern.

How am I going to break in to my own house? Lord, please don't let me get arrested today!

Chapter Three

SQUEAKY WHEELS

Tuesday, August 13th

"Tell me about your church, Mitch." The break room decorated in Caribbean décor at the Rock Springs Regional Hospital was obviously a popular gathering spot for staff as well as guests. After Mitch and Pastor Benton had discussed their families, educational backgrounds, and Bulldogs football, the discussion naturally drifted to talk about ministry.

Mitch fidgeted for a moment, knowing that his church did not compare well with Pastor Benton's. "I've been there almost two years now. Stanton Community is the first church I have served as pastor. My wife, Melinda, and I have a daughter in the second grade, and we really love the community and the schools. The church is pretty small and family-oriented. I love the members but…" Mitch paused, wondering if he should be so transparent, having just met this pastor. He needed desperately to unload on someone who could empathize with him. His face flushed slightly as he continued. "I'm actually struggling a little bit right now."

Mitch was surprised at how much he had opened up after having met Pastor Benton no more than fifteen minutes earlier. Benton seemed to have a very inviting personality that made it easy for Mitch to begin to pour out his heart. The older man had not asked Mitch to make any comparisons although that tends to be the nature of conversations among pastors.

"There is nothing wrong with pastoring a small church." Benton replied. "I have pastored several small churches in my ministry. I learned a long time ago that it is not the size of the congregation that makes a difference but rather the size of our God. Always remember, Mitch, that there is no wrong-sized church. A church of any size can be used of God to touch lives and see people come to faith in Christ."

Mitch paused for a moment, looking down, and then he noticed a small stain on his left sleeve. *Where did that come from?* He covered it subtly with his right hand and looked back at Pastor Benton. "I wish that was the case with us.

Unfortunately, we're not reaching anyone. I don't know if my congregation can spell 'outreach,' and I don't ever seem to have the time myself. Over half of the congregation is made up of senior adults. I'm certainly happy that all of them are there, but we have only a handful of children, a couple of teens, and some weeks we have no preschoolers in our nursery on Sunday morning. Only three other couples are even close to the age of my wife and me. Quite frankly, I am discouraged, and I'm growing more and more concerned."

Benton leaned forward. "Why is that?"

"The fact is that our congregation is aging, our attendance is declining, albeit slowly, and the resources are diminishing at the same pace. Our congregation is very loving, and they really enjoy one another. I don't think they even realize that they're in trouble, and it won't be long before I'm in trouble too if something doesn't change. Already a couple of key leaders are starting to give me a hard time. They won't be able to provide for a full-time pastor within a couple of years the way things are going. They are also very needy."

"Needy?"

"You know. They demand a lot of time, I assume because they are an aging congregation, but mostly because they expect me to be at every meeting, whether church-related or not. They expect me to be in the office when they come by and on call day and night. I am the minister of everything, an ad hoc member of every conceivable committee, head chaplain, and chief bottle-washer. During my second week, I had a deacon ask me who was going to cut the grass. He was expecting me to do it." Mitch shrugged and turned his palms face up, forgetting by now about the stain on his sleeve. "It's not that I'm above it, but I don't know if it's really the best use of my time since plenty of people are capable. He told me that the former pastor always kept the grass cut. I probably shouldn't have, but I jokingly told him that I called the former pastor, and he said he doesn't want to do it anymore."

Benton almost fell on the floor laughing. "I hear what you're saying. God has not called us to be the Ministers of Minutiae. The fact is, though, that high demands on time come with being a pastor. Trust me. It is no different when leading a larger congregation. I once heard a pastor say that ministry would be easy if you didn't have to deal with people! But, ministry requires that we engage people and their problems. I've been exactly where you are; and I feel your pain."

"Sometimes I wish I was in a church like yours where I could really focus and see a lot of people coming to faith in Jesus."

"You don't have to be at Tabernacle church for that to happen. Let me ask you a question. Did God call you to Stanton Community Church?"

Mitch thought about how he should respond. He gazed for a moment at the column in the middle of the room that had been converted to look like a palm tree. He thought he was called there but had been entertaining doubts recently and wondered if a fresh start in another church would get him away from the demands of Stanton Community Church. Without much conviction he responded, "I guess He did."

"Hang on a second. Didn't you and your wife spend time in prayer and meditation seeking to know if God called you there two years ago?"

Mitch knew where this was going, but it would be rude not to go along since he was the one who opened the door to the conversation. He looked down at his hands and realized he was beginning to fidget. "Of course. We prayed about it and really sensed God was calling us."

"Didn't the congregation, pastor search team, and many of your friends likewise pray about whether or not God was calling you to serve there?"

Pastor Benton was looking Mitch directly in the eye as he responded in the affirmative. Benton continued, "God called you there, Mitch, to minister to that congregation and to lead them to make an impact on that community. If God wanted you somewhere else, He would have called you somewhere else. It is not by coincidence, but by divine design that you are in Stanton. Out of several billion people that God could have appointed, He called you. He knew you would be best for the task, and He wants to use you to make a difference. Two years may seem like a long time to you now, but you are just getting started."

"Sometimes I wonder if when He called He dialed the wrong number."

"You are hilarious. You know what I'm talking about. You know God called you there. It's not time to give up, but to get going. You are actually in a good position now because after two years you probably have a good grasp of the personalities, the leaders, and the culture of the congregation. You've been making investments in relationships that you can now call upon to begin moving the church in the direction that it needs to be going."

"I know I need to help them turn it around, but honestly I don't even know where to start. I barely have time to do what they expect of me right now. On top of that, I feel like I've lost some support in the last few months. The honeymoon didn't last long for me."

"Mitch, I think what you are living and learning is what I call the principle of the squeaky wheel."

"What do you mean by that?"

"When someone mentions a squeaky wheel, what do they say about it?"

"They say the squeaky wheel always gets the grease."

"Exactly! Have you received any phone calls lately asking for appointments, counseling, or maybe a request to visit someone in the hospital?"

"I pretty much get calls like that every day and sometimes at night."

"What other kinds of calls and requests do you get?"

Mitch wondered how long of a list he wanted. "Sometimes people needing financial help or invitations to family gatherings. I have people drop by wanting to talk about serious issues and sometimes just to be with a pastor, I guess. I'm also expected to go by the homes of our most senior members on a regular basis."

"You also have responsibilities like preparing sermons and administrative tasks that go with being a pastor with no staff. You have family responsibilities and domestic responsibilities. You add community and the routines of your day, and you have a lot of things crying for your attention."

"Apparently, you've been reading my mail." Mitch took a sip of his coffee and realized it was already getting cold. *Maybe I'll get another cup for the drive home*, he thought.

"Nothing is wrong with these requests and demands in and of themselves, but let me ask you something else. How many people have called you in the past month asking how they can know Jesus as their Savior?"

"I wish! I did have someone track me down after a service when I first started at Stanton Church and did get to lead him to Christ. But, nobody's calling me to ask how to become a follower of Jesus. Do you ever receive calls like that?"

"No, because that's not the way it works. If you and your congregation are not intentional about ministering to your community and reaching out to those who don't know Jesus, then you will be a slave to the squeaky wheel. Do you understand what I am saying?"

"It makes sense to me. We have a tendency to respond and to react to those things that constantly cry out for our attention. Is that what you're saying?"

"That's right! God has called you to Stanton Community Church to lead the congregation to minister to one another but also to reach out to your community."

Mitch thought for a moment. *That's easy for him to say. He's is in a larger church in a larger town with staff to help him out.* He asked, "But how do you do it when no one wants to do outreach and when they expect me to do everything else in

the world? I'm already working fifty and sixty hours a week in a small congregation and barely have time to do what is required of me now."

"Have you ever heard of the *Net Effect*?"

"I'm not sure. I've heard the term before. What are you referring to?"

Pastor Benton leaned forward as if he were telling a secret. "I discovered a
process early in my ministry that God has blessed in every church where I have
served. I call it the *Net Effect*, and I have tried to share it with as many pastors as
I can over the years. But I can't really give it to anyone in one sitting. You have to
work it in a step at a time so that it can change the culture of your church and
become ingrained in your leadership. It will absolutely improve the evangelism
and outreach in your church if you apply it."

"Where can I get it?"

"Well Mitch, it's not packaged. The way I deliver it is by meeting with pastors
one-on-one on a regular basis. We often think of discipleship as something we
do with young believers. God has impressed on me the value of discipling leaders.
We need to grow no matter where we are in our spiritual journeys." Pastor Benton
paused and eyed Mitch as if he were an officer inspecting a promising new recruit.
"I have an idea, and I feel real impressed to ask you this. Would you be open to
meeting for coffee for about an hour or so once each month for a while? If you
are open to it, I would enjoy teaching the *Net Effect* to you, and I hope you would
pass it on to others down the road. I would kind of be like your coach for the
next few months. If you're open to it I would be glad to meet you somewhere in
between like in Southerland or somewhere." Southerland was a small town like
Stanton, which was located almost halfway between Benton's church and Mitch's.

Mitch was surprised, given that they had met less than an hour ago, and he
knew the demands on Benton's schedule had to be high. "Are you serious? Do
you have that kind of time?"

"Mitch, we all have time to do whatever we consider to be important. I'm
not saying that I have all of the answers, but I've been right where you are."

"I would be honored. What would I need to do?"

"I'll e-mail you tomorrow, but I want to be clear. The focus of our time
together will be to help you to lead your church to be intentionally evangelistic.
That is what the *Net Effect* does. The squeaky wheel won't go away, but I think I
can help you deal more effectively with it once we spend some time together."

Mitch replayed the conversation in his mind on the drive back home. One
thing he did possess was a teachable spirit, but it seemed that since he left

seminary he was not connected to anyone who could provide the type of teaching that he desperately needed. He was not too proud to learn from someone who was willing to help him try to turn things around. He could not believe that a pastor of Benton's stature was willing to invest in him as he had suggested. Here was an older pastor with wisdom and experience, and a connection had just ensued in a way that was hard to describe.

Back in seminary a few short years prior, Mitch would have scoffed at the idea. *What does this old dude have that would be of value to me?* he would have thought. Mitch knew back then that the Tabernacle Church was starting to get some attention. He wasn't sure why at first, given that the facility was old and the church long-established. Mitch wasn't sure what the style of worship was at Tabernacle, but surely it was old-fashioned. You could tell just by driving by that it was not contemporary. Or was it? Or did it even matter?

Surprisingly, it seemed like all of the lights were green on the drive back home. Imagine that.

Chapter Four

TWO RAILS OF LEADERSHIP

Thursday, August 15th

Something smelled very good. Ladies were already arriving and beginning to prepare for the monthly gathering of senior saints at Stanton Community Church. The smell of pot roast, baked goods, and something else that Mitch could not quite figure out permeated the entire building including the pastor's office, which was located about midway down the hallway that separated the worship center from the fellowship hall. They called themselves the Young Hearts although their wrinkles betrayed them. A group of teens, however, could not have generated the laughter that you would hear when a couple dozen of these characters gathered. Mitch found it awkward at first, but over the months had grown to love them like extended family. Thankfully, he had survived the scandal of the tieless Sunday and was back in the good graces of most of the senior group. He was at least thirty-five years younger than any person who would be present, but the meal would have been worth attending for the food itself even if he had not grown to appreciate the seniors so much.

The rain on the previous day had been a blessing in more ways than one. It had been almost ten days since Stanton had seen a drop, and the temperatures had stayed in the mid-nineties during the entire stretch of time. Mitch wanted to avoid watering his lawn because the additional cost on the water bill would push the family budget to the brink. Then the steady rain had poured all day and had kept everyone inside. Not only did it water the lawn, but it was just what Mitch needed to catch up on his studies, take some time to tidy up his office, and pick his daughter up from school.

An e-mail from Pastor Benton had arrived within twenty-four hours of their meeting on Tuesday. Within three exchanges over the course of a couple of hours, they had agreed to where and when to meet each month all the way through May of next year. Mitch was impressed at the way Pastor Benton so quickly followed up on their conversation and felt honored that he would give him so much of his time. Mitch had logged onto his Twitter account after dinner on Tuesday and noted that Pastor Benton had several hundred followers. He clicked the follow button and read his latest tweet.

Do not settle for being an average leader unless you are seeking less than average results.

What does that say about me? Mitch thought. *I always thought I was a strong leader until I got to Stanton.* It wasn't in Mitch's nature to have a mental pity party. He was feeling challenged and sincerely wanted to grow. He was hopeful that this relationship with Pastor Benton would give him the boost he needed.

His stomach began to growl in anticipation of the feast he would enjoy within the next hour. *I wonder if Mrs. Hudson will bring some fried apple pies today?* He briefly recalled his adventure at her house back in June. *Maybe I'll rent the DVD of* Snakes on a Plane *and take it over to watch with her sometime.* Mitch had a mischievous grin on his face as he refocused. He recalled Pastor Benton's instruction to be watching for a follow up e-mail that would help them get started on their journey. *This may be it,* he thought as he skipped over three other e-mails and clicked on Pastor Benton's.

From: Marc Benton
Sent: Thursday, August 15, 10:32 AM
To: Mitch Walker
Subject: Let's Get Started
Mitch;
I am so delighted to have the opportunity to spend the next few months equipping and coaching you to lead your congregation to become intentionally evangelistic. I was blessed to have leaders invest time in me when I was younger and it is my prayer that you will likewise take what you learn and pass it along to others (2 Timothy 2:2). I want you to know that I am committed to praying for you daily and consider the fellowship and friendship that we will share to be of great value.

I want to confirm that we will be meeting at 8:00am on Thursday, September 5th at the coffee shop in Southerland at the corner of Highway 8 and Watson Road.

I am going to ask you to read two books over the next few months. I trust these will be in addition to books that you already plan to read. I am an avid reader and have noted that reading books is a common attribute among effective leaders. Ken Hemphill stated in a blog that I recently read that 42 percent of college graduates never read another book upon completing their degrees. You forfeit your right to lead at the point you fail to grow and develop your skills. The world is changing quickly and you must constantly feed yourself information that will stretch and equip you to be an effective leader for years to come. Do not think that I am suggesting that this is a substitute for your spiritual growth. Effective leadership requires that you ride on two rails much like a train that is propelled down a track.

The first rail is your personal spiritual growth. Are you spending personal time with God every day? I am not speaking of the time you spend in sermon preparation although that is certainly advantageous to those of us who are blessed and called to do so. Do you open God's Word each day asking him to speak to you personally? Do you spend time in prayer seeking God's anointing and His power? Do you worship Him privately and publicly? Are you seeking to be intimate with God through a devoted relationship with His Son, Jesus Christ?

You may wonder why I am asking you these things, given the fact that you are a pastor. It is because doing things for God is not the same as having a relationship with God. I fear that many Christian leaders struggle and fail to experience God's touch on their ministries because they inadvertently substitute service to God for a personal relationship with God. Don't make that mistake. Study the illustration Jesus shared in the Sermon on the Mount in Matthew 7:24–27. Many ministries have floundered and failed because they were not built on the solid rock of an intimate relationship with the Father. When the storms arise, and they will come, you will not stand strong if you fail at this point.

The second rail is not as important as spiritual growth and yet it is critical to your effectiveness as a leader. You may recall that Paul told Timothy to "stir up the gift of God that is in you" in 2 Timothy 1:6. Timothy's gifts came from God by His grace. However, Paul reminded Timothy that he had responsibility to develop his gift and not allow it to stagnate from neglect. Reading is one of the ways that you can stir up your gift. The internet affords great opportunities through social networking, blogs, and easily accessible research through search engines and software that any leader would be wise to be acquainted with. I enjoy tweeting and reading the tweets of others. However, 140 characters can only provide me with a taste of what I need. Reading a book is more like enjoying a complete buffet of information that stretches and feeds my intellect, my spirit, my attitudes, and my skills.

If you possess leadership skills but fail to have an intimate relationship with Christ you will lack the power that only God can give that can propel your leadership to levels beyond your human abilities. If you stay close to God but neglect to develop your leadership skills you will touch lives but will be limited by an inability to influence others to grow and lead. Do not limit what God wants to do with you by failing to stay close to Him and do not limit yourself by failing to grow as a skillful leader.

I know this is a lengthy e-mail but I will likely send several like this in the coming months to take full advantage of the task at hand. I want you to purchase a book on the subject of personal leadership development. Let me know if you need suggestions. You may wonder what this has to do with becoming intentionally evangelistic. We will discuss this point when we meet. I need you to do one more thing before we meet. It is admittedly a tedious assignment but you will see the point. For every hour of each day I want you to make a chart and summarize what you did each hour. Don't detail what you do each hour but summarize in one to three words what it was that consumed the greatest amount of your energy for that hour. A few days before we meet, e-mail me what you come up with. I'll see you in a few weeks!

Your Friend,

Marc Benton

Mitch's mind was going a hundred miles an hour. *What have I got myself into?* He was not sure if he was overwhelmed but he knew that he was convicted. He felt good that he was already an avid reader and the e-reader he had gotten last Christmas had actually enhanced that. It was a great tool, although he had not transitioned entirely to the electronic reader and he still had that soft spot for purchasing books whenever he went to the Christian bookstore. Mitch was feeling conviction because of Pastor Benton's comments about spiritual growth. *When had the change occurred?* He had experienced an erosion of personal time with God in the past couple of years and could not say for sure when or why it had happened. Was it the demands of his congregation? A subtle substitution of the time he was spending in sermon preparation and pastoral duties instead of prayer?

"Pastor, are you in there?" Mitch was suddenly reminded that he was not alone in the church today. John Dollar stuck his head in the door.

"Hey Pastor. Are you busy?"

"Come on in, John. You're here early, so I guess you must be hungry."

"Well I am, but I wanted to see what you thought the seven heads and ten horns represent in Revelation 12:3. I'll tell you what I think."

Here we go, Mitch thought. *It looks like I'll be in the back of the line.*

Chapter Five

Not a Fan

Thursday, August 15th

There was no shortage of quantity or quality on the buffet table, although, as he had predicted, Mitch was at the back of the line with John Dollar. Mitch reached out to grab the spoon for the potato salad as his eyes moved down the buffet before him and suddenly realized he was grasping nothing but air. Lester McDonald looked down at him with glee, holding the spoon aloft and grinning as if he had won an arm-wrestling contest. Mitch would have to admit that Lester likely could not only beat him at arm-wrestling but could also submit him, pin him, or knock him out if they somehow found themselves in a mixed martial arts cage match. *I wonder if old McDonald ever had a farm?* Mitch thought. *Forgive me Lord. I shouldn't have thoughts like that.*

Lester McDonald owned a heavy-equipment construction outfit that had done very well and still seemed to be thriving despite the sluggish economy. His son, Thomas, provided the day-to-day management now that Lester was nearing retirement age. However, he was still in fit physical condition and very imposing. He stood over six-foot-four and weighed probably 250 pounds. None of his weight appeared to be fat. Lester seemed to get a kick out of squeezing too hard when he would shake your hand, either as a way to intimidate or to show off. Mitch wasn't sure which, and he imagined it had a little to do with both.

"Did John get you straightened out, preacher?" Lester asked with a smirk as he dipped the spoon into the potato salad.

Mitch opted for the tongs to grab a cob of corn as he looked up at Lester across the table. "Yeah, Lester, he straightened me out." Mitch would prefer not to concede but found that any exchange with Mr. McDonald was a no-win situation. Lester had no formal leadership title at Stanton Community Church, but his grandfather had been a charter member, and that made Lester the key influencer in the church. He didn't need a title. Three of the five deacons would not make a move without consulting him if a major decision was at hand. His son, Thomas, happened to be the deacon chairman. The men who served as deacons had long made key decisions for the church. Although the pastor attended the meetings and could participate in discussion, he was not allowed to vote. When the church held their monthly conference for the members, Lester sat right up front so that people could see how he would vote on any issue.

Lester continued the ritual ribbing of his pastor. "I hope he gave you something. I figured you would surely be preaching better sermons by now," he said sarcastically.

"Well, Lester, this coming Sunday I am going to be preaching on sin, so I look forward to meeting you down at the altar." Mitch, pleased to have been so quick with his retort, could see that Lester wasn't smiling.

"We ain't paying you to be a smart alec."

Mitch realized that although his attempt at banter with Lester may have been clever, it was not becoming of his pastoral role and did not play well with Lester. "I'm sorry, Lester. I thought we were just having a little fun."

"Well, you go ahead and have fun while you can."

Was that a threat? Lester had seemed supportive of him at the outset, but Mitch soon learned that he was not a fan. The pastor search team members that called him to serve at Stanton Community Church were all enthusiastic, and the vote had been over 95 percent in his favor. *I guess Lester wishes he could go back and change his vote…that is, if he voted for me.* Mitch determined to take the high road and he went to sit right next to Lester to eat his lunch. *Bless those who persecute you? I'm learning, Lord.*

Later That Day

"Hey, Pastor Mitch!" Mitch looked across the street and saw two teens riding skateboards on the sidewalk, heading south toward his neighborhood. He had just replaced the nozzle in the filling station pump and was securing the gas cap when he recognized his fourteen-year-old neighbor, Wyatt. Wyatt was one of the two teens who attended Stanton Community Church regularly. The other was Cecilia Ramirez. Cecilia had moved in with her grandparents about the time Mitch began serving as pastor. She and Wyatt were there every week while three other students attended sporadically.

Mitch and Wyatt often played backyard basketball together during the evenings. Mitch had excelled at the sport in high school, but was not quite good enough to play on the college level. Aside from intramural play in college, he had not played competitively since his senior year, but that did not dampen his love for the game. The only organized sport he still participated in was men's softball, and he really enjoyed shooting hoops with Wyatt and some other neighbors, including Wyatt's dad. He had not seen Wyatt with the other teen before, and did not recognize him. He seemed to be a rougher cut than Wyatt; his long hair was uncombed. Without being judgmental, Mitch noted the same air of rebellion that he had seen in other teens.

Mitch shouted back. "Hey, Wyatt, are you ready for me to school you in a game of Horse again?" Horse was a shooting competition that Mitch and Wyatt played at least once a week when the weather permitted. Wyatt seemed to enjoy it when Mitch would talk a little smack during the intervals between their competitions, and was not shy in giving it back.

"You're goin' down Mitch. I'm gonna shut you out next time. I've been practicin'." Within seconds the two teens rounded the corner and were out of sight. *I hope that other kid's not bad news. It's tough enough for teens when their friends are solid.* Mitch had grown fond of Wyatt and become like a big brother ever since he and Melinda had moved in next door. He made a mental note to keep his eyes open. He was still young enough to remember how tough it was to be fourteen.

Tuesday, August 27th

Melinda did it again! That's what Mitch was thinking as he sat in his recliner to unwind following a delicious dinner of grilled salmon. He had promised to read Haley a story, but first he had one task he wanted to complete. The afternoon had gone by too quickly, and he remembered while driving home that he wanted to send Pastor Benton an update. With his laptop sitting on his knees, he opened up his e-mail account and began to type.

> From: Mitch Walker
> Sent: Tuesday, August 27, 7:32 PM
> To: Marc Benton
> Subject: RE: Item You Requested
> Dr. Benton
> I am looking forward to getting together with you next week. I have
> really been focusing more than ever on my personal devotion time and

appreciate the reminder that you provided in your earlier e-mail. Things have continued to be just as hectic, but I feel encouraged on a couple of levels. Not only am I feeling refreshed in my relationship with the Lord, but also something happened last Sunday that really lifted my spirits.

As I was standing greeting members as they exited the Sunday morning service, I was approached by one of our members. His name is James Flynn, and he is a committed and supportive member of my con-gregation. He pulled me aside after everyone left and said that God had really impressed upon him a desire to pray for me as his pastor. He said that he sensed that God had something great in store for our church and that God was going to use me in a great way. It was very humbling and, at the same time, uplifting. He said that he is committed to pray for me personally every morning and I found myself almost in tears as he laid his hands on my shoulders and prayed the most powerful prayer I think I have ever heard. I have never before experienced anything like it.

You will find attached in an Excel document the survey that you asked for that tracks how my days have been spent. I am really anxious to see how you view it and appreciate any feedback you can give. In addi-tion, I purchased a book on leadership as you requested. I apologize that I have not started reading it yet but intend to get started soon.

See you next week in Southerland!

Mitch

Chapter Six

Iron Men

Thursday, September 5th

Mitch was about fifteen minutes ahead of schedule when he pulled into the coffee shop in Southerland. The town, which was only slightly larger than Stanton, was situated almost halfway between his place of residence and Rock Springs. Melinda and Haley were visiting her parents in Lakeland, which was about four hours away, for part of the Labor Day weekend.

The coffee shop was busy, filled with the inviting aromas of coffee and European pastries. The décor was a strange blend of art deco and Rockabilly. Mitch had been inside for only a couple of minutes when Pastor Benton arrived. "Dr. Benton, good morning," Mitch said as he reached out to shake his hand.

"Let's start with dropping the Dr. Benton, Mitch. You can call me Marc. Have you ordered anything yet?"

Both men went to the counter to order coffee and pastries. Mitch and Pastor Benton found a table in the corner that offered some degree of privacy and swapped reviews of their weekend holiday excursions. Mitch ordered a cream cheese Danish, which melted in his mouth. The trip may have been worth the time just to discover the coffee shop.

The conversation was informal. Mitch shared with him about Melinda and Haley, how they had met in high school, their mid-college wedding, and how they had been blessed with Haley within one year of the nuptials. He also shared about his brief career as a high school teacher before heading to seminary and then landing in Stanton as pastor of the Community Church.

"Tell me a little bit about your family," Mitch invited.

"My wife and I will celebrate our fortieth wedding anniversary next year," Pastor Benton replied with a smile of satisfaction.

"Congratulations, Marc. That is a great milestone."

"Well, I am blessed. My wife Betty and I met when I was pastoring my first church. She can sing like an angel. When we fell in love and got married, we agreed that I would not sing and that she would not preach. I want you to know that I've kept my part of the bargain." Marc was grinning. "But when I step out of line she doesn't hesitate to preach to me, if you know what I mean."

"Oh, yeah. I think I've been to the same service but with a different preacher."

Both men were laughing as one of the shop attendants approached their table. "Good morning, you two. It sounds like somebody is in a good mood. You gentlemen need anything?"

Pastor Benton replied, "No, we're good. Thanks for asking."

"Do you have any children or grandchildren?" Mitch asked, as they continued the conversation.

"We have two sons, one daughter, and seven grandchildren. My middle son lives right outside of Rock Springs near us and attends Tabernacle Church where I pastor. My oldest son lives in Texas. He manages a chain of pharmacies and has done real well. Between the two boys I have five grandsons, two of whom go to our church."

"And you have a daughter also."

"Yes. My daughter is the youngest, and she has a daughter and a son. I'm sad to say that we haven't spoken in about a decade. Once she went off to college she married a young man, got pregnant, dropped out of college, and was divorced within three years. But that was not what drove us apart." Mitch could see Pastor Benton's demeanor change dramatically. You could see the pain in his face. He was looking down as he continued. "She had a rebellious streak that hit really hard about the time she turned sixteen, and we could never seem to get a handle on it. Following her divorce, she moved in with us for a while. Initially, I really thought that things were turning around when she moved back." He paused and reflected for a moment as he took a sip of his coffee.

"We struggled knowing where to draw lines of discipline and freedom since she was our child, and yet she was an adult. She could push my buttons like no one I've ever known. Mitch, I hate to admit it, but I didn't always handle things well. I would be embarrassed if my congregation knew all that went on. If it were not for a strong relationship with my sons I would feel like an absolute failure."

"Where does she live?" Mitch asked.

"Quite honestly, I don't know for sure. The last I heard she was living in a trailer park somewhere over on your side of the county, but as I said I have not talked to her in over ten years now. She totally cut us off after a huge blowup. She took the grandkids and off she went. Unfortunately, alcohol was a huge part of the equation. Her mother and I did not tolerate it, and she dug in her heels and grew more antagonistic the more we tried to intervene. She ended up getting married again, divorced again, and last that I heard was living with a man. To make matters even worse, she has severed all contact between us and the grand-kids. I guess she wanted to punish us, and unfortunately it's working. I worry about them like you wouldn't believe."

Mitch was not sure how to respond or what to say. The transparency took Mitch off guard just a bit, considering that they were just getting to know each other. Mitch had shared his church challenges when they met for the first time at the hospital, and now, on their second cup of coffee together, the older man was unloading about the burden of a major family issue. *Maybe all pastors need someone they can unload on without fear of how the congregation will receive it*, Mitch thought to himself.

They continued to talk about their families for the next several minutes, and the mood lightened considerably as they shared more about their loved ones and the summer adventures that both had enjoyed. Mitch committed to himself to pray for the pastor and his family, especially for his daughter and grandkids that he was so obviously burdened over. He also felt encouraged that he could so quickly give something back to this relationship. Marc Benton was a hero in Mitch's eyes, and he did not come into the relationship thinking he had much to offer. It made him think of Proverbs 27:17, *As iron sharpens iron, so one person sharpens another*.

Thursday, September 5th

The conversation shifted as they continued to sip their coffee. Pastor Benton pulled papers out of a folder and laid them on the table. "Mitch, I looked over the survey you did to chart the way your days are being spent. When we talked at the hospital, I shared how I wanted to help you to lead your congregation to be intentionally evangelistic. You can use what I am about to share with you not only to deal with the squeaky wheels that we talked about a couple of weeks ago, but also to begin the process of becoming intentional in evangelism. Now, bear in mind that you will never eliminate all of the squeaky wheels, but your goal is to minimize them so that you can place your focus on the things that will make the most difference."

Mitch was curious to see where this conversation was about to go and slid his coffee cup over to the side in order to get a better view of what Pastor Benton had prepared. "Are you ready to see what I have?" Pastor Benton asked. Mitch nodded as Benton placed a piece of paper between them that contained a chart with a list of percentages.

Sermon/Bible Study Prep	12.6%
Church Services	12.6%
Hospital, Nursing & Funeral Homes	19.0%
Drop-by Visits to Office	10.0%
General Church Administration	4.4%
Committee Meetings	7.2%
Supply Trips to Rock Springs	7.2%
Church Maintenance	4.4%
Counseling	5.4%
Phone/E-mail/Facebook	11.8%
Church Activities, Misc.	5.4%
Total	100.0%

"You see here that I took the information that you provided when you tracked hour by hour how you were spending your time for two weeks. I backed out your day off each week; the hours you spent sleeping and eating; time spent with your family; and any other non-church-related activities. I want to commend you for taking a day off each week because I believe that a Sabbath rest not only honors God but also helps to give you the energy you need to do God's work. You are working about fifty-five hours a week, if these two weeks are representative."

"No two weeks are exactly the same," Mitch replied, "but I would say those two weeks were about as typical as any I would be able to come up with. Maybe I need to have this handy the next time someone makes a crack that preachers only have to work on Sundays."

Pastor Benton beamed a knowing smile. "On top of that, I have many pastor friends who work full-time secular jobs. They pastor churches in addition to running businesses or working forty-plus hours a week. They are the heroes of ministry, in my opinion. I pastored a church when I was in seminary and grew to appreciate early on the sacrifices that those men make."

"Agreed," Mitch responded, reaching over to get his coffee. Pastor Benton continued. "From those 110 hours I tried to place the time you spent in as few categories as possible. You can see what percentage of your time is being devoted to various activities and responsibilities. Let me add that nothing you are doing is bad or wrong in and of itself. But I think the next chart may reveal part of the reason your church is struggling with reaching people." Pastor Benton took a second piece of paper and laid it on top of the first so that Mitch could see it. It also contained a chart with percentages but the categories were different.

Prayer	4.2%
Discipleship	8.4%
Fellowship	15.5%
Ministry	56.3%
Worship	8.4%
Evangelism	0.0%
Other	7.2%

"Do you recognize those categories in the left hand column?" Pastor Benton asked.

Mitch grabbed the paper and brought it closer as he examined the list. "That appears to be the functions of the church described in Acts 2:42–47 with a slight variation. In seminary we were taught that they are Evangelism, Discipleship, Fellowship, Ministry, and Worship. I remember them because I used an acrostic to memorize them in preparation for an exam: Every Dead Frog Must Wiggle. Prayer was not on the list, and I don't remember "other" being on the list either."

"You are right about the five functions of the church, but verse 42 also states that the early believers were 'devoted to prayer.' I believe that prayer is the driver of all of the others."

"That's a great point. I would have to agree."

"Now this is not an exact science, but I took the way you were spending your time and tried as best as I could to determine how your activities applied to these biblical priorities. Quite frankly there were a couple of areas that I could not quantify, and I placed those in the 'other' category. What stands out when you look at the chart?"

"Obviously, the evangelism category pops out since it is at zero percent. But I do try to share the gospel when I preach each week."

"I'll grant you that. Assuming you preached Sunday morning and Sunday evening both weeks, you would have four hours devoted to evangelism if you wanted to make that argument. However, out of 110 hours you would still be well under four percent. We would also have to assume that you had unbelievers in the service each time hearing your message. How many guests were present?"

Mitch may have taken offense at such prodding except that Pastor Benton was not condemning in his tone but more like a father or a big brother who was speaking truth in love. Mitch had agreed to this, after all, and evaluation can be painful. He reflected on a recent visit to the doctor for a physical exam. The doctor told him to watch what he was eating and to begin exercising regularly. He didn't like being told what to do, but understood that the doctor had his best interests at heart. He had conducted no previous evaluation to speak of, and would not grow or be able to make any adjustments unless he was willing to go through this.

"Actually, no guests were present the past two weeks. The evangelism would have to be rated with a zero or a very low percentage at best."

"Let me make something clear. These categories will not all come out to 16.66% with exactly equal distribution. But you can see when part of your focus is way out of balance. I believe that large number in the ministry category is simply a reflection of our conversation at the hospital a few weeks back. It is a tangible affirmation of what you shared with me about the demands on your time by your congregation. What else do you see?"

Mitch studied the chart for a moment and continued. "You mentioned that prayer drives all of the others. It is obvious from the chart that a low percentage of my energy is devoted there."

"In this case, it may actually be higher than that. I did not include your personal devotional time, and you shared that you spent time each morning reading God's Word and praying. The numbers on this chart reflect your work or ministry time. We can assume that is actually a little stronger. That's not to say there's no room for improvement."

"Pastor Benton, I really respect you, and you said you've been where I am before. What's the bottom line here in your opinion?"

Benton leaned back in his chair and placed both hands behind his head. His posture was not confrontational in any sense. Mitch noticed as he looked past him that most customers had gone on their way and, except for a senior couple across the room, they had the shop to themselves now.

"Mitch, I have been studying healthy churches for a long time. It has always been my desire to lead my congregation to be healthy and that means being balanced. But as I study churches that reach their communities and make many disciples, I notice that the pastors have a common quality. Evangelistic churches are led by evangelistic pastors. I have yet to find an exception to that principle. The same is true of a Bible study group. Bible study groups that are evangelistic are led by evangelistic teachers or leaders. I want you to take one key word away from our time together today: *intentionality*. What does that mean to you?"

"I'm not sure about the dictionary definition, but I guess it means to be purposeful."

"That's good. You have to decide how you are going to spend your time each week. If you don't decide, then others will decide for you. You have to be purposeful in the way you spend your time. I go through this exercise personally every couple of years to make sure I am constantly adjusting the way I spend my time to match my priorities. There is much more you can do with this, but what we are doing is directly applicable to helping your congregation become more intentionally evangelistic. Pastors and people in general often tend to find any excuse not to engage in evangelism. The very forces of hell will battle against you to distract and keep you focused on anything and everything else. Apparently, Timothy struggled with the same issue. Remember what Paul said to him in 2 Timothy 4:5? "But you, keep your head in all situations, endure hardship, do the work of an evangelist, discharge all the duties of your ministry." Paul did not commend him for his evangelistic efforts but reminded him to be intentional about it and implied that failure to do so would be failure to discharge all of the duties that God had called him to."

"Give me some ideas of what I should do."

"First, I want to hear you share some ideas."

Mitch and Pastor Benton exchanged a variety of ideas over the next several minutes. Benton listened attentively to Mitch's ideas and gave occasional insight. Mitch began to jot down notes on a yellow lined pad that he had brought with him.

"Let me wrap this up Mitch. Our time is getting away quick. I haven't said much about what the *Net Effect* is yet, but I will get to it. Did you start on the leadership book that you purchased?"

Mitch's face flushed slightly as he confessed, "I'm busted. I told you in the e-mail that I purchased it and that I would start reading it, but I haven't hit page one yet."

"Let me tell you why it is important. The *Net Effect* will not ever take place if you don't step up as a leader. Don't take offense. I'm not saying that you're not a leader. Leadership is a journey, and I'm still growing myself. You remember in my e-mail that I mentioned the two rails of leadership."

"Yeah, spiritual growth and skills growth, if I recall correctly."

"Very good! What is leadership? How would you define it?"

Mitch pondered for a moment. "I guess it means to be a good example for everyone."

"I can't argue that a leader needs to be a good example, but effective leadership goes deeper than that. Suppose someone was trying to be a good example, and no one was paying attention. Would that be leadership?"

"I guess if no one really noticed, then his or her example would not make a difference."

"I once heard it said that 'He who thinks he leadeth and has no one following is only taking a walk.' You have to be a good example, but a leader is intentional about getting people to follow. Remember that the word 'intentional' is what I said I want you to take away from this meeting. I'm going to be talking with you more about how to do that. As we get into the principles and practices of the *Net*

Effect, you will not be able to do it by yourself. You will have to bring others on board for it to happen. Being an example is critical, but leadership is useless unless you are intentionally influencing other people and inspiring them to a greater purpose."

Mitch and Pastor Benton continued on for another ten minutes before departing. Mitch promised to begin reading the book that evening, and Benton assured him that the discussion of leadership would continue when they met again. The hour had gone by quickly, and Mitch did not mind spending an extra fifteen minutes together. He left with three items written on the second page of his notes, which he committed himself to implement as he began his journey of leading his congregation to be more intentionally evangelistic.

1. *Identify three to five people to serve on an evangelism leadership team. Meet with them regularly.*
2. *Build into my calendar at least four to five hours each week to do outreach and evangelism.*
3. *Communicate with my congregation some boundaries on my schedule to free up time for outreach activities.*

As Mitch was driving to the church following his meeting in Southerland, he replayed the key points from his meeting with Pastor Benton. He saw a young lady walking in the opposite direction holding the hand of her young daughter. He was at least a half mile out of town, and he thought of how blessed he was to have a car, albeit an old clunker. He also thought of Pastor Benton's daughter. He could not imagine how painful that must be. He loved Haley, his own daughter, with all of his heart, and he was pained at the thought that he would ever experience that kind of separation from her. *Is that the pain that God feels when one of His children goes their own way?* Within a few moments, he found a gas station, pulled in, and parked out of the way. He bowed his head and began to pray.

Thursday, September 5th

Mitch closed his office door after returning from Southerland later in the afternoon and took a few moments to clear his desk. He had a couple of phone messages to return and took time to respond to some e-mails. That took about an hour, and then he took out his notes from the morning. Without interruption, he could spend time thinking through the three action points he had written earlier.

He felt that putting together the evangelism leadership team might be the easiest task. Although he had struggled in the church, he was still blessed to have advocates. As he thought about them, he wrote down the names of prospective team members. In the past, he would have announced the need from the pulpit and asked for volunteers. Now, he was reminded of Luke 6:12–16 when Jesus had enlisted the apostles. If Jesus prayed before selecting His apostles, it would make sense for him to pray before enlisting this team. He also decided he would approach each prospective team member personally.

The biggest challenge would be establishing the boundaries with his congregation. He turned to his computer and started typing some notes and key points as he continued to think through how to proceed. *Lord, I'm not sure how my congregation is going to receive this. Give me wisdom. I wonder if I may need to buy a helmet to wear in the pulpit after I do this?*

Later that day Mitch pulled into his driveway, mentally and emotionally exhausted from the day. *Amazing…Even with hardly any physical exertion, I feel drained.* At the same time, he felt energized. He had a sense of direction that he had not experienced since his arrival in Stanton. Pastor Benton had been very encouraging. He had also received a text from James Flynn that lifted his spirits:

Praying for you Pastor. Have blessed day.

Mitch replied back:

Thnx James. You r th best. Lot's on my heart. I want to get 2gether soon.

One of the things Pastor Benton pointed out that morning was that the time Mitch had invested in ministering to his members over the past two years could work to his advantage. He had many strong relationships in spite of the fact that a few key members seemed to always be disgruntled no matter what he did.

He noticed his neighbor, Randall, watering plants near the driveway with his back to Mitch as he approached. He was six-foot-six and could still dunk a basketball at forty years of age. Mitch revved the engine and watched as Randall jumped out of the way in fear that he was about to be run over. Mitch laughed and rolled down the window as he pulled farther into the driveway.

"You almost gave me a heart attack!" Randall shouted as Mitch brought the car to a stop. Randall turned the hose toward Mitch, who barely got the window back up in time to avoid a garden hose shower. It was all good-natured, and Mitch walked over without fear of any serious retaliation. "How are you doing, Pastor?"

"Great, Randall, how are you guys doing?"

"Are you ready for some football?"

"That's right. The NFL cranks up this week. How do you think we're going to do?"

"I think we're good for the play-offs again. I sure hope so."

Randall turned the hose off and walked closer. You could tell he had been hard at work cutting his lawn and working in his flower beds. Randall loved working in his yard and could be seen doing something to improve it almost every day. Mitch barely got by with keeping his own grass cut, although he always kept things tidy.

"Where's Wyatt? I may have time to shoot some hoops after dinner."

Randall's countenance changed as he wiped sweat from his brow with his forearm. "I don't know what I'm going to do about that boy."

"What are you talking about?"

"I swear, I believe aliens have invaded his body. Once he got into the eighth grade, he got an attitude that is driving his mom and me nuts."

"Well, he is fourteen now, isn't he?"

"That he is."

"Have you ever heard how we know that Isaac was only twelve when Abraham went to sacrifice him?"

"How's that?"

"They say because if he was thirteen, it would not have been a sacrifice."

Randall laughed and said, "You may be on to something there." He turned somber again. "Seriously, Mitch, I don't want to get into it all, but let's just say we've had some problems lately. He's getting into things that lead to worse things. He decided not to play football this year. I don't think I need to push him, but it is good to have something to keep him occupied. I've noticed that some of his friends have changed over the last few months, and these kids are just not of the same character."

Mitch remembered seeing Wyatt skateboarding in the church parking lot with a teen that he did not recognize from the neighborhood. "I'll tell you, Randall, it hasn't been quite as obvious to me, but I do recall now seeing him with some new friends. I'll tell you what. I'll be a little more attentive to him in the next few weeks. He makes up half the youth group as it is."

"I appreciate that Mitch. Just pray for us. He didn't come with an instruction manual, you know."

"I hear you. You guys mean a lot to Melinda, Haley, and me. The same goes for our church. Let me know if I can do anything."

An evening at home was just what Mitch needed. *This must be somewhat like heaven,* he was thinking as he sat in his recliner after a great dinner with Melinda and Haley. Life gives you those moments that isolate themselves somehow and you wish they would never come to an end. Mitch wasn't thinking about church, ministry, problems, or challenges. Haley was sitting snuggled up on his lap as he leaned back in his favorite chair. The recliner was one of the few pieces of furniture they owned that was not used or handed down. It fit Mitch like a glove and served as the personal throne for his castle, but it was having Haley lying there with her head on his chest that made his day. She had always been a daddy's girl. Melinda was sitting nearby on the sofa reading a magazine, waiting for "Dancing with the Stars" to come on. She was absolutely the love of his life.

The television was playing, but it really didn't matter to Mitch what was on. He cherished moments like this when all was peaceful, darkness had settled in, and it was just the three of them. Haley was their only child. The plan had been to have a house full of children. At least that is what they had discussed when they were young. Haley had arrived just before their first wedding anniversary and three years later, Melinda and Mitch were elated to have number two on the way. It was not to be. Melinda had miscarried. The greatest pain that Mitch had experienced in his life up to this point was the loss of that child. He hurt not only at the loss of his child, but even more as he bore his wife's pain. *What would we have done without the Lord during that year?*

It had happened the very first year of seminary, and he had struggled with why such a thing could have happened within a year after accepting the call to be a preacher of the gospel. He already knew that life wasn't fair, but this was devastating, especially when the doctor told them that it would not be possible to have any more children. In spite of their grief and their questions, they did not let go of their faith. Eventually, God had healed their spirits and strengthened them in a way that would not have been possible had they not experienced such pain in the first place. What could have made them bitter had actually made them better.

Their love for each other was deep, and Mitch loved Melinda now more than ever. That did not keep them from having their struggles sometimes. Melinda often expressed frustration when Mitch came home later than promised because of last-second emergencies at the church, but tonight those frustrations were buried in the warmth of a pleasant evening together.

Haley was such a joy. "I love you, Daddy." *Yeah, she has me wrapped around her finger.* Being with Melinda and Haley seemed to make everything else all right. *I may not be the best pastor in the world, but I love being home with my family.* His thoughts shifted to Wyatt next door and the daughter with whom Pastor Benton had not spoken in years. *I really don't have that much to complain about. Lord, forgive me for having such a bad attitude sometimes.*

"I love you too, baby." *And if heaven is anything close to this, I don't know why anyone would want to miss it.*

Tuesday, September 10th

Mitch sat in his office looking at four names that he had written on a notepad.

Tim Minor
Carly Rooks
James Flynn
Kris Kimmons

He had prayed and asked God to show him whom he should ask to serve with him on the evangelism leadership team. He was not sure what to call the team, but the title would not be nearly as critical as those who would be asked to serve.

Tim was the Bible study director and husband of his part-time secretary, Miss Jerri.

Carly was his wife's best friend. Their relationship went back to their college days and, as fate would have it, they were now living in the same town. Carly was divorced and she had a little girl who was the same age as Haley, making the friendship a great pairing on many levels. She had been the first person to join the church after Mitch was called as pastor.

James was the senior member of the group and was actually the first person Mitch had thought of as he and Pastor Benton discussed enlisting a team. He was one of the five deacons in the church, and he carried a perpetually positive outlook. Mitch always felt encouraged by James.

Kris and her husband, Alan, were also longtime members, and both taught Bible study groups. Kris led the children's group, and Alan taught the youth. Alan would have also been a good choice, but Mitch feared that his business travel would make it difficult for him to attend the meetings. Still, having one of them on the team was as good as having both.

Mitch turned to his computer to access the contact list. His computer table sat immediately behind his desk, allowing him to swivel from the work area on his desk and back to his computer as needed. He looked up each of the four phone numbers. (Miss Jerri could have done this for him, but since she worked only part time, he ordinarily did this type of task himself.) He grabbed the phone and dialed the first number. "Hey, James, this is Mitch. Listen, could I get by and see you one day this week?"

Three of the four answered, and Mitch set a time to meet with the ones he spoke with. "You can't do it by yourself." That's what Pastor Benton said. *I've got to get some help if we are going to turn this around.*

Chapter Nine

BEGIN IN ME

Sunday, September 15th

What a time to be alive! Mitch could not imagine what it would be like not to have air conditioning. *I think we may be spoiled.* A list of blessings scrolled through Mitch's mind: electricity, indoor plumbing, padded seats, heat and air conditioning, clean and carpeted buildings. Mitch remembered a mission trip that he had gone on only weeks before beginning his pastorate at Stanton Community Church. *Those people had none of these luxuries, and yet the believers I met there seemed more content than my congregation.*

No need to start thinking negatively on Sunday morning. Mitch, like most preachers, loved Sunday mornings. He was called to preach, and the largest crowd—small though it may be in Stanton—attended the 11:00 A.M. service on Sunday mornings. Several Bible study groups met the hour before that, but Mitch left their leadership to Tim Minor, his Bible study director.

The worship center was equipped with padded pews, blue carpet, a pulpit behind a table from which communion was served, and a small choir loft behind that. The church had been formed eighty-three years before, but the facilities they met in now looked a little dated, having been constructed about thirty years ago. The congregation did a great job of keeping everything clean and tidy. The worship center was only about half full on a good day, and today seemed to be well attended. Mitch did not notice any guests present. *Looks like I'm preaching to the faithful again today.*

Ordinarily, Mitch was not nervous about preaching, but today was different. He was about to go out on a limb. Thankfully, the Holy Spirit strengthened him as he moved through the introduction, his nervousness evaporated, and he began to preach with more power and conviction than the congregation was accustomed to. He saw James Flynn sitting halfway back on the left side with his wife Darlene. She would lead the music each week before slipping back to sit with her husband. Knowing he had James' prayer support was encouraging.

He decided to take the text that Pastor Benton had shared in the coffee shop almost two weeks earlier: "But you, keep your head in all situations, endure hardship, do the work of an evangelist, discharge all the duties of your ministry" (2 Timothy 4:5). He focused specifically on the responsibility of a pastor to *do the work of an evangelist*. He exegeted, interpreted, and illustrated the text, knowing that he had a responsibility to lead Stanton Community Church to actually do more to reach out to the community.

As he moved toward the end of his message, Mitch stepped to the right side of the pulpit to engage the congregation in a personal manner. "We live in a world that needs the message that Jesus Christ has given us to share. It is a message of hope, forgiveness, a message of salvation. It is a message that not only gives those who trust in Jesus Christ eternal life in heaven one day but also internal life as the Holy Spirit indwells every believer. He walks with those who follow Him in times of blessing and in the darkest hours of tribulation."

Mitch paused and whispered a prayer that God would connect what he was about to share with open and receptive hearts. He continued, "I've got a confession to make." He paused, noting that several members who were looking down suddenly perked up. "I have not been the leader that I need to be for you. I have grown to love this community, and I love each and every one of you. We have spent countless hours together in worship, fellowship, and in ministry over the past two years. But I have allowed us to neglect something very critical. The Great Commission is very clear that we are to *Go and make disciples of all nations, baptizing them in the name of the Father and of the Son and of the Holy Spirit*. As I was preparing this message, I was reminded of something a revered pastor once said at a chapel service when I attended seminary a few years back. He said, 'The Bible does not command lost people to come to your church, but for your church to go to lost people.'"

"Amen," James Flynn shouted. That woke up a couple more people in the back who were caught up in their daydreams. The congregation at Stanton Community Church was not known for being expressive when they worshipped. Mitch continued, "Somewhere I lost sight of that and got distracted. A change has to begin in me. God is working in my life in a way that has not been so strong and so real since I started my seminary training. I want to meet your needs, and I will continue to do my best. But we are missing a huge piece of God's plan for us if we do not reach out to our community with a desire that many would come to faith in the Lord Jesus Christ. Let me share a couple of changes I am making and ask you to consider how God may be speaking to your heart on this matter. The Great Commission is not a pastoral commission but is intended to establish a priority for all believers. We love God, we love our neighbors, and we share the good news by ministering and telling His story."

The room was quiet, and there was a spirit of attentiveness that Mitch had seldom observed in his church. "First, I am committing to devote at least four hours each week to outreach and evangelism. I am not saying that is the right amount or the wrong amount of time. I am not suggesting that I will confine my outreach efforts to a calendar. I just know that is what God put on my heart. I am actually going to place it in my schedule because I know I need the discipline. It will be the priority when it is scheduled, and I hope many of you will take this journey with me. But I will not be available to you during the time I set aside for outreach."

He paused for a moment making sure to make eye contact with several of his parishioners. "Second, I am going to take a couple of hours each morning and at least one full morning each week to study somewhere other than the church office, because I cannot resist answering e-mails, texts, and calls as soon as they come in. I need more than anything else the empowering of God's Spirit, which comes through spending uninterrupted time with Him. I must seek God first in my life and ministry if I ever hope to lead you to make a difference in this community."

Mitch took a deep breath and continued, "Finally, I will continue to visit you in the hospital when needed although I certainly hope that is a rare occurrence. However, I may not always be available to visit your relatives, particularly those who have a pastor of their own, when they are in the hospital, especially those who live outside of our community. I want to add that I will continue to fellowship with you often, but now that I know you all after these two years, I will not feel compelled to accept every invitation that you so graciously offer for the various gatherings. Please do not interpret this to mean that I am not appreciative."

All of a sudden, a tenseness filled the room. Mitch could sense that some members were taking offense at the new boundaries. "Please know my heart. I am going to continue to minister to your needs and I will seek to do so without ignoring what God has called me to do as a preacher of the gospel."

As the invitation song began, James Flynn made his way to the front and took Mitch by the hand. "I'm with you, pastor." He broke into prayer before Mitch could say a word, and when he finished, returned to his seat.

Many affirmed Mitch as they shook his hand at the exit. But not everyone seemed to be pleased. "Pastor, we need to have a talk." It was Lester McDonald.

"Sure, Lester. Why don't you come by tomorrow afternoon, and we'll spend some time together."

"I mean right now." Lester was obviously not happy about the message that Mitch had just shared.

"Lester, right now I have several others to greet, and my wife and I have lunch plans with the Kimmons."

Lester bent down and whispered so that others nearby could not hear. "I don't care what your plans are. When I say I want to talk, then that is what I expect you to do."

Mitch swallowed hard but stood tall and looked Lester square in the eye. "Lester, you feel free to come by tomorrow afternoon." Mitch grabbed the hand of the next person in line. Lester's face turned red, and a vein looked like it was about to pop. Mitch watched out of the corner of his eye as he stomped off. *Lord, I answer to you. Not to Lester. Please get me through this.*

Chapter Ten

GROUNDED

Monday, September 16th

No sign of Lester McDonald, and it was after 3:00 P.M. on Monday afternoon. Mitch had tossed and turned for hours as he tried to sleep on Sunday night. *Why is it that I know I did the right thing, and yet I'm letting him get under my skin? I wonder if he forgot. Surely not.* He turned to his computer and clicked on the inbox. He had an e-mail from Pastor Benton.

> From: Marc Benton
> Sent: Monday, September 16, 1:05 PM
> To: Mitch Walker
> Subject: RE: Leadership Discussion Continued
> Mitch,
> I pray for you daily but want you to know that I was prompted in an even greater way to lift you up as you prepared for services yesterday. I am looking so forward to meeting with you again in a couple of weeks.
> Here is a question I want you to respond to: What is it that you have observed in leaders in the past that motivated or inspired you to do more than you would have done apart from their leadership?
> Marc

Mitch thought for a moment, hit the reply button, and began typing.

> From: Mitch Walker
> Sent: Monday, September 16, 3:13 PM
> To: Marc Benton
> Subject: RE: Leadership Discussion Continued
> Marc;
> I appreciate your prayers. I feel good about yesterday although I do have at least one member who apparently did not receive my message well.

In response to your question:
  –When the leader is enthusiastic
  –When the leader is personally committed or leads the way
  –When the leader expresses appreciation. (That always makes me want
    to do more for a leader)
Is that what you were looking for?
Mitch

Mitch hit the send button and went on to the next e-mail. No sooner had he sent the e-mail than his cell phone started ringing. He looked at the caller ID and noticed it was his neighbor, Randall. "Hey Randall, what's up, brother?"

"Mitch, have you been out and about today?"

"A little bit. Why? What's up?"

Randall was clearly upset. "It's Wyatt. I just found out that he skipped school today. I am going to kill him. And when I get done, I'm going to ground him for life!"

Mitch understood that Randall was talking out of frustration and probably had no idea how ridiculous that statement was. "Randall, I haven't seen him, but I sure will keep my eye out. Do you need me do anything?"

"No. Just pray right now and keep your eyes peeled. We'll track him down."

"I'll check back with you after a while."

"Thanks, Mitch."

Mitch decided to rush through a couple more tasks and head out. Maybe he could track down Wyatt and get him to his dad. *It's so sad that Wyatt cannot see the pain he is causing his dad. Fortunately, he has a father concerned enough to look for him.* As Mitch worked at his desk, he was reminded of the parables that Jesus told in Luke 15. One was about a lost sheep, another about a lost coin, and the other about the prodigal son. In each, something of value was lost. In each, there was great rejoicing when that which was lost was found. In each, persistence resulted in finding that which was lost. In the midst of his concern for Wyatt and his dad, God spoke to Mitch's heart. *Are you concerned for the ones I love who are lost? Are you seeking to rescue them?*

Ouch. Lord, forgive me and teach me. Mitch winced. *I know I have a lot of growing to do.*

Mitch did not drive straight home but headed to the high school and started to drive in and out of streets, hoping that he might spot Wyatt. As he passed by the Three Branches apartment complex, he noticed a group of teens milling around a small courtyard area off to the side. He pulled in for a closer inspection but did not see Wyatt. However, he thought perhaps he recognized the teen who had been skateboarding with him a few days back. He parked and approached the group, feeling more out of place than he could have imagined.

"Hey man, can I talk to you a second?" He was looking at Wyatt's friend and wondered how he could talk with him off to the side.

"Are you a cop?" Wyatt's friend asked.

"No, I'm just looking for someone and thought maybe you could help."

The teen looked at his friends, unsure how to respond, and finally moved toward Mitch. He smelled as if he had just come out of a smoke factory. "Hey, listen, I think I saw you the other day with Wyatt and was just curious if you know where he is. His dad is a little concerned."

"Who are you?"

"I'm his neighbor and a friend just like you."

The teen smirked at that comment, but did not hesitate to respond, "Yeah, he was with us but headed home about twenty minutes ago."

"Did he walk, or was he riding with someone?"

"He walked. Or skateboarded, that is. I know he had it with him anyhow."

"What's your name?"

"My friends call me Dizzy."

"Thanks, Diz. You've been a big help. You take care."

"Yeah. Sure."

Mitch made a beeline for his house, but never saw Wyatt along the way. He pulled into the driveway, parked, went straight over to the neighbor's house, and rang the doorbell. Wyatt's older sister Misty opened the door. She was a sophomore at the community college in Rock Springs, commuting from Stanton. Misty had babysat Haley on several occasions over the past two years. Although she did not attend Stanton Community Church, she was a committed Christian and she attended a church plant over in Southerland that reached out to young adults.

"Hey, Misty. Did Wyatt ever make it home?"

"Oh, yeah. He made it all right. I don't think he had any idea that Mom and

Dad knew that he skipped school today. You may want to go put some ear plugs in because the beat-down is about to begin." She was grinning as siblings are prone to do when their guilty counterparts get caught. Mitch knew she was exaggerating. "Beatings" were not how Randall and Michelle, Wyatt's mom, handled things.

"Tell your dad I dropped by. I'll lift Wyatt up in prayer," Mitch said with a knowing grin about what must be happening in another part of the house.

"You have a good evening, pastor."

"You too, Misty."

Randall called later that evening and brought Mitch up to speed on the "beat-down," as Misty had referred to it. Wyatt was grounded for a month, allowed to go no place but school and church. In addition, he would not be playing, listening, or talking on anything that was electronic. Mitch laughed when Randall told him that he decided to "go Amish on him." Mitch asked if Wyatt's grounding would prevent them from playing backyard basketball. Randall assured him that any time he would give to Wyatt would be appreciated and would not violate his "Amish grounding."

Chapter Eleven

The Doghouse

Tuesday, September 17th

Mitch hunkered down in his newly-made man cave. He had converted the extra bedroom into a makeshift pastor's study by pulling in a table (to serve as a desk for now) along with several versions of the Bible, some devotional and reference books, and his computer, which he used for his sermon prep and Bible studies. Nothing in the room would distract him, except a window that overlooked the backyard. The benefits of the view outweighed his concerns about distractions. Being able to pause and look out for a few moments or simply to have a sense of the day's weather would serve as a way to refresh occasionally.

Today he spent the first couple of hours in his new place of solitude before heading over to the church to check in with Miss Jerri. Once he arrived, he chatted with her for a few minutes, then made his way into his church office. *Let's fire up the computer and get going.* He planned to spend a couple of hours here before going to lunch and then taking two hours he had blocked off to begin his outreach commitment. He still had heard nothing from Lester McDonald. *Lord, is this a miracle? Did you shut him down?*

There's another e-mail from Pastor Benton. Oh yeah. We were interacting about leadership and what motivates. He skipped the other e-mails and went straight to Pastor Benton's first.

From: Marc Benton
Sent: Tuesday, September 17, 10:44 AM
To: Mitch Walker
Subject: RE: Leadership Discussion Continued
Mitch,
Good response. Let me add some more to your list from my experience:
   –Vision (It is hard to follow a leader that fails to express where he is going.)

-Fails forward (Everyone fails. Effective leaders are resilient, and that inspires people.)

-Prayer (Acts 4:31- "And when they had prayed, the place where they were assembled was shaken; they were all filled with the Holy Spirit and began to speak the word of God with boldness.")

Add those to your list of enthusiasm, appreciation, and personal commitment. Do you recall how you initially proposed that leadership is being a good example? I want to stress again how important that is but hope you see that simply being an example is not enough. I want you to take what others do to motivate you and use them as tools to inspire others. You will not find a weak leader at the helm of an effective evangelistic church. God uses men. He used Moses to bring the Hebrews out of Egypt. Yes, he could have done it with the spoken word, but God is gracious in using men. Let Him use you. Grow in your relationship with Him through your daily walk and grow in your skills by applying what you learn as a leader. Are you reading that book?

I'm looking forward to being with you again in two weeks on October 1. We are going to begin working through the six essentials of the Net Effect:

-Praying for the lost

-Personal Evangelism Equipping

-Proclamation of the Gospel Message

-Event Evangelism

-Service/Ministry Evangelism

-Team Evangelism

Note: We may or may not tackle these in the order listed.

Have a blessed week!

Marc

Later That Day

"I'll have the chicken Philly with cheese, mushrooms, and onions." Mitch placed his order in the sandwich shop located on the corner unit of the string of storefronts that made up the business section of Stanton. He referred to this area affectionately as the Stanton Mall. The ten units contained half of the stores in town. A liquor store was also located just beyond the city limits, and Mitch made a point to look straight ahead when passing lest he see someone entering or leaving that would taint his estimation of their character.

"Do you want that toasted?" replied the tall, ponytailed lady in a baseball cap who was taking his order.

I wonder if she is the owner. "That sounds good." Mitch completed his order and paid before turning to scan the small shop. At least a dozen people were seated at the tables with the black and white checkered tablecloths. Mitch did not know any of the customers personally, though he had seen several around town in the past. Going out to lunch was a luxury for Mitch. He and Melinda seemed always to be cutting their finances close, and when he was in town, he would ordinarily go home and have a sandwich with his beloved.

Mitch was on a mission today, however. His intention was to visit all of the stores on the block and introduce himself to as many people as possible. He knew that the first step to opening up doors to share the gospel would be to establish relationships. He smiled at a little boy two tables over who was enjoying a chocolate ice cream. It looked as if more ice cream was smeared on his face than had made it into his mouth. Mitch, enjoying his sandwich, noticed that no additional customers were in the line at the moment. He left his half-eaten sandwich sitting in the basket in which it had been served in order to take advantage of the lull in business to talk with the lady who had served him.

"Excuse me. Ma'am, are you the owner?"

"I certainly am. My name is Dana Hutchison. Can I help you?"

"Sure, my name is Mitch...Mitch Walker, and I'm the pastor at the Stanton Community Church north of here. First, I wanted to compliment you on your sandwiches. The food here is great."

"Thank you so much. I hope you'll tell your friends," she replied with smile of pride as she straightened the baseball cap.

Mitch asked her about the shop and how she came to start the business. She responded enthusiastically to his interest in what she had done. He discovered a few facts about her family before they were interrupted by the bell that rang as a new customer entered the front door. "I've got an idea," Mitch said before giving way. "I would love to introduce you to my congregation on a Sunday morning. I'll take a moment and tell them how great your sandwiches are if you will join us for worship one morning."

"I may have to take you up on that. That is so sweet. What time do your services start?"

Mitch gave her the information before returning to his table to finish the last few bites of the sandwich. He waved and smiled at Dana as he exited and headed next door to the hardware store. He spent the next two hours introducing himself to the owners and managers of the various businesses. Some, like Dana, were enthusiastic, while others seemed to be bothered at the intrusion. Mitch stayed positive in either case and noted as he made his way back down the sidewalk toward his car that none of those he met attended his church. *I'll do this again in a couple of weeks.* Mitch decided that he would drive to some of the other businesses scattered throughout town tomorrow and do the same thing.

Mitch drove back to the church and went to his office to check messages and e-mails. Miss Jerri had already left for the day. If all went well, he would be home in plenty of time for dinner and would go next door to cheer up Wyatt with some backyard hoops.

The next ninety minutes were spent calling all of the church's Bible study leaders. He spoke to as many as possible and left messages for the others to simply express appreciation for their leadership. He was committed to doing this on a regular basis as an application of the lessons in influence and motivation that he was recently learning from Pastor Benton. Some were very appreciative while others were somewhat measured in their response, perhaps sensing that his call was coming from the same place as last Sunday's sermon.

The phone rang as he was walking out the door to head home. *Should I answer it? I'd better, just in case it's an emergency.* It was Deacon Bruce Rollins, and he was emphatic that he needed to come by immediately. Mitch knew if he did not say yes, the tension would deepen even more over the fact that he had failed to attend the Rollins daughter's graduation party last spring. Of course, "immediately" turned into a forty-five minute wait. *Maybe this won't take long.* Finally, Rollins arrived and sat down in the chair across from Mitch's desk.

"Pastor, I think we need to discuss your sermon last Sunday. I've thought a lot about it, and you insulted a lot of people."

A lot of people? I'll bet Lester McDonald is what he means by a lot of people. "I'm sorry, Bruce. It was not my intent to offend anyone. God has been working in my life and convicting me of some changes that I need to make, and I thought it made sense to put them on the table."

Rollins was clearly angry as he continued to grill Mitch over the final points of Sunday's sermon. "You said that you would not feel compelled to accept every invitation for the various activities. I don't know what's new about that. You already missed my daughter's graduation party, and you know how important that was to our family. We called you here as our pastor, and we expect you to be there for us when we need you."

Mitch whispered a prayer asking God for wisdom in his response. He leaned forward with his elbows on the desk. "Bruce, first of all I have already apologized for that. Secondly, I was out of town with my family, and for that I do not apologize. Thirdly, I told you that we were not going to be there soon after we received the invitation. My wife did send a gift, and I am sorry we had to miss, but I need time with my family." Mitch could not believe he was having this discussion almost four months later. The conversation went round and round for the next hour and a half. Mitch could not seem to say anything that would satisfy Mr. Rollins, and he got an earful of complaints. Mitch did pray at the conclusion of the meeting, but the mood remained tense in spite of it.

On the drive home, he was glad that he had kept his composure, but he felt as if he had been beaten up. *I have a feeling that the next deacon's meeting is going to be interesting. Maybe I'll be called to serve in Hawaii by then.*

Haley grabbed her dad by the waist as he entered the front door. *Finally, I'm in a place where I am appreciated.* He hugged Haley and asked her about her day before heading into the kitchen. "Hey, darling, how has your day been?" he asked Melinda as he entered. As she turned, he could tell that something was wrong.

"It would have been great if everyone had been here for dinner. We waited almost an hour before I had to re-heat it. I called your cell three times and texted, and you never answered. And it's not like it's the first time."

Uh-oh. Mitch knew he had blown it. He had not anticipated spending well over two hours longer at the church because of Bruce Rollins before going home, so he had not called, and he had silenced his phone to minimize interruptions. He and Melinda did not fight often, and this would not be a fight. It would be a massacre. He knew she had every right to be upset and went into full apology mode. But he knew that she would feel compelled to have her say before receiving it. *No hoops with Wyatt tonight,* Mitch thought. *I am in the doghouse big time. Man did this day go downhill fast.*

Chapter Twelve

New Focus

Friday, September 20th

"My little girl can shoot better than that!" The trash talk commenced as Mitch made his way around the hedges to get to the paved area where Wyatt was shooting the basketball at a backboard with a chain net that made a unique clanking sound as the ball traveled through the hoop. He and Wyatt had played for about thirty minutes the previous day and had scheduled this showdown once they had finished. Mitch had kept the conversation light the previous day but hoped he could get more serious this time. He recalled a season of mild rebellion in his own life as he was navigating his way through his teen years. Hopefully the connection they had made over the past two years would pay off, and Mitch could steer him in the right direction.

"Then, obviously, she could beat you too since I have your number every time we play." You would think that Wyatt and Mitch were both undefeated the way they talked to each other, but the fact was that Mitch won more than his share of the times they competed.

"What's the game today? Around the World? One-on-One? Double-Clutch? Horse? You name it because I'm feeling good." Mitch bent down to make sure his shoes were tied nice and tight.

"I'm thinking Horse," Wyatt replied. The object of the game was to make a shot. Your opponent had to make the exact same shot or, beginning with *H,* he would be assigned a letter until one of the competitors missed five shots, to spell out *HORSE.* Since his "Amish grounding" left him with no place to go, Wyatt must have been spending a good bit of time practicing because he won the first two games handily.

"OK," Mitch said, "Here's the one that really counts. This one is for the world championship of the neighborhood."

"What're we playin' for?"

An idea suddenly occurred to Mitch. "If you can beat me, Wyatt...," he thought for a moment. "I will go buy you ice cream, or a hamburger, or whatever special treat you want, and bring it back, and serve it to you like I'm your butler."

"That's good because I'm feelin' a little hungry. What if you beat me?"

"If I win, you have to give me a full forty-five minute pastoral counseling session where you answer every question I ask." Mitch said it with a playful grin on his face.

Wyatt pondered his choices for a moment. "You're on."

Mitch was down three baskets before two minutes had passed. He was at H-O-R, and if he missed two more for the S and E, he would be heading to a store.

"Three point shot from the top of the key." Wyatt launched the shot, but it hit the front of the rim and fell short. That put Mitch in control. He shot a left-handed lay-up that Wyatt could not match. *Maybe I've spotted a weakness* Mitch thought. "Left-handed hook shot," he called out. Wyatt did not even come close. After a miss by Mitch, Wyatt took back control and nailed a long jump shot that Mitch could not match to make it H-O-R-S for Mitch and H-O for Wyatt. If Mitch failed to match one more of Wyatt's shots, the game would be over.

Following a missed shot by Wyatt, Mitch took control once again and went back to the left-handed lay-up. Wyatt missed again. Likewise for a left handed hook shot, and now both were tied with H-O-R-S. The next one who could not match shots would lose. Mitch walked out to the foul line. "Left-handed free throw," he called out.

"No way you're making that," Wyatt scoffed.

Mitch surprised himself as the ball made the metallic swish through the chain netting. Wyatt went to the line and readied the ball on the palm of his right hand. It was an air ball meaning that it did not even get to the basket. Mitch extended both arms in the air like a world champion. "Great game! I'll tell you what. Since you won the first two, I'll still go get you an ice cream, but I won't serve it to you like your butler—and you still owe me a counseling session."

"Oh, great," Wyatt said as he stood there with his hands on his hips.

The conversation was not as painful as Wyatt thought it was going to be. In the backyard enjoying the treats that Mitch had retrieved, the conversation was trivial for only the first ten minutes or so. The relationship that Mitch had established with Wyatt over the previous two years seemed to be paying off. He actually opened up as the conversation progressed. Mitch could tell that Wyatt had a good heart and that the Lord was already working on him. He actually seemed genuinely repentant and opened up about the past few months of his life. He promised Mitch that he was going to refocus on doing the right things and getting back on track spiritually. Mitch was wise enough to know that only time would tell if he was sincere or not.

"Tell me about your friend, Dizzy." Mitch asked, as he crumpled the ice cream wrapper and rolled it into a ball.

"I've known him a long time. We used to be in the same class back a few years ago in elementary school. He moved away for a couple of years and then came back last year. We kind of connected back up I guess."

"Does his family go to church anywhere?"

"I doubt it. He's not exactly a churchgoing type of person."

"Man, I don't know what it is, but I really feel impressed to start praying for him. I'm going to be praying for God to open up his heart and asking God to use you to be a good influence in his life."

"Yeah. Sure." Wyatt replied without much conviction.

"But you've got to start flying straight, Wyatt. I know your heart's in the right place, but you've got to be real careful about your choices. You can't jump at everything in front of you. You've been sliding off course, and you know it."

Wyatt would not even look up. He and Mitch had built trust not only from a pastoral perspective but more importantly as friends. Though it was a bit awkward with an ice cream wrapper balled up in his hand and a basketball under his right foot, Mitch bowed and prayed for Wyatt to grow stronger in his faith and for Dizzy to come to faith.

Tuesday, October 1st

The autumn months have a different feel. The leaves are beautiful as they turn from green to red, yellow, and brown. From higher ground, the view looks like a painting by the hand of God. The heat of the summer has passed, the mornings have a chill, and football season is in full swing. Mitch drove through the rain on the way to Southerland for his second coaching session with Pastor Benton. He had a lot to share and did not know how it would be possible in one hour.

The coffee was even better this time, with the cooler temperatures and the rainy weather outside. Mitch jumped right in, telling Pastor Benton about the mixed response to his intentional expressions of appreciation to his leaders, the visits to local businesses that he was making to establish relationships as part of his outreach commitment, the response to his sermon in which he drew boundaries to protect his priorities, and, most recently, two Sundays ago, the visit to the church of Dana

Hutchison from the sandwich shop. Mitch had introduced her to the congregation and "she actually came back with a friend the following Sunday." Mitch shared excitedly. Although none of the other store owners or managers had visited, he could see a difference as he went to many a second time to talk for a few minutes, as time permitted. He also shared about the first brief meeting of the evangelism leadership team although no real plans came out of the first gathering. Pastor Benton encouraged him that teams ordinarily took a meeting or two to lay some groundwork before real action would take place.

"Tell me about the prayer ministry of your church," Pastor Benton asked as he wiped pastry crumbs from the corner of his mouth.

"We have a prayer service on Wednesday nights," Mitch replied. "It was established well before I arrived, and we have continued to meet. About one-fourth of our Sunday morning crowd attends. We take prayer requests during the first half, and the second half I lead a Bible study."

"Anything else?"

"I know our Bible study groups take prayer requests each week, and we pray in our services each time we meet."

Pastor Benton rubbed his face as if he were pondering which way to go. "When you take prayer requests in your prayer service or in the Bible study groups, have you ever audited the nature of the requests?"

"What do you mean by audited?"

"Think through for a moment the different categories of prayer requests that are received. Give me some examples of what you hear."

Mitch thought for a moment. "People ask for prayer for the sick, for people in the hospital, those having surgeries, people who have been involved in some kind of accident, and people who have had deaths in their families."

"What else?"

"We pray for missionaries, church needs, community issues, and we are adamant about praying for our troops."

Mitch opened his notepad as Pastor Benton replied. "That's all good. I'm sure there are other categories you could come up with if we pressed forward, but I think you have given me enough to show you something that can help your congregation."

"Let's hear it." Mitch said with his pen in hand ready to jot down some notes.

"Which category gets the most attention if you were to break it down by percentage of time spent?"

"That's easy. A large majority of the prayer requests are for those who are sick. I would say easily 75 percent have something to do with illness."

"That's not a big surprise, and I've found that to be typical. One thing I have found to be true about congregations that are effective in evangelism is that they are intentional about shifting the balance. You remember that intentionality was a big theme of our previous discussion. Think back to your last prayer service. How many people did you pray for because they do not have a relationship with Jesus? Did you and your group pray for specific people to come to faith in Jesus?"

"I never thought about that. I don't think we have intended to leave them out. But come to think of it, the answer would have to be zero."

"You will find almost without exception that congregations that are seeing many people come to faith in Jesus are intentional in praying for the lost or those who don't have a relationship with Jesus, and they pray for them by name."

Mitch was writing as Pastor Benton continued. Mitch looked up and asked, "Isn't that risky? What if one of the people we are praying for shows up to attend the service?"

"Well first, would that not be an answer to prayer? Look Mitch, you don't put up a banner over the list saying *Lost Heathens We Are Praying For*. If they are on a list you simply call it a *friend's list* or something like that. If they want to know why they are on it, then you share that you and your members pray for their friends regularly and feel honored to pray for the person who is asking."

"I'll be honest, Marc. This has not even been on our radar."

"I had a professor say something when I was in seminary that really stuck with me. He said that we often pray more fervently to keep the sick, our Christian relations, out of heaven a little longer than to prevent the lost from going to hell for eternity."

Mitch felt he had been hit by a brick. "Wow. That is powerful. You know that is true. If a Christian does not get better, then the worst case scenario is they end up in heaven. A person that does not have a relationship with Jesus is in a much more severe situation, even if they are in perfect health." Mitch thought back to his backyard basketball encounter with Wyatt two weeks earlier. "Isn't it great how God brings things together? Just two weeks ago I was talking with my neighbor's son about some challenges he is going through and a friend of his who is not a Christian. The Lord prompted me, and we prayed for his friend right there in his back yard. I guess the Lord is trying to teach me something here."

Mitch made several notes as the conversation continued including a short list of possible ideas for implementation of what he was learning.

1. *Brainstorm with evangelism leadership team ways to get our congregation praying for the lost and unchurched.*
2. *Ask James Flynn to serve as Prayer Leader with specific focus on leading groups to pray for the lost and unchurched.*
3. *Ask James to set up rotation of people to pray in prayer rooms while I am preaching each Sunday morning.*
4. *Ask Bible Study leaders to add category of praying for non-believers each Sunday.*
5. *Share what I learned with congregation when I lead next prayer service and get their input.*
6. *Make a personal list myself and begin praying daily for people who do not know Jesus as Savior.*
7. *Have someone make a prayer board to bring into our prayer service each week with three categories from left to right: those we are praying for, those we have invited and/or witnessed to, and those who have come to faith in Jesus.*
8. *Consider having forty days of prayer emphasis with special attention given to the lost and unchurched.*
9. *Preach a sermon on the importance of praying for the lost and unchurched.*
10. *Lead the congregation to write down names of friends and family who do not have a relationship with Jesus and to carry the list in their Bibles and pray for those people.*

Mitch's mind was racing on the rainy drive back, although he held the speed of his car to under fifty miles an hour on account of the slick driving conditions. Now he had more ideas than he could possibly implement and he was beginning to feel a little overwhelmed. The radio was off and he was deep in thought. It was as if the Lord spoke to him very clearly. *Who said you have to do it all, Mitch? Just take two or three ideas that you can apply quickly and then go back to the list in a couple of months and see if you can integrate another one.* Mitch decided that as soon as he got back that he would create a master list on his computer; then he could simultaneously implement a few ideas and have the others reserved in a place he could return to easily. *Lord, show me the way.*

Chapter Thirteen

Across the Street

Wednesday, October 2nd

"Thanks for taking time out of your schedules to meet with me again," Mitch said to the four members of the newly formed evangelism leadership team. Sitting immediately to his left was James Flynn, consistently one of his best encouragers and prayer warriors. Tim Minor was sitting beside him with his tablet open, scanning something that Mitch could not see. Across the table sat his wife's best friend, Carly Rooks. Finally, to his right was Kris Kimmons, smiling as she always seemed to do. She was one of the happiest people Mitch had ever met. Nothing seemed to get her down.

The prayer service had ended only fifteen minutes ago. As Mitch had led the congregation to call out the names of friends and family who did not have a relationship with Jesus, he noticed a couple of people actually tearing up as the names were offered. The prayer time could not have been more meaningful as James Flynn prayed aloud for their salvation and for the congregation to be sensitive to opportunities to minister and reach out to each one mentioned.

After sharing much of what he had taken away in his last meeting with Pastor Benton, he turned to James. "We really need someone who will take this issue of prayer for the lost and unchurched and lead us to be more strategic and consistent, while keeping the correct balance. James and I have talked about this, and he has agreed to take on this role." Each of the other team members nodded affirmatively as Tim patted James on the back.

Tim added, "I don't know anyone more qualified than James here."

Carly spoke up following the congratulatory affirmations. "Mitch, could we pause and pray right now? I have always been burdened for my mother and tonight's prayer service really spoke to me. My mom does not know the Lord, and I have not been a very good witness to her." Carly paused with tears in her eyes, but maintained her composure as she continued. Kris reached over and placed her hand on Carly's arm in a supportive gesture. "Her name is Wilma Townsend. My dad passed away a few years ago, and I don't think he knew the Lord, either.

We did not go to church when I was growing up, and our family was not spiritual in any way. I came into a relationship with the Lord through the witness and love of friends from school. I love my mom so much, and it breaks my heart that she does not have a relationship with Jesus like I do. I've tried to share with her a few times, but she just will not listen to what I have to say." Carly started to lose her composure at this point. Her heart was clearly broken for her mom.

Mitch stood up and walked over to stand between Kris and Carly, placing a hand on each of their shoulders. "Why don't we pray for her right now? Our Heavenly Father, we come before you this evening in the sweet heavenly name of Jesus to pray for Carly's mom…"

Monday, October 7th

Bitter—Sweet. That was the best way that Mitch could describe what he was experiencing as he sat in his office on Monday afternoon. It was sweet because of the spiritual renewal that he was experiencing in his own heart. His personal time with the Lord each day was more consistent and more meaningful than he could ever remember. The study time in his office at home had minimized the interruptions by at least eighty percent, and he could feel it as he prepared and as he preached his sermons. He was not spending a full four hours doing outreach as he had wanted to do, but he knew he was averaging almost three hours each week, and those were three more than he had been spending before adjusting his priorities. He was also beginning to see some rewards for his labors that he was anxious to share with Pastor Benton.

However, there was the bitter side also. Lester McDonald would not even exit the door where Mitch stood to greet the congregation as they left each Sunday following services. He would go to his Bible study group and sit in his usual place either pretending not to pay attention or looking at Mitch with a smirk on his face. He had not said a word to Mitch since their exchange a few weeks before, following Mitch's sermon on changing his priorities. The morale in the church was strangely mixed between an atmosphere of anticipation on one hand and tension on the other. It was clear that McDonald was talking, although not to his pastor. *Why is it that the harder I am trying to lead this church to be what God desires, the more opposition I seem to get?*

I need to shoot Pastor Benton a note and tell him about yesterday.

From: Mitch Walker
Sent: Monday, October 7, 4:04 PM
To: Marc Benton
Subject: Update on Stanton Community Church

Marc,

I trust you had a blessed Sunday. Thanks once again for meeting with me each month. God is really using our time together to stretch me, and I already feel I have grown more in my leadership in the past couple of months than I can ever recall.

Let me share some good news. Do you remember Dana Hutchison from the sandwich shop? Once she visited, she never missed a Sunday. I found out as I talked with her further that she is a solid believer but had never connected with a church since moving into this area. She joined our church yesterday along with her husband and two children. She said that her ten-year-old son had been asking a lot of spiritual questions since they started attending and invited me over to interact with him. He committed his life to follow Jesus, and he will be baptized on Sunday!

BTW: At least three other store owners or managers have visited our services since I started spending time in the community each week. Each of the three attended only once, but I expressed appreciation and invited them back anytime. I am most excited about the fact that the high school football coach invited me to come by and share a devotion with the team next week, and we are discussing the possibility of my serving as the team chaplain next year. I'm a football fanatic to begin with, and this would be a great way to connect with students as well as many of the coaches. Please be praying for me about this.

I want to tell you about one other person I have been trying to witness to. My neighbor's son, Wyatt, went through a rough stretch recently, and the Lord used me to help him in getting through it. He has a friend named Dizzy (at least that's what they call him). I've tried to share with him a couple of times. He is somewhat resistant, but at least respectful. Please be praying for him and for me as I continue to reach out.

Finally, we have a deacon's meeting coming up this Sunday. Some of our members are not happy about the way I am spending my time, and I have a feeling it will be brought up. Pray for God to give me the wisdom to respond appropriately.

I look forward to our next meeting in November.

Mitch

PS: We are really integrating prayer for the lost and unchurched into what we do and had another great evangelism team meeting recently.

Tuesday, October 8th

"I'm not sure how this is going to go, James, but I sure appreciate you coming with me." In addition to spending much of his outreach time in the past few weeks visiting the businesses in town to connect with the store owners and managers, seeking to build a better relationship with the community leaders, Mitch had also met the local police force, all three of them, along with the school principals and the high school football coach. The coach turned out to be a strong Christian, and Mitch was excited about the prospects of getting involved with the team as the chaplain.

"What do you want me to do when we get there?" James asked.

"I don't really have an organized plan. Just follow my lead." Mitch had divided his personal outreach efforts into three components at this point. He had a list of people he was praying for; he was personally making contact with those guests who had attended on Sunday; and he was spending almost three hours each week casually visiting local businesspeople and others. The number of first-time guests attending each Sunday was only two or three, but that was more than had been visiting each month before he began to shift his focus.

Stanton Community Church was located in a nice neighborhood, where you could see a blend of two-story brick houses on generous lots interspersed with subdivisions where each house sat on its half-acre. Within a three-mile radius of the church could be found other older, white-frame houses, some dating back almost one hundred years. Stanton also had a trailer park and a couple of apartment complexes.

Directly across the street from the church stood an old white wood-framed home with blue shutters and a porch that wrapped around three sides. Three cars sat in the driveway, one of which appeared to have been sitting idle for years. Mitch had often seen people going in and out of the house, but had never gone over to meet them. The front porch was painted grey and it squeaked as James and Mitch stepped up and made their way to the front door. Mitch rang the door-bell. Almost a minute passed without a response. They could hear a television, so Mitch felt certain that someone was home. He rang the doorbell again and knocked on the front door for good measure.

"Can I help you?" A petite lady who appeared to be in her seventies greeted the men.

"Yes ma'am. My name is Mitch Walker, and this is James Flynn. I'm the pastor of the church across the street, and we just wanted to come by and introduce ourselves."

Suddenly a dog came running out the door past the lady's feet, startling them. "Buster, you get back in here." The dog pawed at James' legs and yelped happily as if he were glad to meet a new playmate. She reached down and grabbed the dog, holding tightly with both arms. "I guess by now you can tell he doesn't bite," she said as the dog happily began licking her face. "Lamar. Lamar," she shouted toward a room off to the side. "We've got company."

They were quickly joined at the door by a man whom Mitch assumed was her husband. The couple stood together on the front porch as the elderly gentle-men looked Mitch and James up and down. They reintroduced themselves and shook his hand. Lamar was indeed her husband and they discovered that their son, daughter-in-law, and three grandchildren all lived in the house.

"I've been living here for over four years, and you are the only person from that church to ever walk over here and introduce yourself," Lamar said.

"I am so sorry," Mitch replied. "I'm not making excuses for anybody. I've only been pastor here for two years, but it should not have taken me this long to get over here. All I can do is ask you to forgive me. We want to be good neighbors. "

The lady's name turned out to be Belinda. She spoke up. "We used to go to church when we lived in Cochran, but when we moved up here with the kids, Lamar had some health issues and we just never got back to going. Our grandkids sure need it, I'll tell you, that's for sure. We sure do miss our church back home."

Mitch and James stood out on the porch and talked for almost half an hour. *I cannot believe that I drove past this house day after day for almost two years and never took time to stop and introduce myself. These are some of the nicest people I've ever met and they seem like old friends.* Mitch hoped they would come and visit now that the door was open, and he promised to come back and meet the rest of the family.

The men then walked to six other homes in the neighborhood. No one was home at three of them. They got a very icy reception at two others and felt as if they had intruded on someone. However, they were gratified to meet yet another man who was about as friendly as he could be. He was a member of a church from another denomination but he seemed as appreciative as if his own pastor had come by to visit.

All seven homes were within walking distance of the church. "I was really nervous about this," Mitch confessed to James as they made their way back. "We should have taken something we could have left on the doors of those where no one was home so that they would have at least known that we came by."

"I guess if we are supposed to love our neighbors we can start with our neighbors," James said as they stepped back into the church parking lot.

"I don't know if this is the most effective way to do outreach, but I think it was worth it just for the conversation we had with Lamar and Belinda."

"I agree. I'm going to add their family to my prayer list."

"Thanks for helping me out, James. I'll see you tomorrow night at the prayer service.

Chapter Fourteen

Gutter-Cleaning

Saturday, October 12th

It was rare for Mitch to have an entire day with absolutely nothing formal on his agenda, and the Walker family planned to stay home and do as little as possible. In order to preserve their time together, he and Melinda had politely turned down some invitations to go to various activities, and he had asked the Lord to give them a day without distraction, so they could enjoy each other. Today would be all about family, Mitch had decided, and he would do his best to put church problems aside. He planned to grill out; he knew that he had to clean the gutters, which should take less than an hour; and he expected to watch a college football game in the evening. Anything else on the list of possibilities was a maybe.

Entering the kitchen, Mitch found Haley eating a bowl of cereal and Melinda at the sink rinsing a couple of dishes. He came up behind Melinda and kissed her on the back of the neck, not letting up until she squirmed and screamed for him to quit. "Stop, you're causing me to make a mess!"

"That's all right. Haley will clean it up," he replied.

"Uh-uh. No, I won't. I'm too short."

"You're not too short. You would just rather play than work," Mitch chided.

Suddenly Mitch fell forward and turned a somersault across the kitchen floor.

"What in the world are you doing?" Melinda asked. She looked at Mitch as if he had lost his mind.

"Hey girls, I just want you to always remember."

"Remember what?" Haley asked.

"That's how we roll in the Walker family, girls."

"You are crazy," Melinda said rolling her eyes at Mitch's corny attempt at humor. She secretly thought his humor was funny but, much like a teenager, would never let on. That is one of the things she loved about Mitch. He made her laugh and although he often had to be serious, he also knew how to have fun. He was a great dad and a loving husband. Mitch grabbed a bowl out of the cabinet, sat down at the table, and began to pour himself a bowl of cereal.

"Haley, what do you want to do today? Do you want me to start teaching you how to play basketball?"

"No, I want to play dolls together. Can we do a tea party, Daddy?"

"How about softball? You know I bought you a tee last Christmas, so you can start learning to hit."

"No. Tea party."

"Haley, have you ever thought about wrestling or karate, or at least croquet? You've got to give your ole dad *something*."

Melinda intervened. "Mitch, stop that. You know good and well she doesn't like those kinds of things."

"What about it, Haley? Tell your mom what Daddy's girl really likes."

"Tea party!"

"She's all girl, all right. OK, I'll come to your tea party as long as I don't have to change clothes."

"Yeaaaaah. Oh boy!" Haley said with excitement.

"Let me get going and clean the gutters out first. When I get finished and have a chance to clean up, we can have the tea party.

Melinda grinned. She loved to see Mitch giving Haley this kind of attention. "You're not really going to get up on the roof this morning are you?" Melinda asked.

"Hey, I don't want to, but I didn't do it last year, and I recently noticed water overflowing in the front. I need to take care of it before it gets worse. I'm going to use the leaf blower, and hopefully that will make it quick."

"You just be careful. I don't like it when you climb on things. It makes me nervous."

"You worry too much."

"Can I watch?" Haley asked

"I don't know how much there is to watch, but sure. You'll just need to stand far enough back from the house."

Mitch, determined to get this task out of the way as early as possible to free up the rest of the day for family relaxation, went to the garage to get the leaf blower, a small garden spade in case he needed to dig something out of the gutter, a long extension cord for the blower, and the ladder. He placed the ladder against the house on the higher side of the yard, where the ground was closer to the roof line, giving him the best angle to make his ascent with all of his equipment. The house was a small ranch; thankfully none of the gutters were more than fifteen feet or so off of the ground.

"I'm going start in the back, Haley. You stand away so that none of the debris will fall on you." The blower did its work, causing the dry leaves to blow in the air and float down as a harmless leafy storm while Haley watched. *She sure is easy to entertain sometimes*, Mitch thought.

He made his way to the front in short order where the leaves were wet and packed more thickly. As he approached the troublesome spot he had noticed from the ground, he could see Randall next door working faithfully in his yard. They gave a wave to one another. At the trouble spot, the leaf blower suddenly seemed to be insufficient for the task. He walked back to the other side of the roof, careful to keep his footing, to get the small garden spade that he had set down near the ladder. Making his way back, he cautiously bent forward using the spade to dig through the muck of the leaves. Haley stood out front, watching and waiting for the leafy storm to begin again. Mitch hit something with the spade that was more solid than the decaying leaves. *What is that?* He noticed that the barely recognizable object had a furry tail. He realized that a squirrel had apparently died and found its resting place right there in the gutter.

"What is it Daddy?" Haley remarked at her father's unknown discovery.

Mitch reached down to grab the dead squirrel by the tail. No sooner had he lifted it up when it started flailing in his hand, catching him totally off guard. Without any forethought, he flung it toward the front yard to avoid being bitten. Haley screamed as she saw the furry animal flying through the air toward her. Before Mitch realized what was happening, his feet slipped. Suddenly he was sliding over the side, which made Haley shriek even louder. He somehow managed to brace the heel of his right foot in the gutter as his left leg dangled, and he was not sure if he was going to be able to hang on. Randall dropped his rake and began to sprint to Mitch's aid as Haley continued to scream.

Melinda burst out of the house to find her daughter screaming next to a dead squirrel, and, to her utter shock, her husband dangling over the edge of the roof.

"Mitch!" she cried out, running down the two steps of the porch toward him.

Randall was under Mitch, hoping to break his fall to some degree if he continued to slip over the edge. "Can you pull yourself up, Mitch?"

"I'm already cramping and I don't have anything to get a good grip on."

Randall reached up with his 6 6" frame and could almost touch Mitch's left foot. "Mitch, either I need to go get the ladder or you're going to have to let me break your fall as best I can." Before Mitch could reply his right foot was out of the gutter and he was sliding. Now Melinda joined Haley screaming as Mitch slipped over the edge. Fortunately, Randall broke his fall and Mitch was thankfully a good sixty pounds lighter than his human stunt cushion. Unfortunately, though, both men were lying in the yard with their wind knocked out, concerned about the possibility of broken bones.

"Mitch, Randall, are you all right?" Melinda asked as she ran to where they lay. Mitch's elbow was bleeding but he realized that Randall had taken the worst of it by breaking his fall. He turned his attention to his neighbor who was trying to clear his head. Fortunately the thick Bermuda grass had provided a small cushion. He collected himself shortly.

"I haven't taken a lick like that since I was in the Navy," he said, as he lay there taking inventory of his condition. Fortunately, neither man had any injury that required serious medical attention.

Relieved immediately, Melinda saw that Haley was still whimpering with the creature lying at her feet. Seeing that no serious damage had been done, she ran to comfort Haley. "What in the world happened?" Melinda asked turning toward the men with a still-horrified look as she cradled Haley.

"That stupid squirrel was lying in the gutter and I thought it was dead. I picked it up by the tail to clear the gutter and it went berserk so I launched it away from me."

"Well it's really dead now," Melinda said as she looked at the contorted body.

"Daddy killed the squirrel," Haley lamented.

Mitch struggled to his feet. Randall was still sitting on the grass trying to pull himself together. *It's not my fault he wasn't a flying squirrel*, Mitch thought. *He shouldn't have been passed out in my gutter. It's my gutter, not his.*

"Honey, it's OK," Mitch said to Haley as he got down on his knees, blocking her view of the deceased rodent. "He's in heaven with God now. God will take care of him."

Haley sniffled and looked at her dad with her big brown eyes as she asked, "What does God want with a dead squirrel?"

Mitch looked at Melinda, not knowing what to say. "I told you that you shouldn't be up on that roof," Melinda maintained. "You really could have been killed."

"Hey, apparently it was his time to go, not mine," Mitch replied as he turned and looked at the squirrel. Mitch had been lucky. Randall had been a little less lucky, but no serious damage was done. The squirrel—he had no luck at all. Mitch ended up doing one more thing on his family day that he would have never expected. Instead of having a tea party with Haley he led his first and only funeral service for a squirrel.

Chapter Fifteen

The Hot Seat

Sunday, October 13th

"I make a motion that we call the church together for a vote of confidence."

"I second it."

The deacons' meeting was going even worse that Mitch had anticipated. The Sunday morning service had opened with the baptism of Dana Hutchison's son. Ten first-time guests had been present. Mitch had never smiled as much as when Darlene led the congregation singing "I'll Fly Away," because he could not help but think of the poor squirrel that had flown to meet his Maker the day before. Lamar and Belinda were in attendance along with all three of their grandchildren, although Mitch noted that their son and daughter-in-law did not join them. Lamar had even asked about the process for joining their church as they were exiting, and they stayed around to discuss it with Mitch. *I cannot believe they wanted to join after only visiting once! God is really working in hearts around us.* They discussed their relationship to Jesus, and Mitch was moved by Lamar and Belinda's testimonies. The evangelism leadership team had met the previous Wednesday, and all had affirmed that they were seeing God's hand in lives more than ever since the focus of their prayers had changed.

"Any discussion?" Thomas McDonald asked, following the motion.

The motion had been made by Bruce Rollins, who was obviously unmoved by his conversation with Mitch a few weeks before. The second to the motion came from John Dollar who, as usual, seemed to be reveling in a good disagreement. Mitch pitied his poor wife. *At least I don't have to put up with him each and every day. That would drive me crazy.* Mrs. Dollar was somewhat quiet and reserved. Mitch assumed she had given up long ago trying to argue. He had heard John on more than one occasion having a one-sided debate with his wife as they made their way through the parking lot on the way to their car.

The other two deacons, James Flynn and Tim Minor, sat silently with grim expressions on their faces.

"Shouldn't the pastor step out of the room?" Bruce Rollins asked.

"If you have something to say, I think you should be willing to say it to his face," Tim responded.

Thomas turned to Mitch. "Do you want to hear this, or do you want to step out?"

"I'll stay. I want to hear what these men have to say."

"We don't need to have a vote of confidence." James Flynn was the first to speak up. "All you are going to do is stir up strife and dissension, and I don't have to tell you how ungodly that is. We need to get behind our pastor. If anything we need to go to the church with a unanimous endorsement and affirmation from the deacon board."

John Dollar weighed in. "There ain't no way we can do that. Everybody in this church is upset and dissatisfied with this man. We called him here to be our pastor, and now you can't even find him in his office half the time. He said straight up in his sermon a few weeks back that he was not going to do anything for any of the members anymore."

"Hang on a second. That is not what he said." Tim Minor could not let Dollar's comments continue. "He said he would not feel compelled to accept every invitation to every family gathering and that he would not necessarily visit relatives of our members in the hospitals particularly if it were clear that they had a pastor."

Dollar shot back, "Well, I know for a fact that he has been going all over town visiting with people who aren't even members here while we have elderly people who need attention. Let me remind you that they don't pay his salary. We do!"

"We called him to come to our church to be *our* minister," Rollins added. He was very animated. "We're not trying to be a big church; and, we don't want to be a big church. We like it exactly the way it is and the way it has always been. We've all been here for years, and we'll be here long after he is gone, and I personally think the sooner the better."

James Flynn could not believe what he was hearing and came to Mitch's defense. "Men, you better think long and hard about what you are saying. This man sitting over here is a godly man of prayer and a man of integrity. I have been blessed to spend a lot of time with him, and you are painting him as if he had committed some sin or done something underhanded or immoral. We have had more guests than ever attend our church in the past few weeks. We saw a young man baptized this morning as a testimony to what Jesus had done in his heart. We should be celebrating what Jesus is doing instead of debating how Mitch spends his time. The Bible does not describe a pastor as one who only ministers to the congregation. He is called to equip the saints to do ministry and to lead us to reach out to all nations."

Mitch was encouraged at the support he was getting from James and Tim, but equally disgusted at the accusations and the tone of Dollar and Rollins. He knew that a vote of confidence would not only cause strife in the congregation but could also mean that he would likely be dismissed as pastor if over half of the congregation agreed. He understood there were several who were offended at his change in course, but he also knew many who supported him. And of course the vast majority was oblivious that there was even an issue. How would Belinda and Lamar, Dana Hutchison, and some of the other members be affected if this turned into a public debate?

James and Tim had his back, but Bruce Rollins and John Dollar were both angry and loud. Thomas McDonald had not weighed in, but Mitch assumed he had already been given marching orders from his dad and didn't feel the need to add anything.

"I call for the question," Rollins said as the debate mercifully came to a conclusion. Mitch silently prayed hoping for a miracle. *I guess I can deliver pizzas for a while until we can figure something out.*

Thomas restated the motion. "The motion is to bring before the church a vote of confidence on our pastor at a called meeting next Sunday. I assume everyone understands that if he doesn't get at least fifty percent support in the vote that he will be asked to resign immediately. When I call your name say 'yes' if you want us to have the vote of confidence and say 'no' if you don't believe it is necessary. Bruce Rollins?"

"Yes."

"John Dollar?"

"Yes."

Mitch felt he was at tribal council on the hit television show *Survivor*. He reached for his immunity necklace and came up empty.

"James Flynn?"

"Absolutely not. I support my pastor one hundred percent."

"Tim Minor?"

"No."

The vote was tied two and two. Mitch's fate was in the hands of Lester McDonald's son. *Oh great. I'm about to get my torch snuffed*, Mitch thought as he continued to compare the experience to tribal council on the television show.

"I guess as chairman it comes down to me to break the tie," Thomas said as he rubbed his chin with his right hand. Although he had not weighed in during the debate, it seemed obvious to everyone what his vote would be. Bruce Rollins was grinning like he was about to win a million dollar sweepstakes. Mitch felt a trickle of sweat running down between his shoulder blades. You could hear a pin drop as Thomas appeared to be pausing for effect.

Let's get this over with. Mitch was thinking. *Why is he rubbing it in by inserting this unnecessary pause before pronouncing my sentence?*

"I vote no."

"What?" Rollins shouted. "You mean *yes*. You are *for* the motion!"

"The motion does not carry. No called meeting and no vote of confidence will be made."

James walked over and hugged Mitch as John Dollar went over to Thomas and started giving him an earful.

Mitch was still in shock as he drove home. He would have been shocked if the vote had gone against him just because he knew the potential damage the church would experience. Now he was in shock at the way Thomas had voted. Thomas took him by the hand as they were heading out and said, "Hang in there, Mitch. God is going to get you through this." Mitch could not believe it. *So much for making assumptions.* Rollins and Dollar were both out the door as soon as they had their say with Thomas. James, Tim, and Mitch stayed and prayed for more than half an hour. Although Thomas did not stay, he did not go rushing out the door with the first two.

Mitch was still praying when he pulled into his driveway. Having the support of Thomas McDonald was such an unexpected blessing. *I guess he and his dad don't necessarily see eye to eye on everything.* Mitch began praying for Thomas. Mitch knew that Lester McDonald was not going to be happy with his son.

Chapter Sixteen

MAXIMIZATION

Friday, October 18th

"Look who's been freed from bondage. Did your dad finally take the chains off of you, Wyatt?" Mitch had dropped by the church on Friday afternoon to retrieve a book he needed for sermon preparation. He ended up doing odds and ends in his office for almost an hour before heading out the side door. He was the only person there and was locking the door when he heard the skateboards rolling around the corner.

Wyatt had a big smile on his face. "Yeah, Dad let me off a week early for good behavior," he said playfully. Wyatt and Dizzy rolled right up to Mitch and skillfully kicked up their boards without even having to bend over to retrieve them. Mitch and Wyatt went back and forth for almost five minutes about who was dominating the routine basketball contests of late. Both tried to convince Dizzy that they were undefeated.

"Dizzy, have you given much thought to what I talked to you about last time?" Mitch had done his best to share the gospel with Dizzy, who had not been very responsive. However, Mitch noted, he was respectful. Daily, Mitch prayed that God would soften Dizzy's heart.

"You know, I just can't buy it all. You convinced me that Jesus is a historical figure, and I wasn't sure about that when I met you. I believe he was a good man and moral teacher. I just can't accept, though, that a man could come back from the dead like you say."

"Let me ask you a question then. Suppose you had a friend who conned a lot people out of millions of dollars. He looked innocent to everyone, but you knew the truth. You knew he was a thief and a liar. Unfortunately for you, one of those he robbed had connections with people who wanted to bring him down, so they kidnap you, tie you up, and put a gun to your head. You have a choice to make. Do you protect your friend, or do you tell the truth and preserve your own life?"

Dizzy looked down and contemplated how he should answer. "I dunno. I wouldn't wanna rat out my friend, but if you had a gun to my head I might not have a choice."

"Suppose there are ten of you who know the truth. Do you think all ten would be willing to die to keep the lie going, so your friend could be enriched while you all pay the price?"

"No, at least one would break down. That's for sure, out of ten people."

"I want you to think about something. Jesus had twelve apostles. They are also established historical figures. There is no doubt about that. You may remember that Judas hanged himself after betraying Jesus. We know that John lived into old age.... What happened to the other ten men?"

"You tell me."

"They were all executed. It's a historical fact. Some were crucified, and crucifixion was designed to be the most painful and brutal form of execution imaginable. Let's just take Simon Peter as an example. Suppose he knew along with all of the others that Jesus had conned everyone and the resurrection was faked. His executioners are about to nail him to a cross and crucify him like they did Jesus. It would be like putting a gun to his head but more brutal. If he is in his right mind, and he knows Jesus is a fake, then what is he going to do?"

The answer was logical to Dizzy as he responded, "He's gonna tell them to stop and admit that the resurrection was all fake and stuff instead of letting them hammer nails into his body."

"Absolutely! But what makes it more amazing is that not one, not two, but ten men died, and any one of them could have confessed that it was all faked. What did they have to gain by letting themselves be executed? That is…unless Jesus really was the Messiah and really had been resurrected. I believe what had sealed their faith was when Jesus ascended back into heaven forty days after the resurrection. This settled it if they had any doubts. Even if you argue that the resurrection could somehow be faked, there was no way Jesus could fake the ascension."

Dizzy was taking it all in. Still it was clear that he was not convinced. "I'm praying for you, Dizzy. I'm not trying to make you religious, but I do want you to know that you have been forgiven of your sins. You and I agreed last time that all men are sinners. If that is the case, then we all need a Savior. I believe that it's Jesus and I'm praying you will, too."

The conversation wound down, and Mitch prayed for the Holy Spirit to keep working in Dizzy's heart. He felt that something was happening, and that was a work of God right there, as far as he was concerned. Mitch started the car and noticed the guys were heading toward the highway. He pulled up and asked, "Do you guys need a ride?"

Wyatt yelled back, "No, we're good."

"You guys be careful out on that road. There's a lot of traffic on Fridays." *I'm beginning to sound like an old person,* Mitch thought. It didn't seem like that long ago when adults were yelling things like that at him.

Monday, November 4th

"What are the top-attendance Sundays in your church?" That was the question Pastor Benton put on the table as he and Mitch sipped on their coffee that pleasant November morning at their usual meeting place in Southerland. Mitch had brought Pastor Benton up to speed on the work of the evangelism leadership team and some of the successes and failures of the previous few weeks. They had already spoken on the phone the day after the deacons' meeting, or as Mitch had referred to it, as the "shootout at the doomsday corral." The older pastor had shared that he had gone through a similar experience many years before in his ministry, and he was very encouraging.

Mitch had his notepad in front of him as he pondered the question for a few moments. "Easter Sunday…Mother's Day…The first Sunday when school starts back is always good…Those are the three that come to mind. What about in your church?"

"Christmas Eve services are big in our church. We also have a large attendance whenever we have child dedication services or anything where we involve children. We have hosted patriotic services around the Fourth of July, Memorial Day, or Veterans Day that drew good attendance. You could also add Father's Day, although it does not draw like Mother's Day. I don't know if it's less attended because it falls in mid-June or because the moms are more likely to expect their families to be there on their day. I will point this out, however. You will notice in an older congregation that attendance goes up on Mother's Day, but in a younger congregation it actually goes down because the people travel to visit their moms."

"I never thought about that, but it makes sense."

Pastor Benton continued with his next question. "What does your church do to enhance attendance on those highest-attended Sundays?"

"Why do you need to do anything if they're your best Sundays? Shouldn't you focus on your lowest-attended days?"

"That may sound logical on its face, but let's think through it from the perspective of being evangelistically effective. First, I share the gospel as part of my sermon every time I preach. No matter what the subject is I want to point people to Jesus."

"I agree with that. If you fail to do that all you have is a club and not a church."

"Think about it, Mitch. If the aim is to be more effective, wouldn't it make sense to take advantage of those Sundays when more unchurched people are actually present? Let me be clear. We have much more to talk about in the coming months and evangelism takes place primarily outside the walls of the church. But, take Easter Sunday as an example. If you don't do a single thing as a leader you are still likely to have a number of guests on that day, many of whom don't go to church and are not followers of Jesus. They are there with friends and family. Guests are more likely to attend. If you focus on your lowest-attended Sundays you may not have as many guests even if your congregation tries ten times as hard."

"That's a good point," Mitch replied, soaking up Pastor Benton's wisdom.

"I want you to select your three best-attended Sundays, preferably spread out throughout the year. If you were bi-vocational, with a full-time job in addition to your pastoral ministry, I would recommend doing this only twice each year. Since I have staff to assist me, we focus on four Sundays each year. Now here is the key. While I will continue to preach the gospel every week, on those four Sundays we go all out to get absolutely as many guests to attend as possible. When I say guests I am referring to people who do not regularly attend church, not people who attend other churches. Now if they attend and hear the gospel, that does not guarantee they will come to faith in Jesus. But they are more likely to turn to Him than someone who has not heard the gospel.

Mitch decided to discuss this with the evangelism leadership team, but he already knew for certain that Easter would be one of the Sundays. In order to apply what he and Pastor Benton were discussing sooner than that, he intended to suggest to the team that they apply the plan to a Christmas Eve Service this year.

Wednesday, November 6th

Mitch met with the evangelism leadership team following the prayer service on Wednesday. The group was very enthusiastic and agreed that Christmas Eve would be an opportunity to get members involved in bringing guests. Kris noted that she and Alan would be out of town with their family but committed to do everything possible to assist with preparations. Mitch glanced at his notes one last time before leading the group in prayer.

Christmas Eve (Evangelistic) Service
1. *Have service at 4:00-5:00pm to maximize participation by minimizing conflicts with evening family gatherings.*
2. *Advertise and plan a strict 60-minute service so that families can know how to plan (hopefully this will maximize participation).*
3. *Prayer Coordinator: James Flynn. Will enlist a team to ensure the service is prayed for, beginning Thanksgiving weekend. Team will develop a plan.*
4. *Publicity Coordinator: Tim Minor. Will enlist a team to promote the service to the congregation and the community.*
5. *Childcare Coordinator: Carly Rooks. Team will enlist childcare workers for children five and under. First grade and older will participate in the service. Team will discuss pros and cons of volunteers versus paid workers.*
6. *Worship Team: Mitch Walker. My team will determine the elements of the service and brainstorm ideas to maximize number of guests. I will share a gospel presentation, either as a sermon or a summary of the experience.*
7. *Register everyone present at the conclusion of the service with a survey. Survey will include a place to respond that someone has trusted Jesus as Savior or would be willing to discuss further with someone from our church.*
8. *Enlist someone to decorate the church for this occasion. (Carly said she is willing to do this in addition to childcare.)*
9. *Consider how we can get children involved in the program. Note: Parents will come to watch their children and grandchildren.*
10. *Call every member and past guests two weeks before to extend a personal invitation and encourage them to bring family and friends.*

Chapter Seventeen

Lost Sheep

Sunday, November 10th

I can't wait until Melinda gets home. Mitch parked in his driveway and grabbed the bag of fast food off the console. This day would have been a whole lot different if it had not been for the support of James Flynn, Tim Minor, and Thomas McDonald last month. The deacons ordinarily met the second Sunday of each month. However, Thomas had cancelled it today, as was his prerogative as chairman, due to lack of urgency on any agenda items. The budget team was meeting tonight, and Bruce Rollins (who served as both a deacon and budget team member) could not be in two places at one time. That was fine with Mitch.

The inside story going around was that Thomas did take heat from his father over the decision to break the tie in favor of Mitch last month—obviously one thing his dad did not anticipate. Thomas had inherited his father's fortitude, and when one immovable object encounters another, the result is only a stalemate. Mitch respected that and felt emboldened by Thomas' courage, yet (he had learned from the book on leadership that he had finally completed) he knew one of the secrets of effective leadership is *pace*.

Pace refers to the leader's ability to keep the organization moving forward while remaining sensitive to those who follow; ultimately the right pace aids the leader in getting to the destination. Moving too slowly will mean you never arrive, and you frustrate your leaders. If you move too fast, you overwhelm your followers, and they turn into resisters. You cannot acquire pace by taking a pill. You need wisdom that comes only from God. The counsel of other effective leaders and purposeful relationships with your followers are critical to success.

Mitch unlocked the door and set his food on the coffee table near the recliner. He turned on the television in anticipation of a great NFL matchup. Melinda was on her way home from a weekend at her parents' and should be arriving in the next couple of hours. Her mom had gone through a minor outpatient procedure on Thursday, and Melinda had gone to spend a few days to help her get through the brief recovery. Haley had spent the day and would spend the night at her best friend Emma's house, allowing Mitch his guilty pleasure of fast food and football with no distractions. Melinda had left a message while Mitch was still at the church, stating that she had had dinner before leaving her parents' and had gotten a late start. The three nights she had been gone seemed like three weeks. *I'm glad I don't have to travel like some people do.*

The burgers were long gone by half time, and Mitch was anxious to see his beloved. *I better go make sure the porch lights are on for her.* The game was tied, and it looked like it would go down to the very end. Both teams scored in the third quarter, and Mitch readied for a great fourth. He was sure it would go down to the last possession. *Let me call Melinda. She should have been here by now.* No answer. He left a message to call back. *I don't want to call her parents. I'm sure they're in bed by now.*

Mitch settled back in for the fourth quarter. Melinda had a navigation system and had made the four-hour trek to Lakeland several times on her own. *She is so slow. I could ride a bicycle and make it faster than her.* She was a careful and attentive driver. Mitch did not mind pushing the gas pedal to go a few miles an hour over the posted speed limit, but Melinda obeyed it as if it were a biblical command.

That was an awesome finish. I can't believe that pass.... She should be here by now. She should have been here at least an hour ago. She has a meeting to attend at Haley's school in the morning. He picked up the phone and dialed again. Again, she didn't pick up. Now he was worried. Something was not right. He dialed her parents, and her mom said she had left over six hours before. "Is she all right?"

Mitch lied, "Oh yeah. She told me it would be late. I just wanted to confirm what time she left." He hated to do that, but was trying not to get his mother-in-law in a panic. Mitch himself was not usually one to panic. That is…until now.

Monday, November 11th

It was 1:00 A.M. when he decided to dial 911. Melinda should have been home at least three hours earlier, and she did not answer her phone. The doorbell rang within twenty minutes, and a police officer was at the door. Mitch explained that Melinda was several hours overdue. Less sympathetic, the officer could not be.

"I'm sorry sir, but unless she's been missing at least twenty-four hours, there's really nothing we can do."

Mitch was incredulous. "You cannot be serious. This is my wife that I'm talking about."

The officer remained almost expressionless. "Sir, I'm sorry, but we get calls like this several times a month. Usually they come driving up within the hour, or sadly sometimes it is someone who decides to drive off into the sunset."

"How can you say something like that?" Mitch had not felt like punching someone in years. Even when McDonald and Rollins got under his skin, he was level-headed and maintained his composure. But his nerves had never been on edge like this. *How can this guy be so unsympathetic when my wife is missing?*

The officer finally relented enough to say that he would check with the hospitals between Stanton and Lakeland. As Mitch closed the door, he began to grow nauseated as his mind filled with several possible reasons for her disappearance, and every one made his stomach feel as if a giant hand were gripping it. *I need to call somebody.* He called Randall next door and then he called James Flynn. Randall was at the door within five minutes. When he arrived, Mitch almost lost it.

He had rarely cried in all of his adult life, and now he was embarrassed that he was on the verge of weeping. *I've got to think. I've got to get control of myself.* He was thinking of the horrible things that someone could be doing to his wife. Or… What if she's dead? What if she had a wreck? He called every ten minutes, and still there was no answer.

After a short time, James Flynn arrived and Thomas McDonald was right behind him. Within the hour, James, Thomas, and Randall mobilized a dozen friends and church members. They divided up different routes and began making the trek along any possible path that Melinda may have traveled with Randall leading the way. The police officer called and relayed that no hospital had any patients matching her description. The clock seemed to crawl, and Mitch had never felt so helpless in all of his life.

Thomas McDonald and James Flynn remained at the house, providing their support. Another hour passed, and Mitch could not take it any longer. "I can't just sit here. I've got to go and look for her." They debated briefly the merits of staying put or joining the search. Where would they look? Mitch prevailed, and the decision was made that Thomas would go with him while James stayed by the phone in the Walker's house. As he grabbed a light jacket and put his arm through the sleeve, he said to James, "I'm not coming back until I find her!"

Chapter Eighteen

GETTING DESPERATE

Monday, November 11th

Thomas drove so that Mitch could answer his cell phone if anybody called with news. Mitch did not realize until they got out on the road that an ominous fog had settled in during the evening hours, reducing visibility greatly. They took the route that they supposed Melinda would have taken, looking for anything that might give them a clue about her whereabouts. The radio was off and the car was deathly silent. *What is there to talk about?* Mitch felt as if he were living in a nightmare and could not wake up. Oddly, his mind began replaying vignettes from the life that he and Melinda shared. She was his only true love. Having met in high school, he had never imagined anything other than a lifetime together. She was truly his best friend, and the joy that she had brought him was now rivaled by a depth of pain that he had never imagined possible.

Mitch reflected on the day that Randall had come over, concerned that Wyatt was missing. That paled in comparison to what he was experiencing now. Wyatt was going through a rebellious stage, and his absence had been for only a couple of hours after school. He also remembered an incident when Haley was three years old and she got separated from them in the crowd at the zoo for about three or four minutes, which had seemed like the longest three minutes of his life. None of those times carried anything like the agony he was experiencing at this moment. *Dear God...Please help me find her.* The miles went by. No clues. *This cannot be happening.*

Mitch's reflections turned in a more tormenting direction as another hour passed. Although he was trying to remain positive and prayerful, his thoughts were out of control. Visions of death, living alone, raising Haley alone, and funerals began to infiltrate his mind. He did his best to push them aside. Thomas drove and prayed silently alongside, trying to be as supportive as possible, without trying to explain or justify what Mitch was experiencing. His concerns mirrored Mitch's. The sun would be rising soon, and they had seen nothing that would provide any clue as to where she was. "What do you think we should do?" Thomas asked at last.

"We're almost to my in-laws' house. The sun should be coming up about the time we turn around and head the other way. Maybe that will help us."

A little before 6:30 A.M., Mitch's cell phone rang. He had called James several times during the night only to learn that no one had seen or heard anything new about Melinda's whereabouts.

"Mitch, it's James. The police are here."

Any tension that had left Mitch's body at all came back with a vengeance as he braced for whatever he was about to learn. He could see the blue lights in his mind and tried to take a couple of deep breaths as James put the officer on the phone.

"Is this Mitch Walker?" the officer asked.

"Yes. Have you found Melinda?" Mitch was desperate to get right to the point.

"Are you nearby?"

"No. We're at least a couple of hours away from Stanton. We've been out searching all night. Is she all right?"

"Mr. Walker. I don't like doing this over the phone, but I need to go ahead and tell you that we have found your wife."

Oh God. Please. Mitch was so afraid of what he was about to hear. "Is she OK?"

"Her car was spotted at the bottom of an embankment this morning right after sunup just past the county line on State 77. She is being transported to the emergency room at Rock Springs Hospital."

"How bad is she hurt?"

"I'm sorry Mr. Walker, but I don't have any other details. I was just dispatched to give you that news."

"We're on the way!"

Thomas hit the emergency flashers and pressed the accelerator. If he got pulled over for speeding, he would deal with it then. Relieved because Melinda had been found, but not knowing her condition, Mitch's emotional reprieve was minimal. "I can't believe we drove right by her just a couple of hours ago. I didn't see anything," Mitch said self-reproachfully.

"I didn't either," Thomas replied. "That could have happened even without the fog, but it was impossible, as thick as it was."

Fortunately, the fog had lifted with the morning sunrise. They were making good time and were less than thirty minutes away when their excessive speed caught up with them. Their hearts sank as the blue lights flashed and the police car's siren blared. Once they pulled over, it took about ten minutes before the officer could confirm their story, and then, although delayed, they received an escort for the balance of the trip.

Several church members were already present as Mitch ran from the car to the emergency room entrance. He had called the hospital en route, but they would not give him any information over the phone. Tim Minor walked toward the door to meet Mitch as he entered, and Mitch grabbed him around the neck. He was on the verge of breaking down again as he asked, "Is she OK, Tim?"

"They won't tell us much because we're not relatives, but the hints they've given are encouraging. I don't want to mislead you, though. You need to talk to the doctor. They're waiting on you."

Mitch was ushered back to a small, private waiting room, and within a couple of minutes, a young doctor with a dark complexion carrying a clipboard entered. He looked anything but somber. *Hopefully, that's a good sign.* "Is Melinda OK, doctor?" He blurted out, without waiting for a formal introduction.

"She's going to be fine, but she definitely had a difficult night," he stated, in an accent that Mitch could not immediately place. "She got concussed by the airbag and is bruised badly from the impact of the crash. The most severe injury is a broken tibia and fibula in her lower right leg. It wasn't pleasant being stranded in her car overnight, but she's back there making light of it now. Apparently, her cell phone got projected out during the impact, and all she could do was to wait until someone spotted her. She had a sleepless night, but the meds we gave her for the pain have lightened her mood considerably, if you get my drift."

"You mean she's OK? There's nothing life-threatening?" Mitch was having difficulty comprehending the good news, having prepared himself for the worst.

"No, not at all. Except for the broken leg, she's just bruised up. She's going to be sore for a few days and will likely be on crutches for several weeks. I hope we can have her out of here in a few hours."

Mitch could not believe it. All of his horrible thoughts turned to vapor. "Can I see her?"

"Come with me. I'll take you right there."

"Hang on." Mitch turned and stuck his head out the door that led to the waiting area of the emergency room. "She's OK, guys. She just has a broken leg and is banged up from the wreck. She will be released in a few hours."

His friends in the emergency room celebrated and joined in a circle for prayer while Mitch made his way back past several rooms that had only blue curtains for doors before coming to the examining table where Melinda reclined with her right leg propped up at an angle. First came the lengthy embrace, followed by the kisses, and a couple of tears, but these tears were different. These were tears of joy. The next hour actually turned out to be somewhat amusing. Melinda had never been one for drugs or alcohol, and more than once Mitch had to suppress a grin at her comments, which she would have been embarrassed by under ordinary circumstances. With any luck, she would forget his never-before-used nickname, "Baby Pops," by the time he got her home for a good night's sleep.

Chapter Nineteen

THE MORE I TRY

Sunday, November 17th

"Good morning, Pastor." Mitch was making his way from his office and down the hallway toward the worship center to greet members and guests alike before the service began. As a small way to connect with those in attendance, he routinely went throughout the auditorium, shaking hands and welcoming as many people as he could in the minutes preceding the service. He would remain after the services until the last person was gone, but found the few minutes prior to the worship experience to be of value. Most people seemed to be in good spirits as he made his way down the hallway, and Mitch could not have been more relieved at the way his week had turned out.

Melinda was not present, as her mobility was hindered by the new cast, but she and Mitch were confident that after a doctor's appointment the following day, she would be cleared to walk on crutches. Mitch smiled and greeted people as he approached the door to the auditorium, and everyone reciprocated warmly. However, Bruce Rollins did not appear to have received the memo on how gracious God had been. He was not smiling. "Preacher, I need to talk to you."

Mitch could tell that this was bad news, and it would not be the first time that Rollins had approached him just prior to the service with some perceived crisis or complaint. "Bruce, is this an emergency?" Mitch asked.

"What do you mean is this an emergency? If I need to say something to you, then it doesn't matter if it's an emergency or not!"

Mitch was so anxious for today's service, not only to express gratitude to the congregation but most importantly to give praise to God for his mercy. He had a message to preach and was not in the frame of mind to let anything take away from it. "Listen, Bruce, with all due respect, if this is not an emergency, or if what you need to share is not edifying, then now is not the time."

If looks could kill, then Mitch would have been a dead man. He did not want to come across rude or uncaring, but he knew he needed to establish these types of boundaries in order to have the focus to be able to lead the congregation effectively. Mrs. Jean Hudson tapped Mitch on the shoulder, unaware of the tension of the moment. "Pastor, I put a pie in the fridge in the fellowship hall for you to take home to Melinda. Now don't you eat it all before you get home," she said with a grin. "I sure have prayed for you this week." Rollins was boxed out within a few more seconds as a little girl came up and grabbed Mitch by the leg, hugging it and looking up with a big smile on her face. He made it into the worship center without any further comments from Rollins and put the whole incident aside within moments.

As he walked up to the platform to welcome everyone once the service began, he noticed that the auditorium seemed fuller than he could ever remember for a Sunday unrelated to a special occasion. He was introduced to a couple of guests when he entered earlier and from the vantage point of the platform could see that at least two other families were present that he had not met yet. He could not wait until time to deliver his sermon. As much as he appreciated the music and respected all of the contextual rituals of his church, the preaching was his central focus.

He opened his message with words of appreciation and thanksgiving to all who had aided in the search for Melinda earlier in the week and for all of the e-mails, texts, and calls he and Melinda had received all week long. And meals; members of the church had kindly delivered dinner to the Walkers throughout the week. As he looked over his congregation, he realized how much he loved his flock, and how his love had deepened this week (in spite of the fact that some seemed determined to oppose him at every turn).

He read a text from Luke 15:5–6, about finding what is lost: "...when he finds it, he joyfully puts it on his shoulders and goes home. Then he calls his friends and neighbors together and says, 'Rejoice with me; I have found my lost sheep.'" He shared the story of losing Haley in the crowd at the zoo when she was a little girl and reflected on the relief at finding her quickly. He went on to share about a friend's son who was missing for a few hours and how relieved he was that he was found quickly. He did not call Wyatt by name so as not to embarrass him since he was actually sitting near the back with another teen. But when he shared the emotions he had experienced the previous week, the congregation was moved, like a family reunited after a long time apart.

"God was with me." Mitch proclaimed. "More importantly, He was with Melinda. God drew me close this week. The depth of my love for God, for my family, and for this congregation has deepened because of what we experienced.

I would not wish what we went through on anyone, and I cannot begin to imagine the pain of one who loses someone they love, not knowing if they will ever see them again. Last Sunday was the longest night of my life, and I know there are people who have gone to even darker depths experiencing the pain because someone they love is missing. I think of soldiers missing in action. I think of the faces of children on milk cartons, Amber Alerts, runaway teens, and my heart breaks for families who live with uncertainty. I have a dear pastor friend who has not spoken with his daughter in years and my heart and prayers go out for him every day." Mitch swallowed hard as emotion gripped him; he struggled to maintain his composure.

"In the quietness of reflection this past week, God spoke to me in His still, small voice: 'Mitch, if you could multiply what you felt times thousands, you would know how I grieve for those who reject my grace. I have so many children who are lost.' I didn't hear God speak with an audible voice, but I heard Him clearly in my heart. I don't know why everything happened as it did or why it happened to our family." Mitch looked over at Mrs. Hudson who was wiping a tear from her eye. "But I do have a sense that God wants to use this to do something through me." Referring back to the text, he explained how God rejoices when someone comes to a faith relationship with Him. "Notice how He rejoices, how He calls family and friends to rejoice with Him, and how heaven itself rejoices." Mitch preached with a conviction born out of the emotions of the week but, most importantly, because the Holy Spirit was filling him and giving him the words that so many of his congregation needed to hear.

"I want to invite you to join me on a journey. I want us to connect on a personal level, serve one another, worship together, but also to commit to do all we can to see people come to faith in Jesus Christ. Let's not be satisfied to make a disciple of just one or two. Many of our families, friends, and neighbors are lost and they need to be reached. They are all around us. We all know many who are like the lost sheep in this parable. Let's be as committed as this shepherd to seek out each lost sheep as he did: 'until he finds it.'"

Mitch always invited the congregation to respond at the conclusion of his Sunday morning sermons. The music would play, and those present were invited to come and kneel at the front responding to what God was saying to their hearts, to pray for friends and family, or to pray with their pastor. Occasionally and sporadically, someone would respond. Today, for the first time since Mitch had begun to serve as pastor, the front of the church was filled with people kneeling and praying for friends and family members who were lost.

The hugs and handshakes were plentiful as Mitch stood at the back greeting people as they departed. "We've never had a service like that," was heard more than once. "I love you, pastor," was echoed by more than one, and "That was awesome" came from a young couple that Mitch had never met before this morning. Mitch felt like he was walking on a cloud as he made his way back to grab his cell phone out of his office before getting Mrs. Hudson's pie from the fellowship hall.

He noticed an envelope peeking halfway out from under the office door just before he opened it. *Perhaps a written testimony or note of encouragement* he thought as he picked it up and broke the seal. The note was handwritten.

> *Don't think you're out of the woods just because you got everyone's sympathy this week or because you stirred a few people up. It ain't over.*

Am I still in high school? was the first thought that went through Mitch's mind. *You have got to be kidding me!* was the second thought. The note was unsigned. Leaving an unsigned note like this was so juvenile on one hand and so devious on the other. It appeared to be a man's handwriting. This had to be from Bruce Rollins. It might be Lester McDonald, but based on the incident prior to worship, Bruce was the more likely source. With no name on it, he knew that any accusation he might make could backfire. He thought of the words Jesus once spoke to Simon Peter. *Get thee behind me, Satan.* He was not making an accusation against Bruce or anyone else, merely an acknowledgment that "we do not wrestle against flesh and blood," as Ephesians 6:12 read. *The more I try to lead this congregation to reach out to the lost, the more I am attacked! Coincidence? Not likely.*

From the valley to the mountain top and from the mountain top to the valley. Mitch could not believe how quickly you could move from one to the other.

Chapter Twenty

Business Meeting

Monday, November 18th

The first frost of the approaching winter season was sparkling outside the window of Mitch's study as he sipped on a cup of hot coffee. His ritual of study in the private sanctuary of his home office was now well established, but he could not resist the temptation to check his phone. He noticed that his secretary had sent him a text.

Lester McD called & says urgent to c u 2day.

I might as well get this over with. Mitch did not know the subject of McDonald's request this time, but he could not remember the last time they had interacted over anything pleasant. Mitch was struggling with his attitude toward Lester McDonald, Bruce Rollins, and, to a lesser degree, John Dollar. He could never seem to please them. Although he had concluded that pleasing God was the priority anyway, that decision did not relieve his struggle. He frankly did not like them. But they were members of his flock, and he knew that the Scripture commanded him to love them. *How can I love them when I don't even like them? How can I love them when they seem bent on opposing me at every turn?* Mitch went right down to his knees and began to pray. He prayed for God's wisdom and grace. He asked God not only to help him to love these men and others who seemed to reflect their attitude but also to give them a spirit of unity. After about fifteen minutes, he got back in his chair and replied to the text.

See if 11:00 A.M. will work.

He went back to his sermon preparation and received confirmation back within a short time. After checking on Melinda and giving her a kiss, he headed out into the cool morning to meet with Lester at the church office. After minimal pleasantries, Lester got quickly to the point.

"I heard about the way you treated Bruce Rollins yesterday."

"What do you mean about the 'way I treated him'?" Mitch asked.

"You were disrespectful, and I'm here to tell you right now that we will not tolerate a pastor who is rude and disrespectful to upstanding members."

"Lester, first of all, you were not there and don't know exactly what happened. Obviously, Bruce has talked to you, and he's upset. I did nothing with the intention of causing any offense, but if you must know…I have often been approached by him just prior to the service. I don't know if it is intentional or simply poor etiquette." Mitch assumed it was intentional but wanted to give some benefit of the doubt. He continued, "When I am getting ready to bring a message on Sunday morning, I don't think it is appropriate to be blindsided with church business or some perceived crisis that can easily wait for another day. I wasn't trying to be rude to Bruce, but I decided to draw a line because this has happened at least a couple of dozen times in the two and a half years that I have served here."

"You did the same thing to me a couple of months back after the service one Sunday morning!"

"You may recall that I told you, politely I might add, I had a family commitment and told you to see me the next day unless it was an emergency. As a matter of fact, I never heard back from you the next week, so I assumed it must not have been urgent."

McDonald's face was red as he leaned forward pointing his finger across the desk at Mitch's chest. "Urgent has nothing to do with it. You work for us, and when we need something, you're supposed to respond. That's what we pay you for."

Mitch silently prayed for the right words as he replied. "Lester, I spent a lot of time with the committee that interviewed me prior to being called to serve as the pastor of this church. We talked extensively about the pastor's responsibilities. I agree that I need to be responsive and to minister to every member, but I have a lot of responsibilities ranging from personal time with the Lord, ministering to my own family, and leading this congregation to reach out to the community."

"I don't think you have your priorities straight. You seem to be more concerned about the community lately than you do the people who are paying you. We all see that you're trying to change us, and that's not what we called you here to do."

"Let me ask you a question, Lester. What is your vision for this church?"

"My main vision right now is for the pastor to get his priorities right."

Mitch resisted the temptation to fire back. He took a deep breath and responded. "Lester, I want to be a 'good pastor.' My first priority is to please the Lord. I prayed for you this morning. As a matter of fact, I prayed for the relationship that you and I have. It's not healthy, and I don't think it pleases God. I apologize if you think I've been rude to you or anyone else. That was not my intent. I want us to partner together to make this church everything that God would have it to be."

Lester's demeanor did not change. It seemed that whether Mitch was apologetic, firm, spiritual, or aloof, nothing would change Lester's mind.

"I think we made a mistake by calling you as our pastor. Bruce and I talked last night and we've made a decision to have the budget committee to either cut out your insurance or reduce your salary by ten percent. Maybe it would be better if you just stepped aside. We're also going to bring before the church a proposal to expand the deacon board. You slipped by once, but I'm going to make sure it doesn't happen again."

The lines were clearly drawn at this point. Here he was speaking for the budget committee, of which he was not even a member. Mitch could see clearly that Lester McDonald was maneuvering to force his resignation. Lester may have been expecting that he would resign then and there. Instead, Mitch took the conversation in another direction completely.

"Are you set for Thanksgiving next week, Lester?"

"I guess. I haven't thought that much about it. Why are you asking?"

"Because I pray that it will be a blessed time for you and your family. I know Mrs. McDonald is a great cook. You've got a great family, Lester. I hope you enjoy them very much next week."

Lester took the hint that the conversation was over. He turned and exited without offering a handshake. Mitch closed the door and fell to his knees once again in the middle of his small office. He seemed to be spending a lot of time on the floor in recent weeks.

Tuesday, December 3rd

Mitch's December meeting with Pastor Benton was unlike any of the others to date. Many things had transpired that required extended conversation. Pastor Benton was aware of Melinda's accident and had called the week following. However, today in the coffee shop Mitch gave him the hour-by-hour account of what he had experienced that night. Benton had intended to discuss personal evangelism during this session, but the bulk of their conversation revolved around the crisis that Mitch was engaged in with Lester McDonald and Bruce Rollins.

"How many members support Lester's position?" Pastor Benton asked.

"It's hard to say. He has a lot of influence, and I know now that he pretty much has called all the shots at the church for a long time. When I accepted the call to serve as pastor there, I didn't know that. We have had some new families join in the past couple of months, so I don't think he would have the majority, but who knows?"

Pastor Benton was very sympathetic, having had similar conversations with pastors over the years and having encountered some challenging conflicts himself along the way.

"Sometimes the noise level of those who are dissatisfied can give the appearance of more support than is actually there. Stay focused on doing the right thing, and you can trust that the Lord will take care of you. I even know pastors who did resign or were fired, and as difficult as that was, it turned out for the best. The hardest part is the damage it does to the family. I can't tell you the number of children who have been turned off to church because of the way a congregation treated their dad. That's not to say that some pastors didn't deserve to be released. Neither pastors nor congregations have a monopoly on being right."

"That's true," Mitch replied. "I just want to make sure I do the right thing."

Instead of discussing evangelism this time, Pastor Benton focused on encouraging Mitch. He understood that any plans for outreach that Mitch made would be moot if he could not navigate this crisis. Mitch broached one final subject before they left the coffee shop.

"Have you heard anything from your daughter?" Mitch asked.

"No, we still don't know exactly where she is and haven't had any contact. Her brothers and their families were with us for Thanksgiving last week. We had a great time, but there is still a void without her and her children being there." The older pastor's strong presence seemed to succumb to vulnerability. Mitch did not intend to end on a down note, but was even more sympathetic after the things that had transpired in his life recently.

"I'm praying for her and for your family," Mitch said.

"You will never know how much I appreciate that."

"By the way, I'm going to try to get by to visit with you in worship sometime over the holidays. I'm able to take a week off, including a couple of Sundays, each year for vacation, but we can't go very far from home this year because Melinda's really not up to traveling."

"That's great. Call me ahead of time and remind me. I'd love for you to meet my wife and to take your family to lunch."

Sunday, December 8th

Stanton Community Church held a church conference each month on Sunday evening. Sometimes the meeting would be cancelled due to lack of any items needing attention. The church functioned under a congregational leadership model, meaning that the members would discuss and vote on most items of church business or in some cases elect leaders or committees that would be empowered to carry out their wishes. About one-fourth of the normal Sunday morning congregation would attend ordinarily, but this time it seemed that an undercurrent of conversation regarding the prospective budget had stirred up enough interest to triple the typical attendance.

The budget committee presented their proposal recommending a reduction of spending for the following year, and it included reducing Mitch's salary along with recommending that he pick up half of the cost for his family's health insurance out of his salary. His earlier conversation with Lester McDonald had given Mitch a heads-up, but he had not known the final proposal until he saw it in writing when he arrived for the meeting moments earlier. He looked at Melinda and could see the concern on her face.

The chairman of the budget committee pointed out that the average amount of the offerings for January through October was slightly below the previous year and that the budget would not be met. He conveniently left out the fact that the offerings for the past six or seven weeks had actually increased by almost twenty percent since a couple of new families had joined and the number of guests had greatly increased. James Flynn stood and made a motion to amend the budget to restore Mitch's salary with a slight raise and to restore full insurance benefits funded by the church. Melinda and Mitch were dismissed from the room by the moderator, Thomas McDonald, given the nature of the discussion.

When Mitch and Melinda returned about twenty minutes later, they were pleased to discover that Flynn's motion had passed. What was said and who had said it, they would never know, but they were grateful.

The other major item of business was the proposal to expand the deacon board from five to seven members. Mitch was called upon to express his opinion of the wisdom for such a change. Privately, he strongly suspected that the underlying motive for this move was to stack the board with men who might oppose him. However, he had no reason to oppose the recommendation in principle, since theoretically more leaders should be of value to a pastor. Therefore, he surprised Lester McDonald and Bruce Rollins by speaking in favor of the motion, which went on to pass unanimously. Everyone seemed satisfied as the meeting concluded. Mitch shook James Flynn's hand as the crowd began to disperse.

James whispered, "Let's pray the Lord guides us to two new deacons who can help us move forward."

Mitch looked over James' shoulder, and he happened to see Lester McDonald leaning over and whispering in Bruce Rollins' ear. *I'll bet he's saying the same thing.*

Chapter Twenty-One

READY AND WAITING

Tuesday, December 10th

"Look, Daddy. We made an ornament in school today." With pride, Haley held up a star crudely cut from construction paper, glitter outlining the edges of the cutout. "Merry Christmas" was written in black marker on it.

"That looks great. Let's go put it on the tree," Mitch responded, guiding his pride and joy into the front of the living room.

Mitch loved this season of year and having a child in the second grade made it seem even more magical. He loved the decorations, the Christmas carols, and the special treats. The thought of Mrs. Hudson delivering one of her delectable pies made him salivate like one of Pavlov's dogs, and he was certain she would do so again this year. He could do without the cheap fruitcake that Melinda always seemed to purchase and place among the goodies. They were never the quality of the Claxton fruitcakes his mom traditionally purchased. But he decided he would overlook that letdown so long as she continued to place a sprig of mistletoe over the kitchen doorway. Kissing Melinda was always high on his list of favored activities.

Unfortunately, Mitch seemed to have lost some of the Christmas spirit. He put on a smile for Haley and played his fatherly role well as he helped her to find the ideal place on the tree for the ornament. Although he was doing his best to maintain a positive outlook and knew that things had turned out pretty well at the church conference, the actions of his two antagonists had really nagged at him the past couple of days. He was just shy of being genuinely depressed. On top of that, he did not feel well physically. He had one of those colds that does not include a fever but seems to drain energy, making the days seem long. Mitch wanted so much to kick back in his recliner and do as little as possible this evening.

In spite of how he felt, he had already arranged to make some visits this evening, and Thomas McDonald had agreed to accompany him. It was pouring rain outside. He headed out the door into the winter darkness.

In spite of the pouring rain, Mitch was not one to use an umbrella. He held a vinyl-covered notepad over his head as if it would give him some protection from the elements. Until he stepped into a puddle, he had not realized that the sole of his right shoe had developed a small hole. He could feel his sock absorbing water. *Great!* At least the car started as he dripped and tried to re-warm himself on the way to meet Thomas. He expected the visits to be a waste of time on a night like this, but the time with his friend would be fruitful. Their friendship had begun following Thomas' surprising support at the October deacons' meeting and had grown strong in the hours they spent searching for Melinda the month before.

Beginning with the businesspeople in the community, Mitch had made dozens of visits over the past few weeks. He had been to almost all of the businesses in town, and to some of them two or three times. In addition, he had gone to the homes nearest the church and was now trying to make a point of going to the homes of those who visited on Sunday. The results were mixed, at best.

On average, over one-fourth were not at home when he visited. He had learned to leave a pamphlet in the door so that the residents would know he had come by and could learn more about the church from the materials he left. Even when someone was home, half of the visits seemed to be awkward. While most people were polite, the interactions would last only a few minutes. Occasionally someone was rude, but that was the exception. Most who had no interest in his visit were quick to give a polite "thanks but no thanks" type of response. Being warmly received in the remaining visits did not seem to guarantee that the people would visit the church in the future. Some were members of other churches already, and some would make promises that they would not follow up on. Sometimes he was able at least to pray for ministry needs and offer pastoral comfort, but with the pouring rain and the way he felt, Mitch was not optimistic about this evening's possibilities.

He was right. No one was home at the first three homes. Christmas shopping, kids extracurricular activities, working late? Who knows?

"Why don't we just call it a night?" Mitch asked.

"That's fine. I can tell you're not feeling well. Do you mind if we make one more stop? There's a guy who works for me that's been going through a tough time. He lives less than a mile from here."

"Sure. Let's do it. What's his story?"

"He lost his wife about three years ago. His kids have all grown up, and none of them live in the area. The bottom line is that he needs friends. He keeps to himself, and I've been trying to reach out to him."

They pulled into the driveway, but could not see the house until they drove well over one hundred yards, bouncing and sloshing down a gravel driveway. "This guy has some property," Mitch said. Finally, they came to a mobile home situated deep in the woods. "This looks creepy." The rain was coming down harder than ever, and you could barely see twenty feet beyond the hood of the car as they approached the small trailer that was surrounded by trees in the middle of the woods. Mitch and Thomas jumped out of the car and ran for the door, getting soaked within moments. Thomas banged on the door and started yelling above the pounding rain as it clanged on the metal roof.

"Hey Danny, can we come in?" Thomas shouted. "It's Thomas from work." Mercifully, the door opened quickly, and they were ushered inside, where they stood dripping in front of a short and weathered man who apparently had elected not to bathe in the past couple of days. He had a full beard and a cigarette hung out one side of his mouth. Mitch was not sure he would have approached him on his own, but he seemed to receive Thomas like a family member.

"What brings y'all out here in this monsoon, Thomas? Are you guys trick-or-treatin' still?" their host asked with a mischievous smile.

"Danny, this is my pastor, Mitch Walker. Mitch, this is my friend, Danny Rose."

"Pleased to meet you, Danny," Mitch said as the two shook hands.

"Sit down and take a load off," Danny responded. "You men want anythang ta drank?"

"No, thanks," they said in unison as they cleared some magazines off a couple of chairs that had seen better days. Danny continued to puff on his cigarette, and Mitch knew the smell would follow him home.

Although Rose had a tired look about him, he seemed genuinely pleased to have company. The television was blaring loudly to override the racket of the rain on the metal roof, and Mitch counted at least five cats that made their way in and out of the small living area as they sat and talked. The noise of the rain forced them to practically yell to carry on the conversation.

The small talk quickly passed and then Danny surprised Mitch with a transparent confession. "I've been prayin' a whole lot lately," Danny said, over the noise. "My wife was a churchgoer, ya know, but I regret to say that I stayed home or went fishin' while she and the kids would go to Sunday school and church services. I left all the religious stuff to her. I can't tell y'all how much I regret it. I miss 'er a lot, ya know." His sadness and grief were unmistakable. "I actually rent this place. I made some bad decisions after her passin', and I lost a lot of thangs, including the house where we raised our young'uns. I was mad at God fur a while. I can't explain it, but lately I've been feelin' like I wanna know God and be close to Him like my wife was. So, I pray, but somethin' is missin'. It's like a miracle that you even showed up here tanite. I've been askin' God to show me how I can know Him like my wife did."

Mitch could not believe what he was hearing. His aches and pains seemed to evaporate as he gave total attention to Danny. He had wrongly concluded early upon their arrival that the visit would be a waste of time with too many obstacles and distractions. However, here was a man who was lonely and hurting and God was working in his life. Now, with Thomas in this man's humble home, he had the privilege of sharing how the man could have a personal relationship with Jesus Christ. It was the easiest thing that Mitch had ever done.

All three men got on their knees on a dirty rug as the television continued its chatter, the cats continued to prowl, and the rain continued to clang loudly on the trailer roof. In the midst of the chaos and in spite of Mitch's weakness, God showed up. When they stood up, Danny had a smile on his face as though he had just become a millionaire. Thomas and Mitch stayed for another hour talking about faith, how to grow spiritually, and the purpose of baptism. Danny shook their hands as they made their way out, shouting through the rain as they got back in the car:

"I'll see ya'll on Sunday!"

It continued to pour rain all of the way home. As far as Mitch knew, Lester and Bruce had not changed their minds in the past hour. Melinda was still wearing a cast. The deacon board would still be expanding. Mitch still had a scratchy throat. However, inside his heart the sun was shining, and his recent travails and stresses seemed trivial. *It's amazing how being involved in seeing someone come to faith in Jesus can change your day.*

Chapter Twenty-Two

SOWING BOUNTIFULLY

Wednesday, December 11th

From: Mitch Walker
Sent: Wednesday, December 11, 7:46 AM
To: Marc Benton
Subject: Good News!
Marc;

I had an unbelievable experience last night. I went with one of my members to make some visits, thinking it was a waste of time because of the weather. Quite frankly, I could not have felt less like going. We went to the home of a man named Danny, and it was almost as if he was waiting for us. I was wondering about the value of visiting homes and must confess that this made it all worthwhile. I wish you could have been there. The presence of God was so real in his small trailer and getting on our knees while he called out to God was something I will never forget!

Mitch

From: Marc Benton
Sent: Wednesday, December 11, 10:01 AM
To: Mitch Walker
Subject: RE: Good News!
Mitch;

That is fantastic! It does happen like that sometimes for those who faithfully sow the seeds of the gospel. Do you recall the parable of the sower in Matthew 13? Remember how some of the seed fell on hard soil, some on shallow soil, and other seed fell on fertile soil? The seed is the gospel, the soil is the heart of man, and the sower is the one who shares the gospel. Those who do not sow will never reap. Those who do will not see a harvest every time they sow. But remember 2 Corinthians 9:6. It reminds the reader that those who sow sparingly reap sparingly, and those who sow bountifully reap bountifully.

If you had not gone (or not sown), you would never have experienced this. The challenge in sharing the gospel is that as we look at people, there is no way to discern from their outward appearance how receptive their heart is. Would you have known this man was ready just by seeing him out on the street? The only way to know a person's level of receptivity is to begin a conversation on spiritual issues.

I had a similar experience recently with a waitress named Maria. I made a point to be friendly during the whole meal and when she came to get the check, I asked if I could try a one-minute activity with her, and I promised her a good tip whether she would or not. I asked her to take thirty seconds to tell me about the best thing God had ever done for her and to allow me to do the same. She went along, and her answer was very shallow, and she knew it. I kidded with her asking, "Is that all you've got?" I went on to tell her how "I once lived my life apart from God but came to realize how Jesus, God's Son, was sent to pay the penalty for my sin when He died on the cross. He rose from the dead, affirming He was indeed God's Son. I repented of my sins and placed my faith in Jesus for my forgiveness and my salvation. I now have a personal relationship with God through Jesus, and He is a part of my life each and every day. He is also the reason I know I will go to heaven one day."

I asked her if anything like that had ever happened in her life. She began to tear up and said "no, but it needs to." We ended up talking several more minutes, and she trusted Jesus to be her Lord and Savior. She is now attending our church, and I have a group of ladies who have embraced her and begun to disciple her.

For every time that happens, there are at least ten that seem not to respond. Most will not respond immediately, and those that do have most often already been exposed to the gospel in some way. I'm out of time now, but I'm going to send you another e-mail later because there's more I want to share about this. It fits right in with what I wanted to cover in our last meeting together, but as you know we had other issues that arose that occupied our time. I love you, brother!

Marc

From: Mitch Walker
Sent: Wednesday, December 11, 11:44 AM
To: Marc Benton
Subject: RE: Good News!
Look forward to it. Thanks!

Mitch

Mitch did a great deal of reflecting over the next couple hours. That thought about sowing sparingly and sowing bountifully really grabbed his attention. Reflecting back on his time at Stanton Community Church prior to August, he now felt he had been a chicken running around with his head cut off. Once he started meeting with Pastor Benton at the coffee shop, he began to shift more of his focus and energy into outreach and evangelism activities. Prior to August, he was hardly sowing at all and at best was only sowing sparingly. Admittedly, there were still days and even some weeks when he did not give as much attention to outreach as he intended, but the comparison was not even close.

He was now engaging the church in praying for non-believers by name, spending some time each week visiting local businesses, visiting homes near the church, going to the homes of guests who attended the worship services whenever possible, and was becoming more intentional in building relationships with unchurched people. He had spent a fair amount of time with his neighbor Wyatt and his friend Dizzy. Dizzy, though resistant, was at least willing to talk about spiritual matters. Mitch had pulled together an evangelism leadership team that had met a few times, and the plans they came up with for the Christmas Eve Service were designed to get as many guests to attend as possible.

In the past couple of months, Dana Hutchison, owner of the local sandwich shop, had joined the church, along with her family, and her son had been baptized. Lamar and Belinda from across the street had joined with their grandchildren, and two of the children were later baptized after coming to faith in Jesus. Their son and daughter-in-law had also attended two of the past three Sundays. Danny Rose had agreed to be baptized at the Christmas Eve Service. *How cool is that?* Two other families had also joined the church recently. The number of guests prior to August was perhaps one or two during the month. Lately guests were coming almost every Sunday; like last Sunday there were often three or four families visiting. In spite of the challenges that Mitch was facing, he had to admit that as he began to sow more bountifully, he was certainly reaping bountifully. *We're not exactly setting the woods on fire, but some good things are happening. I just pray the progress doesn't get sabotaged when the deacon board expands.*

Chapter Twenty-Three

A Slice of Pie

Thursday, December 12th

From: Marc Benton
Sent: Thursday, December 12, 8:08 AM
To: Mitch Walker
Subject: Next Step in the Net Effect
Mitch;
Tell me about the personal evangelism training that you have provided at Stanton Community since you have become the pastor.
> Thnx.
> Marc

From: Mitch Walker
Sent: Thursday, December 12, 8:23 AM
To: Marc Benton
Subject: RE: Next Steps in the Net Effect
None. Nada. Zilch. Zero.
The problem we have is that no one wants to do outreach, and I don't have any "soul-winners," as they used to say back in the day.
> Mitch

From: Marc Benton
Sent: Thursday, December 12, 9:22 AM
To: Mitch Walker

Subject: RE: Next Step in the Net Effect
Mitch:

I think we know each other well enough now that I can shoot straight with you. You indicated that "no one wants to do outreach" and that you have "no soul-winners." A couple of points; first, in terms of your leadership as a pastor it is important to understand that you do not wait on your members to "want to do it" before you intentionally begin "leading" them to do it. They won't all get on board, but I do believe you had one of your members with you this week when you visited that man that committed his life to Christ. "No one?"

Secondly, I have found that the churches that provide evangelism training are where the "soul-winners" are found. For example, I have a man in my church named David S. He was attending another church that did no outreach, and he was quite frustrated. We did not seek him out (since he attended another church), but he came to us when he heard about the training we were providing. He is a layman who has a heart for evangelism and desired to be in a church where the leaders had the same passion and priority. I would say that fifteen to twenty of our baptisms each year are the result of his witnessing. I jokingly say that he will witness to a telephone pole if he thinks it might respond. Whenever someone responds during the invitation that he has seen come to faith in Christ, I always think I must have preached a good sermon.:-)

Equip the Saints (your members) to do the work of ministry (including how to share their faith) as all pastors are instructed in Ephesians 4:11-12. It is stated in the imperative and not as an option if you think it may be a good idea. I read some research from a friend in Georgia recently, and they discovered that churches that provided evangelism training baptized 2.5 times as many as those who did not. This should not be surprising. Let me illustrate.

Some pastors only proclaim the gospel from the pulpit. That is the same as fishing in a barrel. If no unchurched people are present, it may be like fishing in an empty barrel. Other pastors share their faith but do not take time to train others to do likewise. That is what I call solo fishing. You can catch fish when you go fishing by yourself. But your members have contact each week with hundreds if not thousands of people who never hear you preach and with whom you never have any contact.

What would happen if they went fishing? Follow me and I will make you fishers of men. Sound familiar? Jesus said that in Matthew 4:19.

Equipping your members to fish (to witness) does not mean that all of them will do it. But, I have found that some of them will if they are trained and challenged to do so. On the other hand, I have noticed that when pastors fail to equip the members to witness, it is almost guaranteed that they won't and don't. Correct me if I'm wrong, but I think you have transitioned from fishing in the barrel to solo fishing. That's good, and the man who came to faith last week should certainly be grateful. I want to challenge you to take the next step.

Let me remind you about the six essentials of the Net Effect that I want you to apply:

–Praying for the lost

–Personal Evangelism Equipping

–Proclamation of the Gospel Message

–Event Evangelism

–Service/Ministry Evangelism

–Team Evangelism

We've spent time on leadership, praying for the lost, and how to maximize the audience for your proclamation of the gospel message on your highest attended Sundays. Next I want to challenge you in the area of equipping your members in personal evangelism. Out of time now. I'll follow up with another e-mail tomorrow with a few more thoughts.

Marc

From: Mitch Walker

Sent: Thursday, December 12, 11:11 AM

To: Marc Benton

Subject: RE: Next Steps in the Net Effect

Convicting! And much needed. Thanks. I look forward to next e-mail.

Mitch

Mitch was looking forward to an evening at home with his family. Several times that evening, he made it a point to guide Melinda through the kitchen door over which the mistletoe hung. She was getting pretty good at navigating on her crutches, though her mobility had been hampered considerably. Fortunately, she was suffering no significant aftereffects from the accident other than the broken leg. Mitch's mood was considerably different than it had been the previous Tuesday night. He played a game called Connect Four with Haley for almost an hour before dinner. He told himself that he let her win three of the games, and whether he did or not, Haley was always proud when she could defeat her dad.

"I almost forgot to tell you," Melinda said from the kitchen as they continued to play. "Mrs. Hudson brought over a pie for us today." At that bit of news, Mitch's day got even better.

"I can't wait. How long till dinner?"

"No more than about fifteen minutes. Wrap up your game and get washed up."

Mitch could smell the aroma of chicken-fried steak and mashed potatoes. Melinda had a penchant for cooking healthy meals, but Mitch also had a tendency to talk her into preparing one of his favorite comfort foods at least once every couple of weeks. This was one of those nights, and everything was right in Mitch's world.

The family talked, and laughed together as they ate. The scene would have made a perfect setting for a Norman Rockwell painting, especially with the Christmas decorations.

"I'm ready for some pie, Haley, how about you?"

"I'm too full. Can I have some ice cream before I go to bed?"

Mitch answered without consulting Melinda. "Sure you can. Hey, I'm going to go grab some ice cream and put some on my pie."

Mitch went to the freezer and pulled out the vanilla ice cream. When he got back to the table Melinda had already sliced him a good portion of pie and placed it on his plate. "Are you going to eat some?" Mitch asked Melinda.

"Of course, but I'm going to let my dinner settle for a little bit. You go ahead."

Mitch took a bite. "Hmmmm. This is good, but I thought she would bake a peach pie again. What is this?"

Melinda looked at it and took a small sample. "She didn't say, and I didn't think to ask. It's some kind of dried fruit. It looks like the dried apples like she puts in her fried apple pies. She must not have had any fresh peaches or apples on hand. It does taste good though. I'll definitely eat a slice after a while."

Mitch finished it off within five minutes and went for slice number two. Melinda gave him that look that wives seem to come by naturally when they disapprove but are trying not to make too much of a fuss. Mitch acted like he didn't see it, but she knew better. Being in the holiday spirit herself, she let it slide. Mitch polished off the second slice and leaned back with his fingers interlocked across his stomach, which had a little extra bulge from eating more than he should have. "That was great," he said. "I'm going to call Mrs. Hudson and tell her how much I enjoyed that."

The phone rang about nine times before Mrs. Hudson finally answered. "Hello," she said in the mild-mannered tone that was more typical of her (except for when she was under attack from snakes on her back porch).

"Mrs. Hudson, this is Mitch. How are you doing tonight?"

"I'm doing fine, pastor. I was just getting ready to watch the W.W.E."

"The what?"

"Wrestling. I like to watch wrestling. My late husband got me hooked on it a long time ago. The Terminator is taking on the Spike Boy tonight. I can't stand him. Which one do you like?"

"I'm sorry, Mrs. Hudson. I can't say that I'm acquainted with those wrestlers, but I hope your man wins tonight. Listen, the reason I called is to say thanks for the pie."

"What's that?"

Mitch spoke a little louder. "I called to say thanks for the pie." He didn't realize it, but he also was speaking slower as well as louder. *Why did I do that?* "That may be the best one you've ever baked!" He felt a bit of pride in the way that he was being so encouraging by flattering one of his faithful church members. "By the way, what kind is it?"

"It was my late husband's favorite. He called it Skip to My Lou Pie."

Skip to my Lou, my darling. The song title stirred up memories from elementary school music classes. "Those dried apples sure do make for a good pie, don't they?"

"Excuse me. What did you say?"

He spoke loudly and slowly again. "Those dried apples sure make good pies."

"Oh, those aren't apples. I was out of those."

"Yeah, we noticed that. The dried apples worked just as good for this one."

"I didn't have any of those either, so I used dried prunes for this one. My husband had me bake one like that for him every year. Said it was good for cleaning out the system. He would always have me add a tablespoon of castor oil like his momma used to, but I didn't know if you would want that, so I only added a half a tablespoon to this one. I never liked it myself."

Skip to my Lou? Uh-oh. Skip–to–the–Loo! Mitch did not know if it was psychological or physical, but he could hear his stomach begin to rumble audibly. "Thank you, Mrs. Hudson. I appreciate it. I've got to run now." Mitch hung up the phone and shouted, "MELINDA!" She could tell by his tone that something was wrong.

"What is it? What's wrong?" she asked.

"Throw that pie away!"

"What are you talking about? You don't want to save some for the weekend?"

"Honey, it's a prune pie!"

"What?"

"Yeah. Throw that thing away. She added castor oil to it."

"Castor oil? What's that?"

"It's what the old timers used for a laxative back in the day."

Melinda laughed until her belly hurt. Mitch could not quite grasp the humor of the moment. He feared that he had a busy night ahead.

Chapter Twenty-Four

Monday, December 16th

From: Marc Benton
Sent: Monday, December 16, 8:02 AM
To: Mitch Walker
Subject: More on Personal Evangelism
Mitch,

I hope Sunday went well for you. I wanted to pick up where I left off last week. Let me share the way that I keep personal evangelism before my congregation. I make sure that we provide training at least twice each year. I plan for one segment between the start of the school year in August and Thanksgiving. I plan the other between New Years in January and Spring Break for our local schools in April. You will note that effective evangelistic churches do not provide evangelism training 52 weeks a year, but they do not let 52 weeks go by without providing training. So you see that I plan two segments of training in two windows of time. I plan one training segment aimed at the entire congregation and one focused on the core.

The reason for this is that I learned early in my ministry that providing training for the core eliminated a large number of my congregation from the training experience. We would provide training for twelve weeks and would do well to get four or five percent of the congregation to participate. The advantage of the core training was the high commitment level. Those who participated would be highly inclined to witness because accountability and commitment was built into the process. Training for the core requires members to sign up, to complete assignments, and to be accountable. What do you do about the other 90–95% of the congregation? Plentiful resources abound to assist with this, but I have noticed that they tend to have a shelf life. They motivate for a season of time but eventually run their course. The bottom line is to find a resource that will motivate and train those who desire equipping in evangelism. Let me know if you need specific recommendations for a product-driven training resource. My staff and I developed a new resource that we recently implemented. The one we are using now is called *iShare*.

I always take another segment of time to train the entire congregation. The point of the congregational approach is to train every member possible whether they expect it or not. No sign up is required. Typically, I do this through my preaching. I once preached a series to our congregation called "I Witness." I witness through my praying, I witness by inviting, I witness with my testimony, I witness with my team (SS class or small group), I witness with my conversations, etc. Likewise, we have provided curriculum to our Connect Groups (that's what we call our Sunday morning Bible study). Everyone that attends gets trained. Admittedly, the training does not connect with 100% of our congregation but it is a whole lot greater than 5%. I have also found that I can use these times of congregational training to enlist for the next core training. Providing the congregational experience does not guarantee that everyone will share, but I have found that "more people" share and witness when we provide the training. We do not see more people come to faith in Jesus because we are smarter, more educated, or have any special advantage. I have made a decision as a pastor not to fish alone.

One other option which can serve as a hybrid of the two experiences is a workshop format on a weekend. The entire congregation will not participate, but you can greatly exceed 5% because fewer weeks are involved. Yet, you can go deeper by providing several hours of training and incorporate an outreach experience.

Give me a plan for your church for the coming year.

Merry Christmas! Look forward to your visit to our worship in a couple of weeks.

Marc

From: Mitch Walker
Sent: Monday, December 16, 10:13 AM
To: Marc Benton

Subject: RE: More on Personal Evangelism

Good word. I think it will be easier to start with a congregational training. I like the "I witness" idea. I have already planned my messages through February but was praying about which direction to go in March. I will begin working on a five week series on "sharing your faith" for the month of March on Sunday mornings.

I have a question though, and we debated this often in seminary. Shouldn't we focus on relationships instead of confrontational evangelism? I'm trusting you on this, but many of my peers are convinced that evangelism should be relationship-driven.

Mitch

From: Marc Benton
Sent: Monday, December 16, 1:46 PM
To: Mitch Walker
Subject: RE: More on Personal Evangelism

Mitch,

My apologies if I gave any impression that would lead you to think relationships are minimized in the approach that I am suggesting. All evangelism is built on relationships. Remember when I shared about the parable of the sower? The seed is the word of God, the sower is the witness, and the soil is the heart of man. What do you do when the soil is hard or shallow? You use a spade to break it up and soften it. Relationships are the spades that make the soil (heart) more receptive to the seed (word of God).

I have noted that some leaders have replaced the seed with the spade. What is the result if you build a relationship but never verbally share the gospel? The spade can supplement the witness but can never serve as a substitute for the witness. Do you have any relatives who are not believers? Have you personally shared the gospel with them? You have had a relationship with them all of your life, and if your relationship would bring them to Jesus in and of itself, then they would have already responded.

Confrontation sounds negative but the design is not to assault people with the gospel but to be purposeful in initiating the conversation. Your relationships should enhance those opportunities. But reflect back on the parable for a moment as well as your experience last week when the man you shared with was waiting to hear how he could know Jesus personally. Some hearts are ready right now. Relationships are critical to each and every essential component of the Net Effect. Just be cautious not to be caught in the false dichotomy that you must be "confrontational" or be "relational." Effective evangelism requires understanding and application of both. Great question! I'm glad you brought it up.

   Marc

From: Mitch Walker
Sent: Monday, December 16, 4:22 PM
To: Marc Benton
Subject: RE: More on Personal Evangelism
Good stuff! That clarifies for me. It's not "either/or."
Pray for me as I continue to witness to my neighbor's friend. You may recall that his name is Dizzy. I feel like I've done both with him in terms of building a relationship and verbally sharing. But, his heart is harder than the man I shared with last week. I think he is going to come to our Christmas Eve service. We've worked hard, and I'm optimistic about the attendance.

   Mitch

From: Marc Benton
Sent: Monday, December 16, 6:36 PM
To: Mitch Walker
Subject: RE: More on Personal Evangelism
I prayed for Dizzy just now, as well as your Christmas Eve service.

   Marc

Tuesday, December 17th

Mitch sat in his office looking over his notes for the evangelism leadership team meeting. The team was scheduled to meet at Tim Minor's home, and Mitch was assigned to bring dessert. They did not have to worry about him bringing *Skip to my Lou* pie. That was for sure! Melinda was making brownies. Mitch had not eaten any dessert since last week, and the brownies were just what he needed. He knew he would continue to enjoy Mrs. Hudson's pies but would always clarify what the key ingredients were in advance. He looked down at the notepad and added some thoughts to his planning list.

Christmas Eve (Evangelistic) Service

1. *Have service at 4:00-5:00pm to maximize participation by mini-mizing conflicts with evening family gatherings.* **Done. Also can-celled evening service on 22nd in order to emphasize Christmas Eve.**

2. *Advertise and plan a strict 60-minute service so that families can know how to plan (hopefully this will maximize participation).* **Done.**

3. *Prayer Coordinator: James Flynn. Will enlist a team to ensure the service is prayed for, beginning Thanksgiving weekend. Team will develop a plan.* **Done. James took care of this one.**

4. *Publicity Coordinator: Tim Minor. Will enlist a team to promote the service to the congregation and the community.* **Done. Team mailed out flyers and produced some (abt. 200) for members to give friends/family. Major social media blast also planned.**

5. *Childcare Coordinator: Carly Rooks. Team will enlist childcare workers for children five and under. First grade and older will par-ticipate in the service. Team will discuss pros and cons of volun-teers versus paid workers.* **Carly has workers enlisted.**

6. *Worship Team: Mitch Walker. My team will determine the ele-ments of the service and brainstorm ideas to maximize number of guests. I will share a gospel presentation, either as a sermon or a summary of the experience.* **Well publicized and promoted since Thanksgiving. Having everyone present fill out guest card at con-clusion. Card to include a place for people to respond that they**

have trusted Christ at the service or to ask for more information.

7. *Register everyone present at the conclusion of the service with a survey. Survey will include a place to respond that someone has trusted Jesus as Savior or would be willing to discuss further with someone from our church.* **See 6.**

8. *Enlist someone to decorate the church for this occasion.* **Carly Rooks taking care of this.**

9. *Consider how we can get children involved in the program. Note: Parents will come to watch their children and grandchildren.* **Children will sing two songs. Our kids enlisted along with some of their friends.**

10. *Call every member and past guests two weeks before to extend a personal invitation and encourage them to bring family and friends.* **Behind on this one. Try to nail it down at last meeting.**

Mitch placed the pencil between his teeth as he stared at what he had written and pondered the final steps. *I've never been this diligent in putting a special service together. Well, if it doesn't work, it will not be for lack of effort.* Mitch began to pray. He knew that all of the planning in the world would be insufficient if God did not bless the service. He prayed for Dizzy, Danny Rose and his baptism, for Carly Rooks' mom who was expected to attend, for God to soften the hearts of Lester McDonald and Bruce Rollins, and for the simple message that he was preparing. God also brought to his mind to pray for Pastor Marc Benton who had become so close in recent months, as well as for his daughter and grandchildren who would be missed so much in a season like this.

Chapter Twenty-Five

Reverse Mentoring

Sunday, December 29th

The steakhouse was crowded, but Mitch, Melinda, and Haley along with Marc Benton and his wife Betty, were seated within fifteen minutes. The families had spoken briefly with each other while at the church, but Mitch was careful to keep a distance to allow Pastor Benton to attend to the needs of his congregation following the service. Most of the formal introductions occurred in the waiting area of the restaurant. Betty Benton was pretty and as friendly as could be. She treated Haley like her own grandchild, and the families were quickly at ease with one another. They patiently waited as Melinda navigated on her crutches. She would be free of the cast by mid-January, if all went well.

"The service was great but was not at all what I expected." Mitch said as the waitress handed out menus.

"What do you mean?" Pastor Benton asked.

"Your church building looks very old and traditional, and the service was blended, but in my experience leaned more toward a current style. Don't take this personally, but based on your age, I expected more of a traditional approach from you."

"Quite frankly, I've wrestled with it a little bit. I hear conversations about style but often they are in the form of debates as if one is more pure or more spiritual than the other. To be honest, I can show you congregations that claim to be cutting-edge but aren't reaching people. Traditional, Blended, Current, you name it. In churches of every style you can find some that are thriving and others that are declining. Don't get caught up in all of that. Do what fits your community, your congregation, and your preferences so long as you don't violate Scripture. Unfortunately, some leaders elevate preferences to the same level as scriptural mandates. I want to hear about your Christmas Eve service. How did that go?"

"I was blown away," Mitch said excitedly as the young waitress returned to take drink orders, after which Mitch picked up his narrative. "First, the auditorium was packed. That is the first time that has happened since I've been there.

Remember that teen I've been working on, Dizzy? He was there. I baptized Danny Rose, and you would not believe how different he looked from when I met him. It wasn't his dress as much as his demeanor. He looked like a burden had been lifted off his shoulders."

"Can I have ice cream for dessert, Daddy?" Haley asked.

"Haley, don't interrupt," Melinda said with a firm but kind voice.

Mitch continued, "Anyway he sat up front and grinned the whole time. We had the children sing a couple of songs, and everyone enjoyed that, but with Danny, it looked like he was watching his own kids perform. We had at least a dozen families visit as well as a lot of relatives of family members who do not ordinarily attend."

"That's great," Marc responded as the drinks arrived. The waitress began to take orders, and the conversation diverted briefly to stories about favorite foods.

"I haven't told you the best part," Mitch said as he steered the conversation back to the Christmas Eve service. "Carly Rooks is a member of our evangelism leadership team. Her mom was one of the first people we started praying for when we started emphasizing prayer for the lost and unchurched. To make a long story short, Carly was in charge of decorations and used it as a hook to get her mom to agree to attend the service. She hasn't been to church in decades. Carly has tried to witness, but she has been resistant. Guess what? She committed her life to Jesus Christ at the conclusion of the service. She wasn't the only one. Two more people said they had done likewise, and two others want to talk more about it. I know I will be baptizing at least two next week, including Carly's mom. I wish you could have seen her celebrating the commitment her mom made. That's what Christmas is really all about!"

"That is great, Mitch! I am so proud of you and your church."

The meal arrived and the conversation transitioned to topics ranging from family to football games. Mitch was thinking of how he needed to cut back after today since he had been eating so heartily over the holidays, but that wasn't going to hinder him from enjoying his meal today. "Let me ask you a question, Melinda and Mitch," Pastor Benton asked as he cut into his steak. "What are young adults looking for in a church in your opinion? Let me tell you why I ask. We are from different generations, and there are differences in the way our generations think, and to some degree in their values or priorities. I learned long ago that if a pastor fails to give attention to young adults, the church will begin to experience decline. Obviously, the erosion of young adults in a congregation also means the loss of children and preschoolers."

"That's interesting," Mitch replied. "I thought your services were better oriented toward young adults than ours. My congregation has a lot of traditions and lots of senior adults."

"You're making progress. Probably more than you even realize, based on the things you have shared with me. I've always tried to be attentive to all groups but have found that I need to have this conversation with younger adults more often the older that I get. If you ignore any generation in the church, you do so at your own peril. So give me your thoughts."

Melinda spoke up first. "My peers place a high priority on family life. I'm not saying that other generations lack family commitment. To be honest, as it relates to the church, I get frustrated at the schedule sometimes. Our church has activities four or five nights some weeks, and we are a small congregation. I get frustrated at the way the schedule and frequency of services seem to be held sacred by some. I would rather spend more nights at home and actually more time in the community doing service rather than attending services."

"I agree," Mitch said. "I tested the waters once about eliminating a service to give families more time together and as a possible window for new outreach opportunities—I thought I was going to get stoned. They thought I was unspiritual simply because I recommended an alternative."

"When you say 'stoned', you do mean executed?" Pastor Benton asked with a grin.

"Yeah. Stoned, shot, stabbed, hanged, and tossed into the river." With a weak impression of Marlon Brando as the Godfather, he brushed his cheek with his right hand and added, "But I'm sure they would have made it look like an accident." Melinda rolled her eyes, but the Bentons kindly reserved judgment of his impersonation skills. "I really wish that I could get our church to be more hands-on in the community and going on mission trips. We give money to missions, but I don't understand why many of our older members don't want to get personally involved doing missions."

"It's interesting that you bring that up. I was planning for this to be the subject of our meeting when you and I get together again at the coffee shop in a couple of weeks."

Melinda added, "Another thing is that we really want the church and its leaders to be transparent. I don't like the politics of churches. We have actually had some friends leave our denomination because of some of the bickering. I want leaders who are honest, personable, and willing to admit when they fail. I appreciate confidence in leaders, but I get turned off by arrogance."

"You and I had a brief exchange in our e-mails a couple of weeks ago about relationships," Mitch said. "I appreciated your response. I feel like some churches are more focused on its programs than relationships. My peers believe in building community. We see life as a journey and believe it should be shared with others. We believe in discipleship, but we do not view it in terms of a course or a class as much as taking the journey with others, helping one another to grow and be accountable."

The conversation went on for another ten minutes, and Mitch and Melinda did not hold back. "I really appreciate that," Pastor Benton said. "Having conversations like this keep me aware of ways I can connect with our younger crowd. The older I get the more attentive I am to young adults. You have helped me a lot."

"I appreciate you asking us." Mitch said.

"Can I ask you another question?"

"Of course."

"You have a lot of older adults in your congregation, and you are only about thirty years old. Have you ever asked this question of some of your older members so that you could have a better understanding of their needs?"

Mitch paused, knowing that Pastor Benton had him right where he wanted him. "The answer to that would be no. I can't say that I have."

"I'm sure they would be as willing to share as you were. Generation gaps have always existed. You and I are leaders. It's our responsibility to reach out to all generations and bring them together for the Kingdom's sake. Hey, I'm ready for some dessert. What looks good, Mitch?"

"Anything as long as it doesn't have prunes."

The Bentons gave Mitch a puzzled look, knowing there was no such item on the menu. Mitch was able to tell the story of the *Skip to My Lou* pie incident, and now, after a couple of weeks, finally saw the humor in it.

Chapter Twenty-Six

STACKING THE DECK

Tuesday, December 31st

Mitch and Haley walked into the Rock Springs bowling alley after stopping for a kid's meal at a local burger joint. The entrance contained an arcade with dozens of video units and games, and it projected a strange blend of electronic music that was in no way synchronized. In the background, you could hear the bowling balls hitting the wooden floors and pins dropping, with pop music playing loudly over the sound system.

"Can I play a game?" Haley asked as she tugged at her dad's jeans.

"You can later. Let's go find our group first." Mitch had brought Haley along for the afternoon activity of Alan Kimmons' youth Bible study group. He spotted them down on the two lanes next to the end. It looked like at least five students were present. He recognized Cecilia Ramirez, who was oldest of the group. She was talking to one of the newer members, Lindy Hutchison. His neighbor, Wyatt, was there, and he was glad to see Dizzy had come along. He did not recognize the other girl who looked to be the same age as Lindy and, in fact, turned out to be one of her friends. "How's it going guys? Who's winning?"

The group exchanged pleasantries and as they returned to the game, Mitch noticed that Dizzy was sitting at a table wearing boots instead of hideous-looking bowling shoes like the others. *There's no way he wants to be seen in public with those*, Mitch thought. Dizzy obviously was not bowling.

"Hey Diz. What's up? You're not bowling?"

"No. I don't bowl. I just came to hang out."

"You can go play some video games if you want."

"I'm tapped out right now. Anyways, that man says I have to stay with the group," he said, referring to Alan.

"Let me see what I can do. Haley, do you want to play a game first, or do you want to eat an ice cream and watch them bowl?"

"I want ice cream first." Haley said excitedly.

Mitch went and talked to Alan, agreeing to take responsibility for Dizzy in exchange for the group looking after Haley while she ate her ice cream. He came back in short order and said to Dizzy. "Let's go. I've got it covered."

"I don't have no money."

"My treat. What's your favorite game?"

"I like Clockdown and BMX Bizarre."

"I'm not familiar, but I'm willing to learn."

Dizzy did not have any trouble trouncing Mitch, although his skills did improve as they went through the tokens that Mitch purchased.

"I saw you at the Christmas Eve service," Mitch said.

Dizzy was concentrating on the game but muttered what Mitch took to be an affirmation that he was indeed there. Mitch obviously knew he had attended and hoped to have a conversation about it.

"What did you get out of it?"

Dizzy's art-rendered motorcycle hit an obstacle and blew up. He reached down to tap the reset button for his next ride. "Not much. I mean it was all right hearing those kids sing and stuff, but I didn't see any real angels or anything."

Mitch could sense that Dizzy had no interest in discussing spiritual matters right now. He changed the subject and kept some distance. He thought he had made some progress in connecting with Dizzy, but if today was any indication, he was not even close. He let Dizzy play for almost an hour before going back to the group. Mitch had spent close to twenty dollars for Dizzy to play games, but received no words of thanks or acknowledgement. This could have made him mad, but instead it made him more prayerful and sympathetic. *Maybe*, Mitch thought, *Dizzy will have a better new year.*

Monday, January 6th

The new year was off to a good start for Mitch. No major crises had developed, and he had spent a lot of time with Haley and Melinda over the past couple of weeks. The first Sunday of the year had been great, with two baptisms. One was Carly Rook's mom, Wilma, who was baptized along with a twenty-seven-year-old named Ben Roland. He and his wife Amber had visited several times, beginning in November. Amber had become a follower of Christ when she was a teenager and had been praying for her husband Ben since they met back in college. Though Mitch wouldn't have advised a believer to marry an unbeliever, it was a moot point since he had only met this couple after they were already married. Now, of course, he could only rejoice that Ben made a commitment to follow Christ.

"James Flynn is on the phone," Jerri Minor shouted down the hallway as Mitch returned from getting a bottle of water from the kitchen area in the fellowship hall. Mitch had come in to the church office for the afternoon to catch up on some administrative tasks that had piled up over the holidays. "Tell him I'll be right there." Mitch made his way to his office and picked up the phone. "Hey, James. How's it going?"

"That depends. Are you asking from a human perspective or from a spiritual perspective?"

"I'm asking from a friend's perspective. You are a friend, aren't you?"

"Of course I am. I've always been drawn to the needy and the helpless," James answered with a hint of sarcasm.

"Well, I need all of the help I can get. What do you have?"

"The deacon selections are in."

The method of selecting deacons at Stanton Community Church was outlined in the church bylaws. The church members made nominations from which the acting deacons made final selections. The church would then vote on the recommendations, but it was a simple formality once the deacons had made their choices. Mitch knew that five had been nominated for two spots. The nominees included Alan Kimmons, the youth Bible study leader; Randall Mullins, Mitch's neighbor; D.C. Palmer, a senior adult member who was already an ordained deacon but had not served in over a decade; Jacob Rollins, brother of Bruce Rollins; and Lester McDonald. Kimmons or Mullins would be great supporters for Mitch. McDonald and Rollins would line up with the opposition. Mitch wasn't sure where Mr. Palmer stood. He participated in church affairs, but had never vocalized any strong opinions that Mitch could recall.

"Give it to me. How did it turn out?" Mitch asked.

"Well you know that Thomas surprised us both by throwing his support behind you, and I know that you two have actually become pretty good friends. But, I suppose he felt he could not oppose his own dad on something like this. It would be pretty embarrassing to the family to suggest his dad is unworthy of serving as a deacon. He went with Rollins and Dollar on this one. Lester McDonald is now on the deacon board."

"Oh, that's just great. Please tell me that Alan or Randall got the other spot."

"Afraid not."

"Did it go to Mr. Palmer?"

"Not him either."

"Who?"

"Jacob Rollins."

"Are you kidding me? Bruce Rollins' brother! He doesn't even come to services half of the time."

"Yes, I know. I'm not endorsing him. I'm just telling you that he has been a member of this church all of his life, and he is well-respected. He's a banker, and he's helped a lot of people in this church including the McDonald family. Their business and the bank are joined at the hip. Thomas was between a rock and a hard place. I'm not exactly happy about the way he voted, but he was under a tremendous amount of pressure."

"Well that gives them four out of seven votes if they want to come back after me again and five of seven if Thomas wavers any further."

"Like I told you before, there is only one vote you need to be concerned about. Remember?"

"Yea, I remember. It's God's. But couldn't God make it a little easier on me and put more of my supporters into leadership?"

"Just because you don't know what God is up to doesn't mean that God does not have a plan. Don't panic."

"I'm not panicking. I'm just freaking out a little bit."

"You worry too much."

"You don't worry enough!"

"Maybe that's why we make a good team."

"Should I put my resume out?"

"No. You should get on your knees and ask for God to be glorified."

"That's becoming a real familiar place for me lately."

"Then God has you right where He wants you!"

Chapter Twenty-Seven

SERVANT EVANGELISM

Tuesday, January 7th

The temperature had dropped to just above freezing, and the wind made it icy-cold. Mitch loved coffee on a cold winter morning. Refreshing. He sat across from Pastor Benton sipping his coffee and telling him the good and the bad from the past two days—Sunday's two baptisms followed by Monday's announcement of two new deacons who could not be counted on for support. Mitch sincerely wanted to be able to rejoice more over the baptisms of the two new believers than to be anxious about the new deacon appointments, but his feelings could not seem to catch up with what his brain was telling him. *Salvation is eternal; deacons are temporary. Why can't my emotions respond with the right balance?* Mitch pondered. Pastor Benton was sympathetic and encouraged Mitch to stay the course.

"Mitch, you stay focused on helping people to grow and reaching out to hurting people. It's all going to turn out just fine."

"That's what I keep trying to tell myself. OK. Let's focus on what's next. I already feel like I'm drinking from a fire hydrant sometimes. I've worked on my own leadership and priorities, adjusted the prayer focus to include prayer for unbelievers, and started planning a sermon series in March to emphasize personal evangelism. And we invested in the Christmas Eve service in a huge way––and man, it really worked! I appreciate your help on that. We're going to do the same thing for Easter and Back to School Sunday in August. Isn't that enough?"

"Well, honestly, Mitch you could stop there. I don't mean stop doing it. What I mean is that if you continue to apply those things you just described, they will make a difference. I believe you can see that they already have. If you were a bi-vocational pastor, I would be hesitant to take you any further simply because I would not want to overtax you."

"I don't want to be overtaxed. The government is already taking care of that one."

"Don't get me started," Pastor Benton replied with a mild look of disgust. "Do you want to keep going, or do you want to focus on applying what you've already received?"

"No, I want to keep going. I know your time is valuable, and I can't believe you've spent this much time with me already. I want to take advantage of everything you have time to share with me while we have time together."

"That's good. Trust me, this time means a lot to me also. I'm not just teaching, Mitch. I'm learning too. You and Melinda shared some great insights at lunch last week. I've already shared with my staff a couple of adjustments we need to start making, based on your comments. I appreciate your transparency. Hearing your heart and what is happening in your church not only helps make me be a better leader but also will help me to assist other pastors in the future. This is not a sacrifice but a pleasure."

Comments like that are what impressed Mitch about Pastor Benton. *What a great role model for pastors of larger congregations*, Mitch thought. He assumed he was the one being mentored, but the older man had just made it clear that, although he had the primary role, the mentoring went both ways. *Lord, I don't know that I will ever pastor a large congregation, but if I do, give me a heart like his.* "OK, what's next?"

"Do you know how most adults come to faith in Jesus?"

"It happens when the Holy Spirit convicts them of their sins, and they respond to the gospel through personal faith in Jesus."

"That's true, but I was thinking more tangibly. What are the circumstances through which the Holy Spirit often works?"

"I'm not sure I follow."

"Jesus said that 'it rains on the just and the unjust.' I think you would agree that no one is immune from problems. What happens when an unbeliever experiences a crisis?"

"I've noticed that some people get upset with God when troubles come. They blame Him, and if they pray and He doesn't respond by bailing them out, then they sometimes use it as an excuse not to believe in God or at least not to trust Him. Other people turn to God in a time of difficulty. If they do believe in God, they turn to prayer even when they are not religious."

"You are exactly right. Let me tell you what research shows us. Most adults who come to faith in Jesus do so when they experience a crisis—and the Christian community is ministering to them. When they are not experiencing crisis, they have no sense of need for the gospel, even when a Christian is nearby. And if they are experiencing a crisis but no Christian steps forward to help, there is no vehicle for the gospel to be delivered. The Holy Spirit indeed is active, but most often He works through people who are believers. Research shows that the point at which most adults come to faith is when a Christian is helping them during a crisis. This was discovered in studies of adults who came to faith later in life, as opposed to their childhood years."

"I never thought about it that way, but it makes sense."

Pastor Benton went on to challenge Mitch to help his congregation in two ways. First, he encouraged Mitch to discover how the congregation could be more purposeful in identifying hurting people in order to be more intentional in reaching out to meet their needs. Secondly, he discussed the value of servant evangelism and community projects. He shared how the projects not only afforded opportunities to minister but also to share the gospel. In addition, he proposed that the reputation of the church could be enhanced in the community thereby, opening up even more doors to share the gospel. Mitch wrote down some notes for discussion at the next evangelism leadership team meeting.

1. *Can we identify at least one need each month from among the prayer requests received on Wednesday nights and work together to meet the need of someone who is unchurched?*

2. *Can we do something to train our Sunday morning Bible study groups to do likewise each month?*

3. *Could we brainstorm some community service projects and get members involved?*

4. *Could we challenge Sunday morning Bible study groups to do some kind of community project at least a couple of times a year?*

5. *What community leaders could we visit to discover needs in the community that we might address? Mayor? Police Chief? County Commissioner? School principals? Other?*

6. *I need to open my eyes to needs of hurting people who do not go to church and be more intentional in either reaching out personally or leading church to do so.*

7. *Right up my alley! This is where my heart has been but too tied up in past couple of years trying to keep my head above water. This is what ministry is supposed to be about!*

Chapter Twenty-Eight

CONVERTS OR DISCIPLES?

Sunday, January 12th

Mitch found himself amazed at how the enthusiasm of a team of friends and leaders could melt away his anxieties and frustrations when they gathered together. Tonight, all of the evangelism leadership team members were present along with their spouses. Melinda, her broken leg propped up, sat with her good friend Carly Rooks. Tim and Jerri Minor, James and Darlene Flynn, along with Alan and Kris Kimmons, were sitting in the Kimmons' living room enjoying coffee and red velvet cake. The mood was joyful as Mitch made a confession. "Kris, did you bake this cake, or did it happen to come from Mrs. Hudson?" he asked. He still loved Mrs. Hudson's pies but had grown a bit more cautious about dessert in the past month.

"I made it myself. Why do you ask? Are you saying you like Mrs. Hudson's desserts better?" she asked with a look that communicated, "You'd better give the right answer."

"Oh no, no, no. This is great, and I figured it was yours, but I just wanted to be sure." By the time Mitch finished regaling the group with memories of prune pie, some of the team members were laughing so hard that they were crying. The group was really bonding from the regular gatherings together, and Mitch now understood that pulling the team together was one of the wisest decisions he had made in his brief stint as pastor of Stanton Community Church. Every idea had built-in momentum, and buy-in had increased most likely because the team was engaged in the process from the outset. When Mitch would communicate actions and ideas from the platform, the team members and their spouses would be supporting, uplifting, and affirming the ideas among the congregation. They never discussed this dynamic as a strategy, but it naturally flowed out of the process of meeting together regularly to pray and to brainstorm how to lead the church in outreach.

Mitch also appreciated the fact that the gatherings were not like some committees that met simply for the sake of the meeting. The group always left with actionable items that the group had prayed over and developed out of the synergy of the group. *I may want to bring a couple of more members onto this team soon to expand this energy*, Mitch thought. The laughter quieted, and Mitch took the opportunity to shift the conversation to the agenda items he had in mind for the evening's gathering. "Thank you guys for all of the hard work in making the Christmas Eve service so successful. I was challenged by Dr. Benton to take our three highest attended services each year and to invest maximum energy in building attendance, so as to share the gospel with more people. You helped me implement the strategy, and you are all well aware of how great it was. I've seen at least two families visit in the past couple of Sundays who were with us for the very first time at the Christmas Eve service, and hopefully we'll see more. I appreciate your helping with the follow-up."

"Do you remember how we stopped to pray for my mom at our very first meeting?" Carly asked the group. "It's a miracle that her heart softened within a few short months. It was kind of hard to get her to attend, but once she did, the Lord and His Spirit caught hold of her. I could not believe the transformation and how she opened her heart to the Lord at that service. Thanks to each one of you for your prayers."

The roomed buzzed with words of affirmation. Melinda grabbed Carly by the hand as Mitch spoke for the group. "Carly, we are so proud for you and proud for your mom. It's great whenever anyone comes to faith and gets baptized, but I've never been more moved than to see a senior adult lady make a profession of faith and follow through." The group voiced their agreement.

"We also had a young adult baptized. Ben Roland is excited but not nearly as much as his wife Amber," Kris Kimmons added.

Her husband, Alan, was sitting on the sofa next to her and asked, "Didn't we have some other responses?"

"Yes, we had one other person who said that they trusted Jesus as their Savior at the service, and three others checked the section on the registration card that said they would like to know more," Mitch replied. "I've followed up on two, and James followed up on two."

"I went by and visited one of the couples who both checked that box, and we talked for over an hour," James replied. "They have not been in church for a while. After discussing what it means to follow Christ, they assured me that they had a personal relationship with Jesus. What do you do? I'm not saying they do or they don't, but they are the ones that have to have the assurance. I did my best to share and clarify. They told me they were going to start going back to a church that they used to attend."

"I have not been able to track down the other person that said they want more information. The good news is that I spoke with Hayden Tolliver. He responded that night along with Mrs. Townsend and Ben Roland that he had trusted Christ."

"When is he going to be baptized?" asked Jerri Minor.

"He already has been, but at another church."

"That's not fair," Kris Kimmons said. "He came to faith at our service."

"I would love to have baptized him, but let's not get sidetracked. It's not about increasing numbers but about faithfully sharing and growing the Kingdom. He belongs to God, and that is what is important."

"You're right. I'm just excited that we're seeing people trust Christ and get baptized. It's just refreshing to see how God is moving in our church. I didn't mean to sound selfish."

"Oh no, not at all. We should be excited."

"What are we doing to disciple these new believers?" Tim Minor asked.

Mitch had intended to introduce servant and ministry evangelism as the main topic of the evening, but Tim's question opened up a lengthy but critical discussion. Three children and three adults had been baptized in the past three months. Jerri Minor, as the church secretary, agreed to follow up and make sure that all were assigned to a Sunday morning Bible study group. Tim and James agreed to take personal responsibility for investing time with Danny Rose and Ben Roland while Kris agreed to take all three of the children through a New Christians class. All agreed that more attention should be given to this issue but time went by quickly, and they left with a plan to give greater attention to those to whom God had given them responsibility.

Chapter Twenty-Nine

Fashion Statement

Sunday, January 19th

The voices of members arriving for Sunday morning Bible study were beginning to fill the hallways of Stanton Community Church. Mitch had arrived by 7:30 A.M. and had spent some time walking through the hallways of the church and worship center, praying for those who would attend. He had also taken a final look at his sermon before people began to arrive. As he tried to interact with as many members as possible in the hallways, he would occasionally be pulled into his office for an impromptu counseling session or prayer meeting. Now Kris and Alan Kimmons were heading his way. "Guess what, Mitch?" Kris asked. "We're going to take all of the children through a New Christian curriculum over the next few weeks, and I've contacted the parents of all three who have recently indicated they want to follow Christ. They are all supposed to be here this morning."

"Awesome, Kris! Thanks for jumping right on that. Where did you get the materials?"

"I ordered them online. They arrived Friday, and I had time to dig into them yesterday to get ready. I called the children earlier in the week. I actually called all of the children that we have contact information on. I figured that this may be a good way to prepare children to become followers of Christ as well as to follow up those who have already made the commitment."

"I like the way you're thinking, Kris. I wish everyone had your enthusiasm and initiative. You and Alan are great examples of the way church members should be engaged with the life of the church."

"You're doing a great job, Mitch, and we appreciate your leadership," Alan replied.

Mitch continued down the hallway and saw Wyatt come in, bundled up against the January cold. To his surprise, he noticed that Dizzy was right behind him, but he was not dressed as you would expect for church—or for cold weather. Mitch was amused to see him wearing shorts, although the temperature was near freezing. He wore a black hooded sweatshirt, black shorts, black socks, and black shoes. Mitch didn't say anything about Dizzy's attire. He was just glad to have him in attendance. He had been afraid that Dizzy had regressed when they had last talked at the bowling alley. He greeted both and turned as John Dollar called out his name from the opposite end of the hallway.

"Good morning, John. I hope you've had a good week."

"It's been all right. I want to ask you a quick question before I get to my Bible study group. I was studying Romans 8:21–30 this week, about predestination."

A quick question? Now that would be refreshing, but how will that be possible if he opens up this can of worms?

Dollar got right to his point. "Now I want to make sure you understand about this because there's a lot of confusion out there, and I've been studying it for a long time."

Hmmm? Predestination? If everything is predestined, I guess we were bound to have this conversation today! Might as well get it over with. Mitch listened attentively and was cautious not to take Dollar's *bait* to engage in de*bate*. The hallways were emptying as the Bible study groups started up, which opened an opportunity for Mitch to interrupt the lecture with a suggestion. "John, I sure appreciate your insight, but your group really counts on you, so you may want to get in there before they get started."

"We'll talk more about this later," Dollar replied as he turned and headed back down the hallway toward his group.

God bless the elect, Mitch thought as he turned and headed the other way. Mitch thought about how amazing the church was. You would be hard-pressed to find the same level of diversity of background, education, experience, and opinion anywhere else but in a local church, but somehow it works. God keeps it all together as people are bound by their faith in Jesus Christ.

The Bible study hour and then the worship service zipped by, and Mitch was pleased as he stood at the back door greeting members and guests alike on their way out. He suddenly noticed Lester McDonald lurking on the other side of the foyer as the line continued to proceed. McDonald did not look happy (but then, Mitch could rarely remember a time when he ever did). He noticed that Lester's right foot was tapping up and down as if he were revved up and ready to pounce as soon as an opportunity availed. Mitch saw him coming as soon as the line came to an end.

"Do you see that?" McDonald asked with a clear sense of disgust.

"Excuse me?" Mitch asked.

"Do you see that over there?"

Mitch looked around but could not discern what McDonald was talking about.

"Lester, I have no clue."

"Look at that boy over there," he said pointing to Dizzy on the front porch. Dizzy was talking to a couple of other teens in the cold, wintry air wearing his black shorts.

"What about him?"

"You see what he's wearing, don't you?"

"Sure, Lester, what about it?"

"He's wearing shorts to church!" McDonald went on a diatribe for the next couple of minutes, regarding appropriate dress for church and making a clear case for why Dizzy's wardrobe selection was unfitting and unspiritual.

"Well Lester, he didn't call me and ask. I don't wear shorts to church and my wife doesn't wear shorts, so I don't know why you are getting so worked up with me like I've done something wrong."

"What are you going to do about it?" McDonald demanded.

"What do you think I should do?"

"I think you should go over there and set him straight. You're the pastor. Tell him not to come back if he's not going to dress right!"

"Can I ask you a question, Lester? What is that boy's name?"

"I don't know his name. I can't say I've ever seen him before."

"Do you know his parents?"

"No."

"Have you ever talked to him before?"

"I don't need to talk to him. You do."

"Before I do, let me ask you one more thing. How long has that boy been a Christian?"

"I don't know if he is one, and I'd have to say he's not one, just looking at 'im."

"So let me get this straight. You're more concerned over the fact that his calves and knees are showing than whether he knows Jesus or not?"

"That's not what this is about!"

"Lester, I do know him. His name is Dizzy, and he's not a believer. God is more concerned about changing his heart than his pants. God works inside out.

If he comes to faith in Jesus, the other things will take care of themselves in time as he grows and matures."

"This church is going to hell in a handbasket under your leadership, and I'm not going to let you talk down to me."

"I don't appreciate your language, and I think you need to pray for that boy. I know I'm going to be praying for you."

McDonald huffed and walked away. Mitch never considered himself "Mr. Confrontational" and wondered where that just came from. McDonald was not used to being stood up to, and Mitch wondered if he had gone too far. *God, you sure are good, but your children sure do get on my nerves sometimes.*

Chapter Thirty

ALMOST PERSUADED

Saturday, February 1 st

The game clock showed only 1.9 seconds remaining. The coliseum was buzzing as the home team huddled for their final timeout. The game had gone back and forth as the two evenly matched rivals had fought in what would have been known as a classic had it been shown to a network television audience. No one was sitting down. Mitch, his neighbors Randall and Wyatt, and Dizzy had made the trek to Rock Springs to see one of the four state universities' basketball teams seek to keep their season record unblemished.

The noise was deafening as the ball was in-bounded on the far end of the court. Would there be enough time for the home team to go the length of the court and make a three-point shot? No one was open downcourt, so the point guard took the shorter pass and began dribbling at breakneck speed, skillfully navigating around two defensive players along the way. "He's not going to have time!" Wyatt shouted. As the point guard reached the mid-court stripe with no time left to continue his drive, he launched the ball toward the basket, hoping for a miracle shot. As the ball arced, the horn sounded, but it had been released in time. It tracked high and long toward the basket. Would it get there? Swish! It dropped through the middle, hitting nothing but the bottom of the net. The home crowd went crazy with excitement. Students rushed the court to celebrate with the local team that had barely kept their undefeated streak intact.

Mitch, Randall, Wyatt, and Dizzy gave each other enthused high fives. Dizzy grinned as he received a hug from a good-looking girl sitting next to him whom he had never even met before. Dizzy, blushing, had the biggest smile on his face that Mitch had ever seen. He was still somewhat of a mystery to Mitch. Through his tough exterior, Mitch often caught glimpses of a different person who genuinely wanted to fit in. Normally, Dizzy would barely acknowledge that he liked sports, but he was obviously caught up in the excitement of the victory like everyone else. No one was in a hurry to leave, but after the celebration began to wane, the foursome loaded up to head back to Stanton. Although Dizzy did not know it, Mitch silently prayed for him for the entire forty minutes of the drive home.

Randall was driving, and Mitch sat up front in the honored "shotgun seat." After they dropped Dizzy off at his apartment complex and headed toward their own neighborhood, he turned and asked Wyatt, "What's going on with Dizzy nowadays? Is he doing all right?"

"Yeah, I guess so."

"No. I'm serious, Wyatt. I don't want a Sunday school answer. How is he doing, really?"

"You saw the apartments where he lives. They're not the nicest place in town. A lot of the kids there seem to get in a lot of trouble, and he's got a lot of friends there. I was starting to hang around with some of 'em, but we talked about that. I realized how they were pulling me down and stopped hanging out. But I still like to hang with Diz because we both like skateboarding, and he doesn't try to get me in trouble."

"What do you know about his family?"

"I've met his mom a couple of times. I don't think he has a dad who lives with him. At least I've never seen 'im, and Diz doesn't talk about 'im. He also has a sister, but I don't really know her. His mom seems to let him go just about wherever he wants."

"I believe I recall you telling me that his family is not exactly the churchgoing type?"

"No, they don't go, but Dizzy has come with me a few times lately."

"I appreciate you reaching out to him, Wyatt. I really like him, but he just seems like he's struggling. I don't know if he's been hurt, or if his family life is tough or what. I just know the Lord has given me a burden for him for some reason."

Wyatt did not really say anything in response to that. He didn't necessarily seem to disagree in any way, but perhaps the conversation was going a little deep for him. They pulled into the driveway and exchanged pleasantries before heading their own ways. Mitch walked in his front door and got a warm hug from Haley. "Who won, Daddy?" she asked.

"We did on a miracle shot from half court with the buzzer going off."

"What's half court?"

Mitch had forgotten that his daughter wasn't totally oriented to all of the basketball terms, and he gave her a brief explanation. Continuing to look for Melinda, he finally found her in the bedroom talking on the telephone. It was great to see her standing there without a cast on her leg although she still had a slight limp. "I'm so sorry, Carly," Mitch heard her say. "We'll be over in a few minutes." Melinda hung up the phone. "You got here just in time," she said. "We have to get over to Carly's house right away. Her mother just passed away."

Mitch, Melinda, and Haley were out the door within a couple of minutes. "I can't believe this," Mitch said. "She was sitting right there with Carly last Sunday and looked like she was having the time of her life." Mitch had baptized her barely more than a month ago.

Melinda recounted her conversation with Carly from a few minutes earlier. Her mom had collapsed right in Carly's living room. A 911 call went out immediately, but she had died before the paramedics arrived. They tried to revive her and had rushed her to the hospital, but it was too late. It was not clear, at this point, if Carly's mother had suffered a heart attack, a stroke, or something else. They did their best to get Haley ready for what she was about to experience when they got to the Rook's home, where her best friend, Emma, would be grieving the loss of her grandmother.

"Can you believe she trusted Christ barely a month ago, and now she's in heaven?" Mitch mused.

"I'm so thankful that God worked in her life. I know Carly is going to be heartbroken, but can you imagine how much deeper the hurt would be if her mom had not trusted Jesus for her salvation? I'm so glad that my parents know the Lord. I wonder if people really think about what they do to their children or their spouse when they don't prepare them for eternity. I want Haley to know after we're gone that we will be in heaven because of our relationship with Christ and that we can be together again someday."

"Amen to that. These next couple of days, as tough as they will be, will not be nearly as difficult as it would have been a couple of months ago." *Thank you, Lord, for hearing our prayers and saving Carly's mom, and thank you that she is with you now and for eternity.*

Tuesday, February 4th

The funeral service was held at the Stanton Community church on a bitterly cold February day. Afterward, Mitch, Melinda, and Haley joined Carly, Emma, several church members, and a few of Carly's family members, including her brother, Burton, at Carly's home afterward, where they quietly talked and grazed on the dozens of dishes of food brought over by church members. The service had been somewhat celebrative as Mitch shared a eulogy for Mrs. Townsend, including the testimony of how she recently came to faith in Jesus. He unapologetically talked about the need to prepare for this moment. His message pointed out that even though it is difficult to be ready for death, it is easy to be prepared because of what Jesus did on the cross when He died for the sins of the world. He encouraged everyone who had any doubt about their eternity or their relationship to Jesus to come before the Lord in a spirit of repentance, placing their faith in Jesus for forgiveness of sins and for salvation. Privately, he had prayed that someone attending the funeral would be convicted by the Holy Spirit and would fully devote his or her life to Jesus because of the testimony of Carly's mom, Wilma Townsend.

Mitch found himself alone later in the day with Carly's brother, Burton, as the houseguests began to depart. "Burton, I've enjoyed getting to know you these past couple of days, but I hate it had to be like this," Mitch said as they sat in the living room together.

"Me too, pastor, but I appreciate all that you've done. I know that Carly thinks the world of your family."

"When are you going to be heading home?"

"I'm going to head out tomorrow afternoon. I want to make sure Carly has everything she needs. I'll come back next weekend and help her begin to deal with mom's estate and start working through those details."

"You let me know if there's anything we can do to help."

"I appreciate it."

"I was honored to preach at your mom's funeral, Burton. I'm glad she came to faith in Jesus, and we know she's in heaven. Did I understand Carly to say that you don't have a church where you attend?"

"No, I've never been much of a churchgoer."

"Do you have anyone you consider to be your pastor?"

"Not really. I guess I don't even know a preacher other than you."

"You mind if I ask you a personal question?"

"I guess not. It's just you 'n' me sittin' here."

"I hope you live to be ninety-nine, but let's say something did happen, like with your mom, and you died. Who would preach your funeral?"

"That's the kind of thing I try not to think about. I guess since you're the only preacher I know, you might just get nominated." Burton said that with a hint of a grin as he tried to lighten what he could sense was a serious conversation.

"That's probably true, and I want you to know that I would be honored if that circumstance ever presented itself. I told everybody today that your mom is in heaven, and I told everyone why we know that to be true. If I ever had to do your funeral, what would you want me to tell them? Where would I tell them you would be?"

Burton looked as if he had just seen a ghost. He did not get angry or defensive but was sober and reflective. "I don't know. I hope I go to heaven. I've never done anything that was really that bad."

"Have you ever broken any of the commandments? Have you ever lied or stolen anything?"

"I've never been arrested."

"That's not what I asked. Have you ever done anything that would violate the commandments or the word of God?"

"Of course, I have. Who hasn't?"

"The Bible teaches that we have all sinned and come short of God's glory. It teaches that the consequence of sin is death. Death in this context means eternal separation from God. God is a loving God, but He is also a Holy God. He cannot overlook your sin or anyone else's. You cannot go to heaven if you die in your sin. That's why Jesus died on the cross. He died a sacrificial death for your sin. We know He's God's son because of the resurrection.

"That may be true, but I've got too many questions. Don't get me wrong. I respect you, but quite frankly I think the church is filled with hypocrites."

"A lot of people would agree with you, but does that change whether or not Jesus died on the cross for your sins? He either did or He didn't. Don't let a hypocrite come between you and God. I heard someone say once that if a hypocrite stands between you and God that places him closer to God than you are."

"I'm just not ready for something like that. I told you that I'm not a church-goer."

"Well, I'm not saying church is not important, but I am saying that church attendance is not the issue. People don't go to church to get to heaven. They go because they're going to heaven, and they desire to worship and serve God in a community of other like-minded believers. I'm not asking you about church. I'm asking if you would be willing to turn from your sin by seeking Jesus' forgiveness and choosing to follow Him as Savior and Lord."

"I can't do that right now. I'm not ready."

"Burton, just remember that God is ready. Your mom is going to be waiting for you on the other side. It would be tragic for you to miss it. I want you to also think about your wife and children and the pain that you will cause them if they didn't know that you had made things right with God."

Mitch sensed that Burton was under conviction and was perhaps close to taking the step of faith. He allowed Mitch to pray for him and expressed sincere appreciation although he did not respond to Mitch's witness. Mitch was reminded that sometimes the seed falls on harder soil.

Chapter Thirty-One

HOME RUN HITTERS

Tuesday, February 11th

The roads were icy during the early morning hours, and Mitch questioned the wisdom of making the drive to meet Pastor Benton for their monthly engagement to discuss evangelism and leadership. A few text messages back and forth, internet weather reports, and a test drive to the church and back gave him the confidence that the trip would be safe enough. He did not want to miss these opportunities, knowing that their time together was valuable, and limited. He had already learned more than he had time to apply, but he was trying to document as much as possible so that he could refer back in future years to make deeper applications. The church seemed to be moving forward, though the pace seemed to be hindered by the continuous opposition of that handful of key members. It was amazing how so few could serve as such a heavy anchor on the progress of the majority.

The cautious drive to Southerland was tedious, but Mitch managed to make the trip without damage to vehicle or pedestrian. He was glad to get inside, and anxious for a cup of hot coffee. Pastor Benton had already arrived, and their pleasantries quickly gave way to a continuation of their monthly discussion on intentionality in evangelism.

Mitch took a brief moment to share about the loss of Wilma Townsend, the disappointing conversation with Burton Townsend, whom he felt had been close to surrendering his life to Christ, and his continued concern for the teen named Dizzy of whom he had grown so fond and for whom he felt such a burden. Pastor Benton asked Mitch to pray for his wife. Their prodigal daughter had actually been born on Valentine's Day, and the upcoming holiday was a painful reminder to both of them that they had lost her along with the grandkids and did not know if they would be in contact with her ever again. They prayed and then launched into the topic of the day.

"How would you assess the value of the investment you and the congregation made in getting ready for the Christmas Eve services back in December?" Pastor Benton asked.

"It was hands-down worth all that we did. We had many guests present, had a great service, and most importantly, we were blessed to see people come to faith in Jesus as a result of it all."

"I'm glad you and your congregation experienced that, and I hope you're sold on the value of intentional prayer and preparation. Let me review with you again what I call the six components of the *Net Effect*. You will be hard-pressed to find a church that is not reaching people if they fully integrate all of these:

- Praying for the lost (intentionally and by name)
- Personal evangelism equipping (for the core and the congregation)
- Proclamation of the gospel message (maximizing attendance and guests present at your best-attended services)
- Service/ministry evangelism (helping and serving the needy and hurting in your community)
- Team evangelism
- Event evangelism

"We're going to talk about event evangelism today, and we'll talk about team evangelism sometime in the near future. I know this is elementary, but do you have a basic sense of what I mean when I say 'event evangelism'?"

"Sure, it's somewhat self-descriptive. I assume it means that when our church sponsors various events, we should use them to an evangelistic advantage. Would that be accurate?"

"Not bad! Your Christmas Eve service was a proclamation service similar to the one you provide every Sunday morning. Of course, I encouraged you to ramp up the top-attended services in order to take advantage of more guests being present. But think about this...would it be true to say that there are people in your community whom you could not even pay to come to your church services?"

"Sure. We wish they would but they have no interest in church. We have definitely improved in inviting people and attendance has reflected that, but not everyone responds."

"Exactly, but that doesn't mean that you don't have other options to connect with them. Last month we talked about service and crisis ministry evangelism. That's one tool, but you still limit the number of people you will connect with if you stop there. I know you like basketball, but how about softball? Do you ever play?"

Mitch's eyes brightened as they always did when sports were the theme of the conversation. "I love to play, but it's been a few years since I played on an organized team."

"Let me tell you what I learned about evangelism through church softball several years back. Our church had a team, and we had a pretty stringent requirement that all of the players attend church at least three out of four Sundays. We had a good team, and they represented our church well. At least they did most of the time. It's amazing how competitive church softball can be."

"You're telling me. I actually got in a fight at a game one time. Let's just say that my opponent didn't appreciate the way I slid into second base and broke up a double play. I was getting pounded for a minute there."

"Are you serious? You got in a fight and got beat up?"

"No, I didn't get beat up. She was pretty scrappy, though," Mitch said with a grin that let Benton know that he reeled him in on a joke.

"You're killing me. Seriously, let me tell you what happened. We decided to have two teams, and I pulled the men together and told them we were only going to have nine men on each team. They began to object knowing that you need at least a dozen members, and I told them to hear me out. I suggested that we open three spots on each team for guests only. I explained that we would give the guests a discounted price, but we would expect them to pay. If it were free, they might show up for a couple of games and then drop out. Having them pay ensured a greater level of commitment."

"How did it work?"

"I explained further to our men what I meant when I said that we wanted three guests on the teams. I told them that 'guest' was a code word for 'heathens who can hit home runs.' I asked them to work together to find three unchurched friends to play on each of the teams. We weren't looking for members of other churches that did not have teams but rather for men who were not Christians. The way I figured it was that heathens are going to play softball somewhere, so why not with us?"

"Are you serious? Didn't you have to put up with some stuff? I mean if the members are competitive, I can't imagine how you dealt with unbelievers when they got bent out of shape over something."

"Well, we did have to confront some challenges. We had men who were swearing, fighting, yelling at the umpires, and bringing things to drink that I would not approve of."

"How did you handle that?"

"I told our deacons to stop acting like that and to be a better example!"

Mitch laughed out loud. "Touché. You got me back on that one."

"Seriously, we did have to confront some issues, but it should not be surprising when people who are not Christians act un-Christlike, but here is what happened. Now mind you that I do not intend to devalue worship by making this statement. Those men spending two nights a week with our men was the closest thing to worship they had experienced in their adult lives. They were hearing testimonies of how God changed the lives of the men on the teams, hearing men pray for one another, and having a great time. Many of them had the perception that Christians don't know how to have fun. Not only that, but their wives were in the stands with the wives of our men. We started seeing several of these men show up for Bible study and worship, and ultimately several decided to become followers of Jesus. In addition, several of the wives followed their lead. We saw women coming to faith through men's church softball."

"That's an awesome story."

"Here's my point. The same people that you could never pay to come to church will pay you to play softball, or eat barbeque, or to attend a couples' banquet. The possibilities are limitless. Dozens if not hundreds of activities are available that both Christians and non-Christians enjoy, and they are spiritually neutral. But here is the key—no event is inherently evangelistic. Softball can be evangelistic in one church and not in another. The same could be said for fish fries, golf outings, youth sports leagues, revivals, seasonal banquets, or any other activity."

"We have activities and social events at our church, but honestly they are all geared toward the fellowship of our members."

"Here's the great thing about changing the focus. When you prepare for these weekday and weekend social activities in the same way as you did the Christmas Eve service, you enhance the possibility of guests participating, but the fellowship of the members is not adversely affected. It is a win-win situation."

Mitch had made a list of ideas to take back to the evangelism leadership team before he left the coffee shop.

1. Work with evangelism leadership team to identify four to six events that we do (or could do) and change them to evangelistic opportunities.

2. Evaluate our upcoming Vacation Bible School to see if we are taking full advantage of the evangelistic element.

3. Develop a checklist for preparing events to make them more evangelistic. Include:

- Prayer strategy
- Tasks that must be accomplished
- Completion date for each task
- A leader or team for each task
- Promotion strategy
- Delivery strategy (how the gospel will be shared)
- Follow-up strategy

4. Always begin planning at least six to eight weeks out to enhance member participation, preparation, and promotion.

5. Could we apply some of this to the upcoming Easter egg hunt in April?

6. Develop a method where we register guests, keep information, and invite them to events that follow.

7. Invite a vocational evangelist to come and preach for a harvest day, special event, or a series of services.

Chapter Thirty-Two

ODE TO TAMMY

Wednesday, February 19th

The meeting was held in a Bible study classroom near the pastor's office. Everyone stayed after the Wednesday night prayer service for an hour of prayer and continued planning to implement evangelism and outreach strategies for the congregation. Committee meetings are not always the most exciting endeavors in the life of the church, but the members of this one looked forward to gathering each month. The meetings were based on a clear purpose, and the team was seeing progress that flowed from their efforts.

Two additional members were attending for the first time tonight. Mitch had invited Cecelia Ramirez to join and provide the perspective of a teenager, along with Danny Rose who only recently trusted Christ. Mitch felt that he would provide yet another perspective, having been unchurched until recently.

The evangelism leadership team was of critical importance to Mitch. They gave him prayer, partnership, wisdom, great ideas, support, and built-in involvement. His investment in this team was paying great dividends, and he had learned a very valuable lesson in leadership. That lesson was that leading people to be leaders was more fruitful than leading a group of followers. The members of the team were growing in their own leadership as they spent time together and implemented the strategies they developed.

"I'm not a pessimist, but I thought Sunday was going to be horrible because of the treacherous driving conditions," Mitch said to the group.

"Ordinarily I would be disappointed when attendance was less than half of the norm," James Flynn replied.

"Isn't it amazing how much someone publicly acknowledging their commitment to follow Christ changes perspective," Mitch continued. "I would have been depressed over the attendance a year ago even though I understood the circumstances that caused so many members to stay home."

"I'm really pumped about this," Tim Minor said with a wide grin. Tim and Jerri had always made a point of praying for all of their neighbors but were never quite sure how to share their faith, particularly with a Chinese couple named Chan. Then a crisis had opened up an unexpected opportunity. One night, the Chans' convenience store in a neighboring town caught on fire. It was not destroyed, but the damage was significant. The Minors rallied a couple dozen church members to volunteer an entire Saturday to assist with cleanup and repairs. The Chans saved what would have been thousands of dollars in labor costs and several days of labor because of the good graces of members of the Stanton Community Church family. As a way to express their appreciation, the Chans had felt compelled to visit the church several Sundays ago, and they had not missed a Sunday since, not even on the snowiest day.

"I wish all of you could have been with me on Saturday," Tim continued. "I was in their living room, and they were so hungry to hear more about the Lord. I couldn't believe how easy it was to share the gospel with them. To be there when together they trusted Jesus for their salvation was unbelievable."

"It was awesome to see them come down the aisle when Mitch gave the invitation," Carly Rooks added.

"It really was," Mitch replied. "I was reminded of the passage in Luke 15 where Jesus talked about the one hundred sheep. Do you remember how one was missing, and the shepherd left the ninety-nine and went after the one that was lost? The Scripture teaches that there is more joy in heaven over one sinner who comes to repentance than over ninety-nine just persons who need no repentance. I was reminded that God takes more joy over one couple professing their faith in a half empty worship center than a full service of believers where no one is saved."

"Amens" came from several of the members. Tim added that he and Jerri would take personal responsibility for discipling the Chans, who were already scheduled to be baptized on Sunday.

Mitch guided the group to zero in on plans to make the Easter service the next target of evangelistic focus, much as had been done with the Christmas Eve service. In addition, he led the group in discussion about how to apply the same principles of preparation for other events and they agreed that an Easter egg hunt the day prior to Easter services would be a great opportunity. The one-hour meeting took ninety minutes. However, no one noticed, and no one complained.

Sunday, March 2nd

Mitch felt like a celebrity walking in public as he made his way from his office to the worship center for the forthcoming service. However, it was not his autograph that people were seeking. He was excited about his message, as he planned to begin a series today to equip the congregation to share their faith and had settled on the theme of "I Witness" for the five Sunday mornings in March. That is, if he ever made it to the worship center. Seven or eight people surrounded him, seeking answers to questions or simply wanting his attention. The clamoring seemed unusually high compared to most Sundays. *Just a coincidence, I suppose, or maybe it's this new cologne that the commercials suggest makes a man irresistible.*

"Pastor, can you play a song for my husband again this year?" It was Mrs. Hudson. She had wedged her way between a little girl and two other ladies that all seemed to be trying to talk to Mitch at the same time.

"I don't know if we can play a cassette, Mrs. Hudson," Mitch said as he reached out and took it from her hand. Mrs. Hudson lost her husband the year before Mitch was called as pastor, and she always requested a tribute song in his memory on the week of the anniversary of his passing. Deference was given to her request because Mr. Hudson had served as the music director for many years. Mitch was sympathetic but felt pressed for time. Fortunately, he saw Darlene Flynn, who now led the music each week, exiting the choir room. "Darlene," Mitch said over the buzz of the small crowd in the hallway. "Can we still play cassettes on our system?"

"Sure, we can do that. What do you need?"

"Mrs. Hudson requested we play a memorial song again this year in honor of her husband."

"Actually, Joy West was supposed to sing the special music today, but she's sick. How about if we play it while the offering is being received?"

"That's fine. You take care of it." Mitch looked at the cassette to catch the name of the song. It was not marked, so he assumed it would be *Beulah Land*, just like last year. He hoped it was not *Precious Memories* as she had requested the first year. That was much too somber and had made the time of worship feel like a funeral service.

"My grandson made sure it was already cued up," Mrs. Hudson said to Darlene as she took the cassette and headed to the worship center to make the adjustments to the order of service.

Mitch made it into the worship service just in time to go to the platform to make the church announcements before the service began. At least there had been no crisis situations or distractions to take his attention away from his message; it was just one of those days where several people happened to converge on him at once.

He was very excited about his message and the potential impact of getting more members committed to personally sharing their faith. The congregation seemed to be singing with a bit more enthusiasm today, and the service was made to order as it set the stage for his message.

He called the ushers forward to receive the morning offering. "This morning before we pray for our tithes and offerings, I want us to remember Mrs. Hudson on the anniversary of the death of Mr. Hudson three years ago. I did not know him personally, but I know that he was well-beloved by this congregation and faithfully served as music director in addition to many other leadership roles for many years. We thank God for his faithfulness, his testimony, and the knowledge that he is in a better place, serving in the presence of the Father. As the offering is received, we will prayerfully reflect as we listen to one of his favorite songs. Tim, would you lead our offertory prayer?"

Mitch quietly stepped down from the platform and sat next to Melinda on the front row as Tim prayed. He bowed his head and began to pray his own prayer, seeking God's blessing on all he was about to share. *God, let your words shine forth through me with clarity and conviction that your people might faithfully carry forth your gospel into this community.*

"Amen," Tim said as he concluded the offertory prayer and the ushers turned with offering plates in hand to pass throughout the congregation. The service was packed, in stark contrast to the snowy day only three weeks before. *Thankfully no snow this week,* Mitch was thinking. *Thank goodness it's not "Precious Memories" again* was his next thought. At least *Beulah Land* has a little pep to it. It was not Mitch's preferred song, but it was at least tolerable. *Wait, it's not "Beulah Land" either....* It was evidently going to be a Southern Gospel favorite or something with a country flavor, Mitch could tell, as the guitars twanged the opening bars of the song. He kept his head bowed to affirm the dignity of such a moment as this. These types of spontaneous moments were what made small congregations special, and he was glad that he could oblige Mrs. Hudson. He also knew it would give him credibility with many of the older members.

A very pretty country voice kicked in the opening lyrics. "Sometimes it's hard to be a wu-maaan," the song began. *Huh?* "Givin' all your luv to just one ma-an." *Is that Tammy Wynette?* "You'll have ba-ad times, and he'll have good times."

Mitch's eyes opened as he recognized the number one country song of all time that was being played just before his sermon. "Doing thangs that you don't understa-and." *Oh no!* Mitch looked over at Melinda. Their eyes met in looks of disbelief as the recorded voice belted out one of the most famous lines in country music history. "Stand by your man. Give him two arms to cli-iing too, and sumthin' warm to come to, when nights are cold and lonely. Stand by your man…"

This cannot be happening. Some smart alec near the back shouted, "Amen." Melinda looked at Mitch and grinned.

"Stand by your ma-an, and show tha world you lu-uv him…" Melinda's grin turned to a quiet giggle. Mitch was trying not to laugh. Within seconds, Melinda was giggling uncontrollably. From the back, they may have assumed she was sobbing, but she was on the edge of losing it and suddenly bolted for the door so that she would not laugh out loud. Thankfully she was not still on crutches, or she would not have made it out. As she dashed out the door next to the piano, the song came to its crescendo. "Keep givin' all the luv you caaaaaaaan. Stand by yower maaaaaaan!" More amens were heard. *Smart alecs!*

Mitch stood and made his way to the platform, going as slowly as he could, trying to figure out how he could possibly segue from the song to his message. He turned and saw Mrs. Hudson wiping tears from her eyes. "Mrs. Hudson, that was a beautiful song," he began. *I might as well just go with it,* he thought. "And you were faithful and did stand by him through all of your years together. We wish he was still with us, but we are thankful that we know he's with the Lord. Let me ask all of you. Isn't that what we want to be able to say about any of those we love who precede us into eternity? How do we stand by those we hold most dear?"

Somehow he managed to transition from that point to his opening illustration. By God's grace he rescued the message—and had a story that he would repeat dozens of times to other pastors in the years to come. Melinda did make it quietly back into the service. She knew how important it was to stand by her man, whether or not she was reminded to do so by Tammy Wynette.

Chapter Thirty-Three

INTO THE LION'S DEN

Friday, March 21st

Mitch liked to take Fridays off but had learned long ago that pastors rarely got a full day off. More than once a critic had sarcastically suggested to him that pastors have it easy because they only have to work on Sundays. *If only they knew,* Mitch thought. Rarely did he go through a week without dealing with a crisis or the problems of one or more families in the church or the community. The congregation would never know about the counseling, encouraging, and responding that he did because of confidentiality on the one hand and, on the other, the simple fact that it would be tedious to give a day-by-day account of everything he did each week.

Besides guiding the congregation in weekly worship and the study of God's word, he served as an ad hoc member of practically every team or committee. Hidden factors that weighed heavily on him as a pastor also included the responsibilities he felt to live a life above reproach, to lead the congregation to grow in their faith, and to reach the community. He could not shut down when five o'clock came, or on a supposed day off.

He appreciated firemen and law enforcement officers and viewed them as heroes, working long shifts for less-than-generous compensation. But Mitch had no shifts. He was always subject to calls to serve his congregation. He was not a martyr about it and would never complain. He was honored to serve the Lord and felt very blessed to do so on a full-time basis. At least Fridays were more leisurely. His Sunday sermons were almost always completed by Thursday (now that he had defined boundaries and had committed to the study time in a place with fewer distractions).

This Friday, he was driving back from Rock Springs after making a hospital visit to Bruce Rollins' wife. Loretta Rollins had been admitted on Thursday night, and they were still running tests. Mitch had prayed with her and with Bruce. Mitch could tell that Bruce was concerned, and any former contentiousness seemed to melt in these circumstances. He was not very talkative, but at least

Mitch had spent time with him without hearing any complaints, for the first time in months.

As he approached the city limits sign, he came upon the one business in town he had not visited to meet the owners. The Stanton Package and Spirits Store was a white block building that could not have been more than a thousand square feet in size, obviously in need of a fresh coat of paint and a new sign. Although meeting the owners of the other businesses in town had yielded some positive results, Mitch had presumed that the owner or manager of this one would have no interest in spiritual conversation or church. It wasn't because of the alcohol per se. While many of Mitch's contemporaries would think nothing of drinking alcohol in moderation, he took a more conservative view and opted to abstain. Like many teens, he had given alcohol a try in a time of spiritual lapse but was just not comfortable partaking like others.

Today for some reason, he felt the Lord urging him to pull into the parking lot and to introduce himself to the owner. *Should I back in to a parking space so that no one will know I'm here?* he thought. *No, I'm just being paranoid. It's the middle of the day, and there's only one car here.* As he entered, he was indeed the only customer and saw a bearded and tattooed man sitting behind the counter, reading a magazine. George Jones was crooning over the stereo speakers, and the smell was a little musty for his taste. *Maybe we can get George to sing "He Stopped Loving Her Today" for Mr. Hudson's memorial song next year*, Mitch thought mischievously.

"What can I get for you?" the man asked from behind the counter. He set down the magazine and took a pack of cigarettes from his shirt pocket to get a smoke.

"Hi, I'm Mitch Walker, pastor of Stanton Community Church in town, and I just wanted to drop by and introduce myself."

"Would you like something to drink, preacher?"

Mitch did not know if he was sincere, or if he was just testing his reaction.

"Oh, no. I just finished a soft drink a few minutes ago. Are you the owner?"

"Yeah, my name is Justin Gravely."

"Pleased to meet you, Mr. Gravely." Mitch reached out his hand and received a firm handshake. To Mitch, Gravely looked like a character you might associate with a hard-core motorcycle club. "Are you from this area?" Mitch asked.

"No, I was actually born in Canada. I moved here about ten years ago. My only son works over in Rock Springs. My wife and I moved here to be close to the grandkids." Mr. Gravely had a "grandpa gleam" in his eye.

"That's great. I've got a little girl in the second grade. My parents love her to death and have a twenty-four-hour ice cream policy for her. I know being a grandparent must be fun."

"Oh, yeah. We would have moved anywhere to be near them."

"Well, I just wanted to come by and introduce myself. I don't know if you have a church or a pastor but I wanted you to know that our church would be glad to serve you in any way we can."

"Is that right? I can't say I've ever had a preacher say that before. I'll be straight with you, though. I don't like church, I don't like religion, and I don't like preachers." As he said that, he was looking Mitch in the eye with a sense of pride. His demeanor changed from the way he looked when talking about his grandkids just a few moments earlier; now he seemed to be looking for a good fight.

"It appears we may be on different sides of that opinion. In any case, I would like to invite you to visit our church sometime. I'd also be honored to pray for you or your family if you have any needs." Mitch had not intended to jump so quickly into a churchy conversation but was following his gut instinct, or more specifically, the guidance of the Holy Spirit. He sensed that this might be his only chance.

"Buddy, I don't need prayers, and I don't need a preacher. What I need are customers. If you can send a few more of those over from your church, I'd appreciate it."

Mitch felt awkward but looked Mr. Gravely in the eye and was careful not to let him get the impression that he was taken off guard by his comments. He did not know if, by "a few more," Gravely meant that some of his members were already his customers, or if he was just trying to get a reaction. "I don't think I can help you there, but I did want to come by and say hello and get to know you." Mitch started to make his way out, moving slowly so as not to look like he was being run off.

"Yeah, whatever."

Mitch was just about to push the door open when Mr. Gravely called out from behind him. "Hey, preacher. I'm not going to any church, but if I did, I'd go to yours. You're the first person that's ever even invited me and the first preacher that's had guts enough to come in here and even try."

"Yes sir, Mr. Gravely. I hope you don't object because I'm going to pray for you anyway."

"Knock yourself out, son. Nice meetin' ya."

"You too. Have a good weekend."

Mitch headed to his car, feeling unsure if anything had been accomplished on this visit. He was about to enter his car when he looked up and noticed a truck passing by, headed south into town. It was a red and white Chevrolet with mud caked on the tires. He could not mistake that truck anywhere. The driver slowed just a bit, and their eyes locked briefly just before Mitch slipped down into the driver's seat. It was Lester McDonald.

Chapter Thirty-Four

ACCUSED

Saturday, March 22nd

Spring fever had captured everyone in Mitch's neighborhood, it seemed, on the first warm weekend of the year. At this time of year, Mitch loved going to the park with Haley, shooting hoops with Wyatt next door, going for walks, filling out brackets for NCAA March Madness, and cooking out. On the other hand, there was one rite of spring he didn't love so much—he had to start working in the yard. As he cut the grass for the first time, he thought, *I wonder if Haley might like cutting the grass this year?* He knew that thought was a waste of mental energy, though. Mitch was not sure which would bring the greatest ire from Melinda, asking an eight-year-old to cut the grass or announcing that he had to climb back on the roof for the next gutter-cleaning. Wisely, he decided to do the work himself and to contain his efforts to ground level.

As he pushed the mower toward the road, he thought he heard his name above its roar. "Mitch!" someone was shouting. He turned and saw Melinda standing on the front porch, waving the phone. "You have a call." Mitch shut down the mower and grabbed his cell from the holster on his belt as he walked toward the porch. He looked and noticed that he had a couple of missed calls. The vibration feature on the phone did not always get his attention when he was walking or working. "It's James Flynn," Melinda said.

Mitch took the phone from Melinda. "Good morning, James. How's it going?"

James got right to the point. "What are the deacons meeting about this morning?"

"What are you talking about?"

"Thomas called late last night and said we have a called meeting at eleven this morning."

Mitch did not like what he was hearing. There was no reason for the deacons to meet without including him. His understanding of the function of the deacons from Scripture was to serve in partnership with the pastor to share the ministry load. "James, I don't know anything about it. Why are they meeting all of the sudden and not including me? They can't conduct any business like that, can they?"

"I'm not sure what's going on, but, technically, our procedures allow for two or more deacons to call for an unscheduled meeting to deal with a crisis situation."

"What kind of crisis do we have? I don't know about any crisis."

"Thomas would not give me any of the details but only said that it was a personnel issue."

Personnel issue? That kind of narrows it down since I'm the only "personnel" the church has. "This is ridiculous, James. It's not right for them to try to meet behind my back."

"That's why I'm calling you. I wouldn't do that. I don't know what they're up to, but you know I'll stand up for you."

"Did you say they're meeting at eleven?"

"That's right."

"Well, they're going to have a special guest. I'll see you there."

Mitch did not even bother to shower or clean up. He still could not get a handle on where Thomas McDonald, the chairman of the deacons, stood on his leadership. Thomas had supported him in some tight situations but lately seemed to be wavering. *His dad must finally be getting to him.* Mitch told Melinda that he had to make a trip to the church but did not get into the details about why he was leaving the yard work undone and heading over. He did not think it necessary to raise her concern. He was paranoid enough for both of them at this point. He left immediately and actually drove around for a short while so that his arrival would not take place until time for the meeting to start. He was wearing shorts, a T-shirt, and a ball cap, looking like anything but a pastor.

He made his way into the church and could hear conversation coming from the room where they ordinarily gathered. "What are you doing here?" Lester McDonald asked as soon as he walked in the room. Mitch noticed that only four of the seven deacons were present so far.

"Are we having a deacons' meeting?" Mitch asked.

"We are, but you weren't invited."

"This is not a birthday party, Lester. I'm a partner with the deacons, and I don't need an invitation. As the pastor, I am a member of the team."

"Just as well. Maybe this will help us speed things up, so we can get this church back to where it used to be."

Mitch held his tongue and made his way in, standing next to James. He looked over at Thomas. They greeted each other, but Thomas would barely look him in the eye. The other deacon present in addition to James Flynn, Lester McDonald, and Thomas McDonald was John Dollar. "Where are the Rollins brothers?" Lester asked out loud.

Thomas replied, "Jacob said he could not leave the bank this morning. I didn't hear back from Bruce Rollins or Tim Minor. I left them messages.'

"I can tell you where they are," Mitch replied. "Bruce Rollins is at the hospital with his wife, and Tim and Jerri Minor went to the mountains for the weekend. They left on Thursday."

"What's wrong with Bruce's wife?" Thomas asked.

"They don't know yet. She's been having nausea all week that they can't account for, and she was pretty much dehydrated when Bruce took her to the doctor. I don't think you'll be seeing him this morning unless you drive over to Rock Springs."

"We can't really do any kind of business with just four people," James pointed out. "Why are we here anyway? What's the emergency?"

John Dollar spoke up. "I'll tell you what the emergency is. It's come to our attention that our pastor may have an alcohol issue." Mitch could not believe what had just come out of John's mouth. That may have been the most ridiculous thing he had ever heard Dollar say, and he had a lot of comments to choose from.

"What in the world are you talking about, John?" James Flynn asked.

"He's been seen frequenting the liquor store lately, and you know where our church stands on the alcohol issue. The Bible is clear that the pastor is not supposed to be a partaker of spirits. You can read it for yourself in 1 Timothy 3:3."

"That is absolutely a crazy accusation," Mitch said, with a look of disgust.

James immediately came to Mitch's defense. "When have you ever seen Mitch drink anything with alcohol or even give the appearance of being drunk? We don't even use real alcohol in our juice when we take communion."

"People have seen him at the liquor store right outside of town."

Mitch suddenly realized what was going on. Lester had seen him coming out of the store the previous day and apparently used it to stir up John Dollar, who served as the self-proclaimed theological watchdog for the congregation. McDonald was just leaning back in his chair, watching it all happen with a smirk on his face.

"I'll go ahead and confess to you, John," Mitch responded. He paused, and it got quiet as you would expect when the word *confess* comes from a pastor's mouth. "I went to the Stanton Package and Spirits Store yesterday. It was the first and only time I've ever been there, and for your information, I didn't even buy a pack of gum much less an alcoholic beverage. I haven't had a drink of alcohol since I was a teenager."

"Then what were you doing there? They don't sell anything except for alcohol, and they don't have gum."

"How do you know they don't have any gum?"

"I—I—uhhh…just know that they don't sell gum in a place like that. What were you doing there if you weren't buying alcohol?"

"Well, if you must know, I went to meet the owner and invite him to church. His name is Justin Gravely, and I don't think he's going to attend, but I sure did extend an invitation. I just wish you were as concerned about getting someone like him into this church as you are about trying to get me out! That is the one and only time I've been there, but I'll tell you that I do intend to go back again sometime."

"I cannot believe we are wasting a Saturday morning like this," James Flynn said. "I will tell you this. If any of you men try to take this and smear our pastor's reputation in any way you can be assured that I will call you out on it. I won't call you out in here, but I will bring it before the whole church publicly. Some of you remind me of the religious leaders who complained when Jesus forgave the sins the paralytic that they let down through the roof in Mark chapter four. God is doing great things in this church right in front of your eyes, and you can't even see it. Thomas, I think this meeting is over. Don't you, Mr. Chairman?"

Thomas looked embarrassed. He would not even look at his dad. "Yeah, it's over. Mitch, I apologize. This should not have happened this morning." Lester McDonald just sat there with a defiant look, arms folded. Mitch knew that Lester had a competitive nature and was not likely to give up. He also knew that if God didn't change Lester's heart, this type of harassment would continue. *Thank God for men like James Flynn*, Mitch thought. *I would resign tomorrow, if not for men like him.*

Monday, March 31st

From: Mitch Walker
Sent: Monday, March 31, 8:19 AM
To: Marc Benton

Subject: Sermon Series Fruit

Marc;

I preached the series called "I Witness" this month. It is the first personal evangelism training that I have provided since being called to serve as pastor. I took the macro approach as you suggested and provided it for all members by preaching it on Sunday mornings. I know that not everyone responded or applied it, but several did. Here is what happened. I shared the gospel with a young man that came to me for counseling recently. He was referred to me by one of our members and had just gone through a heartbreaking break-up with his fiancée. The good news was that God had his attention, and he made a commitment to follow Christ.

One of our students, a high school senior named Cecelia Ramirez, was able to bring a friend to Christ who goes to school with her. Also, Danny Rose, who is a new believer, led his younger brother to Christ. We baptized all three yesterday! Coincidentally, or not, we recently added Danny and Cecelia to the evangelism leadership team. It was interesting to see this unfold. Others told me about their efforts to share their faith personally with family and friends. God blessed the efforts, and I thank you for challenging me to do this.

Getting ready for Easter weekend and looking forward to it!

Mitch

From: Marc Benton
Sent: Monday, March 31, 3:02 PM
To: Mitch Walker
Subject: RE: Sermon Series Fruit

Mitch;

Your experience reflects what we formerly discussed from 2 Corinthians 9:6. When we sow sparingly we reap sparingly; and, when we sow abundantly we reap abundantly. It is a simple principle that the more the gospel is shared the more of a harvest your congregation experiences. I've seen the same thing happen in my congregation literally every time that we provide evangelism training. That is the net effect of equipping and mobilizing your members. Keep it up. See you the week after Easter.

Marc

Chapter Thirty-Five

A Swing and a Miss

Tuesday, April 22nd

Mitch sat in the coffee shop waiting for Marc Benton to arrive. He was early, and he ordinarily looked forward to these meetings, but he was not quite as eager today as in the past. He had anticipated that the activities of the Easter weekend would surpass anything that Stanton Community Church had ever experienced, but nothing could be further from the truth. He saw Pastor Benton enter with his usual winsome smile and make his way to the counter to order coffee before joining Mitch.

"Do you need anything?" Pastor Benton asked as Mitch read his lips from across the room. Mitch shook his head and held up his cup of coffee to let him know that he had already ordered. He noticed that his mentor had a green and white book in his hand, along with his tablet computer.

"What a beautiful morning it is," Pastor Benton stated as he approached and joined Mitch at the table that had become their favored spot to gather each month.

"Man, it sure is. Quite a contrast to the weekend, isn't it?"

"You've got that right. I was afraid the river was going to overflow and give us one of those floods we get every decade or so. I believe we got over ten inches of rain this weekend."

"I don't how much we got, but that's the first time I've ever seen ducks swimming in our front yard."

"Are you serious?"

"No, but I wouldn't have been surprised."

"I'll tell you. I was worried about how it would affect our Easter services," Pastor Benton said. "But, our members came through, and we had a great day. I'm sure you folks did, too."

"Well, not exactly," Mitch replied. Our attendance was up and that was good, but the evangelistic event we planned for Saturday was a flop, and we didn't have anyone respond, trusting Jesus as Savior, at our Easter service."

"Don't be too hard on yourself, Mitch. Remember that it is God who saves.

We just need to be sure we are doing all we can to sow the seeds. Did you do all you could?"

"We sure did, more than we have in the past. A whole lot more."

"I'm not surprised if you didn't get a huge response during the invitation at your Easter services. It's not because I'm a pessimist. It's just that a lot of guests are present, and it can be awkward to respond in an unfamiliar place and for those who have not experienced a worship service or a responsive invitation like that. Let me ask—Did you have some guests? And did you register everyone who attended?"

"Actually, we did. In spite of the rain, I would say we had at least twenty guests, which would be the largest number since our Christmas Eve service. I think we would have had a whole lot more if they hadn't had to travel in a monsoon."

"Did they hear the gospel?"

"Absolutely."

"Then you did what you were supposed to do. You and your congregation worked to get guests present, you shared the resurrection story, and you gave people an opportunity to respond to the gospel message. It may be possible that some have responded, and you just don't know it yet. They may follow through in another church, or perhaps in yours in the coming weeks. Keep praying, and do good follow-up. Keep inviting every one of them to future fellowship and worship opportunities in the coming months and continue registering guests that attend. You will be able to develop what I call a "prospect snowball." Do you have a follow-up plan?"

"Yes, I sent a personal letter to each guest yesterday, and one of the members of our evangelism leadership team divided up the names among the group so that all of our guests received a phone call last night. We are also going to try to visit some of them tonight, and we're asking the Bible study group leaders or teachers to make a contact also."

"That's good. The key there is to utilize multiple attempts and means to follow up and to do it fairly quickly. It sounds like you're on target. Don't get discouraged that there was no response when you gave the invitation yesterday. I believe it is an important part of the worship experience, but it cannot be used as the total measure of what God is doing."

"That's a good word. I guess I just had high expectations."

"Don't apologize for that. I think you should have high expectations, trusting

God to work and move in every service whether it's Easter Sunday or Arbor Day weekend."

"I don't think I have an Arbor Day sermon," Mitch said, with a grin.

"Well, you just keep studying son, and I'm sure God will give you one."

"No, seriously, that's what I needed to hear. I guess between having no one respond to the invitation and our flop on Saturday, I was a little discouraged."

"What happened on Saturday?"

"Well, we applied all of the prayer and preparation principles for an evangelistic event this weekend. We planned an Easter egg hunt and some other family activities, but as you know it's hard to hunt Easter eggs wearing scuba gear."

"Oh yeah, that's right. It poured all day Saturday like it did Sunday morning."

"We didn't even consider that it might rain while we were planning and by the time Friday rolled around we were scrambling for a plan B. It was too little too late. We moved it indoors, but between the weather and the poor communication about an alternative, we were literally washed out. We only had about ten people show up and that include my wife and daughter. We were expecting fifty or hopefully even more if everything went right."

"I know you're disappointed, but sometimes you swing and miss. I've had a lot of flops in my ministry. I traveled with our student pastor along with a busload of students to Adventure Land Amusement Park during spring break a couple of years ago. We drove almost two hours and pulled into an empty parking lot. Somebody forgot to check to confirm that they were open. We assumed it was, and we had some unhappy teens that day. They weren't the only ones who weren't happy. It was embarrassing."

"You're not serious. That kind thing doesn't happen in a church like yours."

"It can and did happen, but we learned from it. The thing that separates successful leaders from the unsuccessful is not whether or not they fail. Everyone fails. Leaders learn from their failures and keep pressing forward."

"In retrospect, I think we may have been trying to do too much in one weekend. I think we tried to put too many eggs in one basket."

"Was I supposed to laugh at that?" Pastor Benton asked.

"I couldn't resist. Anyway, we were essentially planning two big events in two days and then to top it off, we didn't think through alternatives or develop a secondary plan to account for bad weather. I'll debrief with the evangelism leadership team."

"What's next on your agenda for evangelistic efforts?" Pastor Benton asked.

"We're gearing up for Vacation Bible School in June, Back to School Sunday as our next high-attended worship service in August, and personal evangelism training in the autumn months. The next training will be for the core. We are going to have an eight-week evangelism class that will meet on Tuesday nights, using the *ishare* materials that you recommended."

"That's great. Let me know if I can help as you prepare. Listen, there's one more component of the *Net Effect* that we haven't covered yet. It is the issue of team evangelism, but I'm not going to give you much on it at this point. Instead, I want to give you a book to read. You've got a lot on your plate, and this would best be applied as you move into the new school year next August."

"Tell me again what you mean by team evangelism?"

"You have Bible study groups that meet together prior to worship. Is that correct?"

"Sure. We do."

"They are probably organized to some degree by life stage. Let me ask you. Who is best at reaching young people?"

Mitch thought for a moment, trying to get a feel for where this was going. "I guess other young people."

"Exactly. Who do you think would be best at reaching young couples?"

"Other young couples?"

"That's correct. A middle school student might reach a twenty-eight year old, but they are more likely to reach their peers. You can go through all the life stages and see it at work. Who is best at reaching senior adult men?" Benton did not wait for Mitch to respond. "Senior adult women, but that's another story." Mitch laughed as Benton continued. "You have teams already organized to some degree. Are your groups doing outreach and evangelism?"

"No. Honestly, they are built on Bible study and fellowship."

"I want you to read this. A friend of mine wrote it, and it effectively tackles the issue. It's called *Sunday School That Really Works: A Strategy for Connecting Congregations and Communities*."

"But we don't have Sunday school. We have Bible study groups."

"Don't let that mislead you. The author uses the word Sunday school in the descriptive sense based on a historical perspective. It applies to Bible study groups by whatever name they go by that generally meet before the worship service on Sunday but with understanding that some groups may choose to meet during the week. I'll follow up in our future meetings and through e-mails, but go ahead and get into it."

"Sure, I'll get right on it." Mitch left the coffee shop feeling much more encouraged than when he had arrived. Pastor Benton had a way of doing that. He was a great encourager, and Mitch prayed that he was likewise a blessing to his mentor.

Chapter Thirty-Six

Friday, May 9th

Having found himself indoors almost all week, Mitch had developed a severe case of cabin fever. He had taken extra time in his study all week to get a jump on sermon preparation for the upcoming summer months. Today, the spectacular weather beckoned him to knock off early and get outside. He and Melinda had already planned to cook out on the grill tonight. Melinda's best friend, Carly, and Haley's best friend, Emma, would be coming over along with Randall and Michelle Mullins from next door. Their son, Wyatt, was invited, but Mitch understood that teens were sometimes difficult to nail down for such events. He seemed to prefer to keep his options open. Nonetheless, he and Mitch had agreed to an afternoon basketball game after Wyatt got out of school. Mitch hoped that Dizzy might also come along so that he could be invited at the last moment.

Mitch closed his eyes and could smell the aroma of the barbequed chicken and the fresh vegetables he would prepare a few hours later. He loved cooking what he called "chicken on the grill" for which Melinda always gave him grief. It's "grilled chicken" not "chicken on the grill," she would say. He didn't know why he called it that, but by now he just did it to aggravate Melinda in a good-natured way.

Wyatt must have grown about three inches in the past year and put on at least twenty-five pounds. He was starting to hold his own this spring, as he and Mitch battled in their one-on-one grudge matches in the concrete coliseum, as they called the backyard basketball court. As Mitch made his way over, he saw that Wyatt was alone. "Hey, are you ready to get stomped again?" Mitch asked as the trash talk began.

"You didn't stomp me last week. You hit a luck shot at the end and never did admit that you fouled me on that last shot that I missed."

"Fouled you? You didn't see any blood. Did you?"

"You better loosen up. I know you're about to turn thirty, so you might need to take some extra time since you'll be going downhill from there."

Anyone who did not know better would think they didn't like each other. It was quite the opposite. Their jabs at each another were the way they related, and they actually never got mad although they played each other very hard. Mitch would not admit it, but he had lost a step, and Wyatt had gained one over the winter. "Where's Dizzy at today?" Mitch asked. "I was hoping he might come over tonight for the cookout."

"I guess you haven't heard."

"Heard what?"

"He's in juv-e," Wyatt said referring to a Juvenile Detention Center where teens are incarcerated when arrested.

"For what? What happened?"

"I heard he was arrested for burglary. He was caught breakin' into a garage, and they said he stole some stuff."

"What did he steal?"

"I dunno. But, the garage he broke into was the home of a police officer."

"Oh, great. Not that he should have broken in, but that was not the smartest thing to do, breaking into the garage of a police officer. What's going to happen?"

"Dude, I don't know. I just know he's in trouble."

"Has he ever been arrested before?"

"Well, I know he gets in trouble sometimes, but I don't know that he's ever got arrested before."

"Where's the detention center?"

"It's over in Rock Springs."

"Isn't his last name Carver or Carter, something like that? I may see if I can get over and see what's going on."

"It's Carver, but Dizzy is not his real first name. It's Johnny."

"Heck, I never even thought about that. Makes sense I guess that Dizzy is a nickname. Where did he pick that up?"

"Some kids in his neighborhood. A long time ago. Because he liked to like go round and round until he couldn't stand up. I guess it stuck. He's not like a druggie or anything, but I know he's also tried a few things that make people dizzy, if you know what I'm sayin'."

"Man, I hate that. I thought he might be coming around."

"He's back and forth. He doesn't have a dad, or he left or somethin'. I told you he lives in a bad area in that apartment complex. He doesn't do that kind of stuff when he's around me."

"I'm not going to give up on him. Let me know if you hear anything else. I'll make some calls, and see if I can get over there. I'm sure he needs a boost. In the meantime, you might want to go get a handkerchief since you will be crying when this game is over."

"Yeah, right. Bring it on, old dude."

Tuesday, May 13th

Mitch had no idea that it would almost take an act of Congress to get permission to visit Dizzy in the Juvenile Detention Center. The forty-minute drive to Rock Springs turned into almost an hour with heavier-than-expected traffic. He actually enjoyed the trip that he was compelled to make for one reason or another at least three or four times a month. The hospital, the mall, the restaurants, and a variety of other resources were located there, including the county jail and the detention center. He enjoyed music but often turned the radio down so he could think. He had a lot to think about.

He went through a personal debrief of the Sunday activities. The worship center was almost filled to capacity. James had actually suggested that they begin praying about adding another service. The congregation on the whole seemed to be somewhat oblivious to the power plays behind the scenes being led by Lester McDonald. Most of the members were happy to see the crowd growing, lots of guests attending, and people being baptized. Mitch tried to calculate in his head and could think of at least ten who were baptized since last summer. Most of all, you could tell a difference in the spirit of the services. The passion for worship had increased, and the enthusiasm was heightened. He thought the *Stand by Your Man* catastrophe a few weeks earlier would be a problem, but everyone pretty much laughed it off. *Why are they still after me when things seem to be going so well?* He was still amazed at how a small handful of antagonists could drain his energy even when God was so clearly moving.

Marc Benton had been a godsend. He was very gracious, and Mitch could not be more thankful that he took time each month to drink coffee and talk about ministry with a young pastor from a small, obscure church in a small town. The conversations they shared in the coffee shop were not profound, and Mitch had heard much of the same information in seminary, but the monthly meeting with a pastor who lived it helped make it tangible and motivated him to make application—and it was working. The church was never going to be big, and that was not Mitch's goal. People were coming to faith in Jesus, and they were making disciples. That was the goal. That was what Jesus commanded the church to do in the Great Commission. *Two services on Sunday mornings?* That was hard for Mitch to envision, but he was willing to do whatever it would take to reach people in his community.

The evangelism leadership team had also met on Sunday. They debriefed about Easter weekend and worked on ideas to maximize participation in Vacation Bible School. Mitch also proposed an idea that was well received by the team. It occurred to him that there were six elements to the *Net Effect,* and that the team consisted of six members. He suggested that each member take ownership of one element and serve as somewhat of a captain or an advocate for that component. All members would work together, but one person would provide primary leadership. Prayer was James Flynn's passion, so he was assigned *Praying for the lost.* Tim Minor was the Bible study director and was assigned *Team Evangelism.* Mitch had consumed the *Sunday School That Really Works* book and passed it on to Tim. They had already scheduled a time to sit down and talk about it once Tim finished.

Cecilia Ramirez was assigned *Service/Ministry Evangelism.* Like many younger leaders, she had a passion for service. Mitch knew that Cecilia might be going off to college but thought it best to engage her in leadership in any way possible while she was still present. Mitch was surprised when Danny Rose spoke up and asked for his assignment to be *Personal Evangelism Equipping.* He was a new believer and had never received any formal training himself. However, seeing his younger brother become a follower of Jesus through his witness lit a fire in him to learn more about sharing his faith and helping others to do likewise. Kris Kimmons was assigned *Proclamation of the Gospel Message* which focused on maximizing attendance at key services, and Carly Rooks took leadership of *Event Evangelism.* Kris and Carly discussed coordinating these two elements because of the similarities in preparation. Mitch shared with the team that he would serve as the coordinator for all components to keep the flow of evangelistic emphasis spread throughout the year. *This is a great way to get us to be more intentional,* Mitch thought. Every good idea eventually degenerates into work. Mitch knew that unleashing the team on these tasks would be hard work, but the souls of men, women, boys, and girls would be worth the effort, if and when they heard the gospel and responded.

Mitch almost drove right past the detention center as he pondered these things. He made his way into the facility, taking almost fifteen minutes to go through all of the security screening procedures that it took to visit one of the detainees. He found himself sitting alone in a common area with tables and chairs. They could not meet privately and would be in sight of a security desk where an officer sat reading a book or a magazine of some kind. The officer seemed oblivious to Mitch. Soon another officer escorted Dizzy into the area and said that he would return in thirty minutes. Dizzy appeared to be very humbled in his demeanor.

"Hey, Diz. Are you all right?"

Dizzy sat down with his fingers interlocked with both arms on the table. "Yeah, I guess," was his typical brief and to-the-point reply.

"Any idea about how long you'll be here?"

"I gotta go to court next week. I hope they'll let me go."

"Has anyone been to visit you already?"

"Yeah, my mom's been here a couple of times, and I have a P.D. that came to see me."

"P.D.? What's that?"

"Public Defender or sumthin' like that."

It occurred to Mitch that Dizzy's family could not likely afford any legal counsel. They talked for a while about the detention center and its strict routines. One of Dizzy's big concerns seemed to be what he judged to be the poor quality of cuisine, and the fact that they could not drink Cokes. Mitch did not ask about the burglary. He was not there to judge or to offer any amateur legal counsel. His primary goal was to let Dizzy know that he had a friend...someone who cared about him and would be there for him. Although the conversation was awkward, Mitch pressed forward, knowing that he could not judge the value of his visit solely by the immediate response. There was not much to joke or laugh about in a place like this.

"Dizzy, man, I have talked to you about the Lord several times. I know you have a lot of questions and a lot of doubts. Can I ask you something?

"I guess."

"Is this what you want?" Mitch said as he swept his arm in a circle, pointing at the different sides of the room. "Do you want to live life in a place like this? I know you probably won't be here long. At least, I hope not. But the choices you make, if they don't change, could cause you to live in a place like this."

"I hate this place."

"Dizzy, I'm not wanting to preach at you, but you have to understand. This is a vacation compared to a real prison."

"I'm not planning on going to prison."

"Nobody does. But some people live a life where they make decisions that have horrible consequences. I know you're not there, but you may be on that road. You don't want to stay there. You can get on another road. Choosing to become a follower of Jesus Christ will put you on another road."

"Maybe so, but I don't want to be a church guy. I mean I don't mind visiting with Wyatt and all, but I just don't like to do some stuff. I'm just not religious. I remember goin' to church some when I was real little. But that was different."

"Man, I'm not asking you to be religious. I'm asking you to trust Jesus Christ with your life. Let me ask you a question. Do you like ice cream?"

"Sure."

"What's your favorite flavor?"

"I dunno. I guess strawberry."

"When did you decide to start liking it?"

Dizzy pondered for a moment not knowing exactly how answer. "I've always just liked it, I guess."

"That's right. It's just in you to like it. I'm not asking you to like church or to like doing certain things. I'm asking you to put your faith in Jesus. The Bible teaches that His Holy Spirit will begin to fill your life once you do. He will change the things you want to do. Imagine what it would be like if you wanted to go to church or to read the Bible. What if you looked forward to it, and it was actually fun to you? Have you noticed that a lot of people really do enjoy it? To some people, it is like eating strawberry ice cream."

"I can't believe I would ever like it."

"I'm not asking you to believe it. I'm asking you to believe in Jesus and to leave it up to Him. You don't need to change to come to God. You need to admit that you can't change. I told you before that we're all sinners. We all fall short of God's standards. You need to come to God like you are. God doesn't want you to live your life in prison. I'm not just talking about a building. Your sin and disobedience imprisons you, and it will continue to do so for all of your life and even for eternity if you don't commit your life to Jesus Christ."

"I just don't know if I'm ready."

"You may not be ready. But God is."

"Well, I'm not."

Mitch was heartbroken. He thought that he could convince Dizzy in a place like this that he needed the Lord. As he drove back to Stanton, God spoke to His heart. It was as if the Lord reminded him that it was not his job to convince anybody but to be faithful to share. He shared with Dizzy, but he feared that he would never be reached. *But I'm not giving up.* He prayed all the way back to Stanton.

Chapter Thirty-Seven

DOCTORS AND NURSES

Thursday, May 15th

"Hey, James. How are you?" Mitch had just returned from lunch and was planning to spend the afternoon catching up on some things in the office when his cell phone rang.

"Not too good. Did you hear that Bruce Rollins had to take Loretta back to the hospital yesterday?"

"I had not heard. What's going on?"

"You know they couldn't find anything wrong last month when they took her for some tests. Bruce took her to the emergency room last night. He didn't call or let anyone know, but Jacob just called from the bank and said Bruce told him they're about to take her in for emergency surgery."

"What's going on? Did they find something?"

"I don't have any idea, but I thought you would want to know. I'm going to head over to the hospital and see what's going on."

"I'll see you over there. I'm leaving right now."

Mitch went straight to his car to drive to Rock Springs. He called Melinda on the way and asked her to contact the ladies who were part of the prayer chain, and to let her know that he might be late getting home. He prayed for green light grace and violated the posted speed limit most of the way but was careful not to get too aggressive. Upon arrival, he made his way to the surgical waiting area, where he had been on many occasions. He found Bruce Rollins sitting by himself. James had not arrived yet, and no other family members were present.

"Bruce, what's going on with Loretta?" Mitch could see that Bruce's eyes were red and wet. It was obvious that he was afraid, and things were not going well.

"I'm not sure. When we were here a few weeks ago, they said they couldn't find anything wrong. They just gave her some kind of prescription to help her nausea and boost her energy, and it helped for a little while, but the last couple of days she's been ailing again. I brought her to the emergency room last night because it seemed like she was on the verge of passing out. I could tell something wasn't right. I didn't call anybody, not even our daughter, because I didn't want to cause a stir if there wasn't much to it. We were in the emergency room all night, and they started some tests this morning. They did a CAT scan and found something in or on the brain. I'm not sure, but the doc said they have to get in there and check it out right now."

Mitch took Bruce by the hand and asked if he could pray. "Please," Bruce said. "This is pretty scary." As Mitch began to pray, James entered the waiting area and joined them in praying for Loretta. After praying, they sat down and waited. Conversation was sparse, and the time went slowly by. After less than an hour, a nurse called out, "Bruce Rollins? Is there a Mr. Rollins in here?" Bruce stood up and made his way to the nurse. He stood there talking to the nurse for a moment, then he turned and motioned for Mitch and James to follow him. They went into a small, private, waiting room. "She said the doctor is coming to talk to me," Bruce told them.

They waited there silently for about ten minutes before the doctor entered with a grim look on his face. "Mr. Rollins, she's still in there, and they are finishing up. I'm sorry, but I've got some news that's not good. We saw something on the CAT scan that obviously did not belong, but we knew we would need to get in there and see what it was and to see if we could remove it. We will need to confirm with more tests, but it looks like there is a tumor and any attempt to remove it would be hazardous."

"What does that mean?" Bruce asked, hoping it was not as serious as it was sounding.

"I can't say with certainty until I hear back from the lab. We have one on-site, and we went ahead and sent a sample, so we'll know within a few hours. I know it's good to hope for the best, but you need to be prepared. It may not be good."

"What do you mean?"

"I don't want to jump to conclusions until we hear from the lab, but my experience tells me that this is going to be very serious. That's all I can say until I hear from the lab."

Bruce turned pale and looked like he was on the verge of breaking down, but he somehow held it together. The doctor left Bruce, James, and Mitch and they had the private waiting room to themselves. A hospital attendant came in as soon as the doctor left and said that they could stay in the private area until they heard back from the doctor. "Would you like to request a visit from a chaplain?" the attendant asked.

"No, my pastor is with me," Bruce replied.

Mitch could not remember a time when Bruce had referred to him as "my pastor" with any affection. He sat there with Bruce and James for the next four hours. He left the room once to grab soft drinks for all and to visit the restroom. The conversation was trivial and sparse. Mitch did not attempt to explain or suggest any reason for what Bruce and Loretta were experiencing. Bruce's brother, Jacob, arrived along with his wife, Fran. Once Loretta was out of surgery, Mitch accompanied Bruce into the recovery room to see her briefly. Her head was totally shaved, and she was still unconscious from the surgery. Mitch almost wept himself as he stood behind Bruce, who held his wife's hand and sobbed. He had his problems with Bruce, but he knew that Bruce loved his wife as much as he loved Melinda.

"I don't know what I'm going to do if she's not all right," Bruce quietly said. Mitch led him to pray for Loretta as she quietly lay there amidst the tubes and cords and monitors.

Back in the small private waiting room, the clock seemed to run even slower as they waited for news from the doctor. The time finally came, and he entered with a somber expression. "I'm sorry, Mr. Rollins, but it's what I feared. It's malignant."

You could hear the gasp from his sister-in-law, Fran, as Bruce said, "Oh no. It's not bad though, is it?" The denial was immediate as he heard news that was turning his world upside-down.

"I'm afraid it is. This type of cancer is very aggressive. It's already spread to a point that surgically there was nothing we could do. It's already stage four."

"Stage four. What does that mean?" Bruce asked.

"I'm sorry, Mr. Rollins. It will be terminal."

"You mean that she's going to die?"

"Apart from some unforeseen miracle, I'm afraid that she will. I'm so sorry."

"How long?"

"This is a very aggressive form of cancer as I said. I've never had a patient live more than six months once they got to this point. That's not even likely. We're talking just weeks."

"Can you do anything? Please tell me there's a cure."

"We can do radiation, but I'll be honest. It would still take a miracle."

Mitch and Jacob had to prop Bruce up as he crumpled and started to weep. Everyone was crying quietly. Bruce could not be quiet. He had just gotten the very worst possible news. After the doctor had left and things had settled, James volunteered to go make some calls. "Hang on a second, James," Bruce said. "Somebody has to go and tell Tonya." Tonya was the only child of Bruce and Loretta, the child who had graduated the previous year, and whose graduation party Mitch had failed to attend. "She doesn't need to hear it through the grapevine."

Mitch offered a solution. "Bruce, would you like for Melinda and me to drive over and talk to her?"

"Would you, Pastor?" Bruce asked.

"Sure. I'll go get Melinda, and we'll go tell her and bring her back here if she wants."

Tonya lived about an hour and a half away from Stanton. It would take nearly three hours for Mitch to drive home to pick up Melinda, arrange for someone to stay with Haley, and to get there. They all agreed to hold the news until they heard back from Mitch, confirming that Tonya had been informed.

It was after nine o'clock when Mitch and Melinda showed up at her door. They had prayed that she would be there and had decided that they would not call her cell phone unless she was not in her dorm. Mitch was so glad Melinda was there because Tonya needed a female presence as she learned the horrible news about her mom's prognosis. Melinda drove Tonya's car as they made their way back to the hospital, not arriving until after midnight. Tonya embraced her father, and they wept for a long time. Mitch could not remember watching others cry so much in one day as he had in the past dozen or so hours. Melinda headed home, and Mitch stayed at Bruce's side all night long.

Thursday, May 22nd

A week had passed since Mitch spent the entire night in the waiting room with Bruce and Tonya Rollins. He had gone back on Sunday afternoon and assured Bruce that the church was praying for Loretta's complete healing. He also had the opportunity to visit with Loretta that afternoon. She was fully aware by that point of all the doctors had said. Mitch was amazed, however, that although physically weakened, she had a peaceful and confident appearance. She said more than once that she knew that God was in control. Mitch had gone back on Monday and Tuesday and was surprised when they sent her home on Wednesday.

A visiting nurse was attending to Loretta in her bedroom as he and Bruce sat in the living room drinking glasses of sweet tea. The counter and the refrigerator were filled with dishes of food brought over by church members to assist with the days of recuperation from the surgery.

"Would you like some pie?" Bruce asked.

"No thanks, Bruce. But you help yourself."

"I'm not really hungry right now. Have I ever asked you if you knew Pastor Harris?"

"No, but that name's familiar. Didn't he pastor Stanton Community Church at one point?"

"Yeah, he did. He was here for almost ten years. We were about the same age, and we were really good friends. He was the best pastor we ever had."

Mitch did not take any offense and could sense that he was remembering his friend fondly. "Whatever happened to him?" Mitch asked.

"I told you he was a good friend, and he was, but he and his wife started having some problems. No one could prove it, but the rumor was that he was running around on her at one point. I tried to defend him, and I'm not going to say all I know, but I'm afraid it was true. He was having an affair. He resigned, and not everyone knew the real reason why, but I knew. He really let me down. He was not only my friend. He was my pastor."

"Man, I hate that Bruce. I had no idea." Mitch was surprised at Bruce's transparency. They had never had a conversation that was so personal.

"I never gave up on God. I know some people see a preacher or a Christian fail and then stop worshipping or serving the Lord. I never understood that. It's not God's fault when someone falls. I guess some people are just looking for an excuse. I'm afraid though that I may have been soured toward preachers. I haven't exactly been the best supporter of our pastors since then."

Mitch nodded but did not respond. He had no idea that Bruce had been hurt so deeply by a former pastor. It may have explained a lot about why he could never seem to please Bruce even though many things were going well. Mitch thought that missing Tonya's graduation party was trivial but now understood a little better about why Bruce had magnified it. He wasn't mad at Mitch. He was just mad at pastors in general, and Mitch happened to be within striking distance.

"You're a good pastor, Mitch. I know that now. I would not have expected you to spend the time with me that you have this week after all I've said and done."

Although Bruce did not technically apologize, that was the way Mitch received it. "Bruce, you're a good leader, and I know you love the Lord. Right now we just need to focus on Loretta. Tonya, too. I'll do anything I can to help you guys get through this."

Mitch stayed for a couple of more hours and went by every day after that. As the days progressed, he felt that he had gained a genuine friend. That was a miracle. Now he prayed for another miracle—for Loretta to be healed.

Chapter Thirty-Eight

THE EYE OF THE NEEDLE

Thursday, May 29th

Tim Minor was already seated when Mitch walked into Dana Hutchison's sandwich shop. Mitch ordered chicken with bacon and pepper jack cheese topped off with pepperoni. He went to the fountain to pour his soft drink and joined Tim who, apparently, could not resist the temptation to take a few bites from his own sandwich before Mitch sat down. He may have been considered rude to do so in a formal setting, but in the man world an "eat when ready" philosophy prevailed.

"How's Loretta doing?" Tim asked as he wiped the corner of his mouth with a napkin.

"Her attitude is amazing, Tim, but she's not recovering. Physically she's getting worse instead of better. Do you mind if we have a blessing for our food and pray for her?" Mitch and Tim bowed and went before the Lord on behalf of the Rollins family.

"Did you guys have a good Memorial Day holiday?" Mitch asked, as he began to take his sandwich out of the wrapper.

"We sure did. We went to the parade over in Rock Springs and then came home and cooked out with our family."

"We cooked out too. It would not be Memorial Day without eating something grilled outside." The two men ate their sandwiches and talked more about their week. Mitch finally got to the point of their meeting. Today represented a Bible study director and pastor meeting. They had met in the past, but the conversation always revolved around curriculum concerns and administrative issues. Both men had read *Sunday School That Really Works* by this point, and the time had come to consider how to implement team evangelism through the Bible study groups.

"I'll tell you the key thing that struck me," Tim said. "Did you see the research that the author did on leadership training? The study clearly showed a direct correlation between meeting with the Bible study leaders on a regular basis and the potential growth of the congregation. The fact is that we never meet with our leaders. We just enlist them, give them materials, and send them to teach."

"That was an eye-opener. He sure made a strong biblical case also from Ephesians 4:11–16. I can't believe how many times that I have read that text and never connected the dots to the underlying principles. We have good Bible study leaders, but they put all of their energy into teaching, and I see now that we have been missing opportunities in at least three areas. We have not utilized our groups for ministry, for outreach, or for leader development."

"I agree, and the fact that we have not provided any training is likely the reason that they haven't done it on their own. I'll be honest and admit that I've never received any training for my role as director. I understand now that I'm not called just to count the attendance on Sunday. My role is to work with you to motivate and equip our leaders to fulfill the Great Commission."

"I'm kind of in the same boat. The things I learned in seminary about small groups either didn't stick or were more technical than practical. I realize now that I need to work with you to equip our leaders to engage their groups in all elements of the Great Commission and not just teaching. The premise of the book was easy to grab hold of. 'A Sunday school that really works is one where the lost are being reached, lives are being changed, and leaders are being sent.' You and I need to meet at least every couple of months and really make our Bible study groups a priority. I've noticed that most of our newer members have been coming to the worship service but have not connected with a group."

"Where do we get started on this?"

Mitch had a lot on his plate but felt that having Tim as an enthusiastic and committed partner would allow him to lead the groups to become more purposeful and more outreach-oriented. He left the sandwich shop with several ideas written on his notepad.

1. *Schedule and begin promoting training for Bible Study Leaders. Schedule one for August, one for October, an appreciation banquet for February, and one for May.*
2. *Begin talking about the Bible Study groups more from the pulpit to elevate importance and priority. Take more responsibility for promoting and leading small group Ministry.*
3. *Purchase "Sunday School That Really Works" for all Bible Study Leaders.*

4. *Make sure all new members are assigned to a group. Make sure all regular worship attendees are assigned to a group.*

5. *Ask leaders to report total number of ministry contacts made each week. Begin tracking to see how total contacts correlates to weekly attendance.*

6. *Ask all groups in student and adult areas to enlist an outreach leader.*

7. *Help groups organize to get more people involved in leadership.*

8. *Start a new young adult group in August.*

Monday, June 2nd

From: Marc Benton
Sent: Monday, June 2, 11:26 AM
To: Mitch Walker
Subject: Next Steps
Mitch;

I want you to know how much I have enjoyed our time together each month since last August. I imagine that your summer is much like mine, and I regret that I cannot make any appointments during these months. Let's plan on getting together one more time around August or September for a final debrief. I hope you have plenty to keep you occupied as you continue to implement the principles of the Net Effect.

Please pray for us. We've actually seen fewer people come to faith in Jesus this year than in previous years. It's hard to put our finger on why, but I do know we have continued to pour as much energy into evangelism as in the past. I am reminded of how the Scripture teaches that Paul planted, Apollos watered, but God gave the increase in 1 Corinthians 3:6. I am working with our leaders to evaluate and ensure that we did our part. I do know that our community is changing, and we must seek to determine what adaptations we need to make to respond to those changes. We are open to anything and any adjustment we need to make, so long as it does not violate the Scripture.

I have been pondering this issue of why fewer people seem to be open to the gospel in our nation today than in years past. Although we have had good results in evangelism, I am sure you are aware that baptisms have been declining in our denomination. I am wondering if it is because we live in the eye of the needle. Do you remember how Jesus said that it is easier for a camel to pass through the eye of a needle than for a rich man to inherit the Kingdom of God?

I fear that the prosperity we have experienced in our country has had a negative consequence. Although our economy is struggling, we live in the most prosperous nation in the world. Even some of the poor among us have homes, cell phones, televisions, vehicles, and more. I am not complaining or minimizing their plight. I am just pointing out that in the midst of our prosperity, it may be that a larger majority feel they have no need for God. It is burdening my heart because I love this nation and do not wish ill on anyone. We must be faithful to proclaim the gospel message and to seek to fulfill the Great Commission throughout the world, but beginning right here in the eye of the needle. I pray God will continue to bless your leadership and your congregation, and I have enjoyed the time together over the past nine months.

Sincerely,

Marc

From: Mitch Walker
Sent: Monday, June 2, 2:07PM
To: Marc Benton
Subject: RE: Next Steps
Marc;

You will never know how much I appreciate the time you have invested in me. I cannot tell you how much my leadership has grown because of the time we have spent together in the coffee shop in Stanton. We are still struggling in many areas but have definitely made progress. Please pray for me because I still have a couple of people who oppose me at every turn. They are in the minority but are very influential in our church.

We are gearing up for Vacation Bible School in a couple of weeks, and I have no doubt it will be the best we have ever provided. In past years, we threw it all together to minister to the few children we had with no strategic plan in mind. This year we are promoting and inviting like never before and have been praying that God will use it to bring boys and girls to faith in Jesus.

I have been burdened for you of late in a way that is hard to describe. I can't say why I have been compelled to pray for your estranged daughter and grandchildren in the past couple of weeks. I know you love them and miss them very much, and I am praying for reunion and healing one day soon. Don't give up. I know you won't.

I love you, friend!

Mitch

From: Marc Benton
Sent: Monday, June 2, 5:00 PM
To: Mitch Walker
Subject: RE: Next Steps
Mitch,
Your last note was very meaningful. Thanks for caring and for praying. I am too!

Marc

Chapter Thirty-Nine

Answered Prayer

Thursday, June 26th

The crickets were chirping on a warm summer night. As Mitch drifted off to sleep, he replayed in his mind the events of the past three days. The preparation for Vacation Bible School was paying huge dividends. Instead of having a handful of children divided into two groups as in the past two summers, they had six groups this year and more than four times as many children in attendance. Well over half of the guests were from unchurched families.

Mitch could not wait until tomorrow, as he was assigned the task of sharing the gospel with all groups of children first grade and older. He had been praying and planning with sensitivity to share in such a way as to open the door for a response without being manipulative or coercive in any way. He knew that caution was the order of the day and had oriented the leaders to be diligent in follow-up to ensure that those who did choose to follow Christ were ready for the life-changing decision. He understood that children at a very young age were fully capable of responding to the leading of the Holy Spirit and he had plenty of testimonies and examples to support that premise.

He was also pleased at the way so many of the congregation had stepped up to leadership. Several of the students were also engaged, providing assistance with the groups and with recreational activities for the boys and girls. To his surprise, Dizzy had showed up on Monday with Wyatt and was enthusiastically helping out. He came dressed in black from head to toe but seemed to be a bit more cheerful now that he survived his recent encounter with the law. He had been granted mercy by a judge as a first-time offender and had been released on probation. He and Wyatt would skateboard into the parking lot every morning and skateboard out at the conclusion, to the admiration of many of the younger boys.

Is that the bell? It must be time for class to start. But I'm not in school anymore. Suddenly, Mitch realized that he was dreaming something about school and a test that he was late for. It was not a school bell, but his phone was ringing, interrupting his dream.

"Hello," he said in his raspy 3:30 A.M. voice, still not sure whether or not he really had a test to take.

"Pastor, this is Bruce. I hate to call like this in the middle of the night. It's Loretta. I don't think she's going to make it much longer. Would you mind coming over here to pray with us? I know that's what Loretta would want."

"Sure, Bruce. I'll be right there. If you want to unlock your door, I'll just come in when I get there. It should be about twenty minutes or so."

"Thanks. It's already unlocked."

"Who was that?" Melinda mumbled as she turned over, readjusting her pillow.

"That was Bruce. I need to get over there. Loretta's not doing well."

Those words shook Melinda out of her slumber. "Do you want me to go with you?"

"No, we don't need to wake Haley up. You know how these things go. She may pass on, or she may hang on for several more days or weeks. You just never know."

Mitch dressed as quickly as possible and made his way to the Rollins' home. Mitch had been by four or five times every week since the Loretta had been diagnosed with brain cancer only six weeks earlier. The radiation treatments did not appear to have any effect at all. She seemed to deteriorate more every day and though they prayed for a miracle, it appeared that she would not be healed. At least she would not be healed physically, that is. The Rollins' faith had strengthened, and they understood that heaven is the ultimate healing for those who follow Jesus Christ. The turning point occurred over the weekend when Bruce asked Mitch to begin praying for God to take Loretta home. He could not stand to see her suffer and knew that once she passed over into God's presence, there would be no more sorrow and no more pain. Bruce knew that Loretta was prepared for death because of her faith in Jesus. It was clear that her faith gave him the willingness to release her. The pain of holding on was now greater than the pain of letting go.

Mitch arrived in short order and found the door unlocked as planned. Making his way back to the bedroom where Bruce and Tonya were along with other family members, Mitch gave a curt acknowledgement of the others' presence and focused his attention on Loretta, Bruce, and Tonya. Loretta's breathing was shallow and labored. Mitch did not have to ask permission. He grabbed Tonya's hand and placed the other on Bruce's shoulder as he began to pray. A peaceful spirit permeated the room, and when he said "Amen," their eyes opened, and all could tell that Loretta had gone into the presence of God. She looked for the first time in days as if she had a smile on her face. They all wept, and then Mitch led everyone in a prayer of thanksgiving. Before he left, he patiently helped them walk through the steps of making the needed phone calls to prepare Loretta for her final farewell.

Mitch never made it back to bed, but he was able to go home to shower and shave before going to the church for the Vacation Bible School activities of the day. Dizzy and Wyatt were skateboarding into the parking lot when he arrived, and he could not remember ever seeing an expression on Dizzy's face like the one he had today. He looked *free,* which in a sense, he was, since slipping through his brush with the law with minimal consequences. *I just wish he would give his life to the Lord*, Mitch thought, as he put the car in park.

He shared the gospel message carefully and clearly with the younger boys and girls. Those who indicated that they wanted to follow Christ would be given additional counsel in their homes, which would not only help establish their readiness but would also serve as a way to share Jesus with the parents who were not believers.

His last group would be the fourth and fifth graders, and to his surprise, he saw that Cecelia Ramirez, Wyatt Mullins and Dizzy Carver were seated in the back along with the adult group leaders. Apparently, they had just completed a recreational activity and were sipping on water as Mitch shared with the children. He told a story to grab their attention but soon got to the crux of the application.

"Boys and girls, the Bible teaches us in Romans 3:23 that all have sinned. You are old enough to understand that no one is perfect. Only God is perfect. Our sin, when we do bad things, separates us from God. The Bible also teaches in Romans 6:23 that the wages of sin is death. Do you know what wages are?"

A fourth-grade girl responded, "That means you get paid."

"That's exactly right. Sometimes you may do a chore for you parents, and they may pay you for that good deed. There is also a payment you must make for sin. The Bible says it is death, and as you get older, you will understand that death means separation. It causes separation from the God who created us and loves us. We cannot be close to God, and we cannot go to heaven if we have sin in our lives. The problem is that it is impossible not to sin."

Mitch looked at the boys and girls and quietly prayed for God to give him clarity. "So we know that all have sinned, and we know the wages of sin. But there's good news, and it is this: Jesus paid the price for our sins. John 3:16 says that *God so loved the world that he gave his only begotten son that whosoever believes in him will not perish but have everlasting life.* The Scripture teaches us that Jesus never committed any sin. He was God's son, and when he died on the cross, he did it willingly to make sacrifice for our sins. He took the punishment that we deserve. We know that he is God's son because after dying on the cross, he rose from the dead three days later. It was a miracle, and it was part of God's plan."

He continued on, "It does not end there. Here's the best news of all. John 1:12 tells us *that as many as received Him, He gave power to become the children of God.* Jesus wants to live in you. If you are willing to admit you are a sinner and to turn to Jesus for your forgiveness, he will forgive you of your sin. That is called repentance, and you can't have a relationship with God without repentance. Has Jesus forgiven you of your sins? Have you trusted him for your forgiveness? That is called salvation, and when that happens in your life, God's Spirit begins to live in you. I want to invite you to turn from your sin and to place your faith in Jesus for your salvation. I want you to become a follower of Jesus for all of your life and to know that you will spend eternity with him in heaven someday. If you would for a moment, sit quietly with your heads bowed, and let me pray for you."

Everyone bowed their heads, including the students who were seated behind the children as Mitch prayed for them to understand what God wants to do in their lives. "If you want today to become a follower of Jesus, I want you to look up at me," Mitch said. "Everyone else just keep your heads bowed for a few moments more." One boy and one girl looked up at Mitch. The boy was not in the fourth or fifth grade. It was Dizzy. Mitch took a few more moments to lead the young girl and Dizzy in committing their lives to follow Jesus.

After all of the follow up was completed, Mitch asked Wyatt and Dizzy to come with him to his office. After they entered and closed the door, Mitch turned to Dizzy and said, "Tell Wyatt what you just did."

"I just trusted Jesus to be my Savior and Lord. I wanna follow Jesus."

"Now you understand, Dizzy, that this is not just a game. You are committing your life to God. Is that what you're saying? Do you want to be baptized and become a follower of Jesus?"

"I do. I'm serious."

"Man, I'm proud of you. What changed, Dizzy? What made you want to make that decision today in that room with fourth and fifth graders when you weren't willing to do it in the detention center?"

"Do you remember talking about strawberry ice cream?"

Mitch was puzzled. How could that have helped Dizzy understand the gospel? "Yeah, I remember."

"I didn't want to become a Christian. I told you that, but I prayed and said 'God, if you are real, make me want to follow you,' like liking strawberry ice cream. I can't exactly explain it, but I've wanted to be here every day, helping these boys and girls and being around church and stuff. It's been fun. I want to. God answered my prayer. I want to follow Jesus."

"Dizzy, that's great. I know exactly what you're talking about. God through His Holy Spirit began working in you when you prayed, and now He has fully brought you into a relationship with Him. Do you want to be baptized?"

"I wanna do whatever I need to do."

"You talk to your mom, and let's see if we can set up a time to get by there and share with her about your next steps."

"I don't know if she's gonna like this. She used to go to church a lot when she was little, but she's kinda sour on it now."

"Well, let's pray that God will make her open to it. If God can change my heart, and your heart, he can change her heart too."

Mitch watched Wyatt and Dizzy skateboard across the parking lot as he cranked up his car to go and meet the Rollins family to assist with funeral arrangements. *What a day, Lord! Within eight hours, Loretta Rollins went to be with you and then Dizzy Carver gave his life to you, along with some other boys and girls. It's been a good day for the Kingdom and for Stanton Community Church.*

Chapter Forty

ΠOW OR ΠEVER

Sunday, July 13th

"I baptize you in the name of the Father, of the Son, and of the Holy Spirit. Buried with Christ in baptism and raised to walk in newness of life." The congregation applauded as the third child was baptized. All three had come to faith at Vacation Bible School. Although the previous Sunday had seen sparse attendance because of the Fourth of July holiday weekend, the leaders of Stanton Community Church had spent the two weeks following Vacation Bible School, including the holiday week, visiting the homes of all of the children who had indicated that they had a desire to trust Jesus Christ as Savior and Lord. Mitch oriented the leaders, and with much diligence they had counseled, prayed, and shared with several families. They discovered that most of the children who had responded to the call to follow Jesus were interested but not yet clear in their understanding of what that really meant for their lives.

It may have been easier to baptize them all, but Mitch wanted the emphasis to be placed on continued conversations to ensure that the children were clearly being convicted of their sin and ready to follow Jesus. He was confident that others would come to faith in the coming weeks and months as a result of the diligent follow-up.

In contrast to the weekend following the holiday, the attendance was excellent on this Sunday. The auditorium was filled as many family members came to celebrate the baptisms. The evangelism leadership team worked together to make the service meaningful for the children and their families, including the addition of a special reception to be held following the worship service. The spirit of the service was great, and Mitch felt that the congregation may have finally broken through to be a truly intentionally evangelistic church. A church conference was scheduled for the evening, and he looked forward to allowing the evangelism leadership team to report and share future plans to keep the momentum going.

Dizzy was in attendance for the baptisms, but Mitch had not yet been able to connect with Mrs. Carver to discuss his baptism. He discovered that she did not have a phone, and trying to schedule a time to visit seemed like trying to nail Jello to a wall. He was a little frustrated but knew that patience was in order since he was dealing with an unchurched family. Dizzy, on the other hand, had not missed a service. Mitch had especially enjoyed a personal Bible study that he had undertaken with both Dizzy and Wyatt, with plans to meet again next week. He was determined to personally disciple the young new believer. Dizzy understood baptism and was ready for it. He only needed permission from his mom to follow through. Mitch maintained a personal conviction that he should not baptize a child or a teen without a parent's consent.

Mitch announced to the congregation, at the conclusion of the service, an invitation for all to move to the fellowship area to celebrate the baptisms of the children and to meet and greet their families. He was about to call on someone to pray when Thomas McDonald stood and raised his hand. "Mitch, if I may, we will have a called deacons' meeting this afternoon at 4:30 P.M. in advance of the church conference." *What is that about?* Mitch wondered to himself. He was able to corral Thomas as the crowd filed past, moving to the baptism reception.

"Thomas, why do the deacons need to meet?" Mitch asked.

"I don't know, Mitch. My dad and John Dollar caught me right before the service and said they have some urgent business. They didn't say what it was, but I assume it has something to do with tonight's conference."

Mitch did not press because he trusted that Thomas was good for his word and sought out James Flynn as soon as the opportunity availed. "What's going on with the deacon's meeting, James?" he asked.

"I was going to ask you the same thing. I assumed you knew." James rubbed his chin contemplating what might be so urgent. "I don't like this. I'm going to go dig and see if I can figure out what they're up to. I'll keep you posted."

Mitch went back to his pastoral functions and interacted with the guests and families until everyone was gone. He left the church having not heard anything back from James. He was determined to go home, to rest, and not to worry. It didn't work. He was not able to rest, and he did worry. Something was not right. James finally called a little after 3:00 P.M.

"I've got the scoop on what's happening," James said as the phone conversation commenced. "McDonald and Dollar are going to call for a vote of confidence from the deacons so that they can bring it right into the conference for the congregation to consider tonight."

"Are you kidding me? This is the third time they've tried to do this. Why this time? What's going on?"

"It's the same old stuff, Mitch. Here's the bottom line. Lester McDonald has always been the power player in this congregation. He sees his control slipping with all the new families visiting and with the new people joining. He knows it's now or never to squeeze you out of here. I think he's desperate, quite frankly. I've got a feeling they brought this up at the last second, knowing attendance at the conference would be low in July, but you can bet that he's lining up families to be here to vote his way during the conference."

"Am I sunk, James? You remember what happened back in October. John Dollar and Bruce Rollins voted against me while you and Tim Minor voted for me. Thomas McDonald surprised us and pulled me through by voting in my favor, but in January we added Lester McDonald and Bruce Rollins' brother, Jacob, to the deacon board. They've got the votes now to bring me before the church. If he has the deck stacked tonight, I may be ousted when this thing is done. I can't believe this. We just had one of our best days ever. We baptized three people just today, and we weren't able to do that in my first two full years."

"Do we need to start calling people to get them to come to the conference?" James asked with a voice of frustration.

"I don't think it would be right for me to do that. I'm not a politician. I'm a pastor."

"I have less than an hour until I need to head to the church. I'm going to make at least a couple of calls before heading over. I'll tell you this. If they really try to do this, you may have to pull me off of McDonald."

Mitch could not believe what he was hearing. James was a godly man, and he knew that it would be like David facing Goliath if a physical confrontation took place. Mitch had never heard James so worked up. *I hope this doesn't get out of hand*, he thought. He began to pray. *Lord, give me wisdom. Deliver us from any evil, and do not let Satan have his way. I pray for your will to be done, and I'm not sure how you're going to do it, but deliver me. I need you.*

Mitch pulled into the parking lot just before 4:15 P.M. He had not ceased praying. He noticed that Dizzy and Wyatt were taking advantage of the empty parking lot, skateboarding and doing some unbelievable tricks. Mitch walked over and chatted with them briefly before heading into the church. All seven deacons were present this time, unlike the Saturday morning fiasco back in March when only four showed up in the attempt to use the liquor store visit against him.

219

Thomas called the group to order and noted that there were no agenda items but opened the floor to those who had business to introduce. John Dollar jumped right in and immediately got to the point.

"You men might recall that we had a vote of confidence last year on the preacher, and it barely failed." A vote of confidence by the deacons was the first step in dismissing a pastor. If a majority of the deacons agreed, the entire congregation would be called to vote for or against their pastor in a regularly scheduled church conference. If the majority of those present at the conference failed to give the pastor a vote of confidence, he would be asked to resign. It was essentially the congregation's method for firing a pastor.

Dollar continued, "I'd like to make a motion that we vote to bring the pastor before the congregation this evening for a vote of confidence, and I want to speak to my motion."

"Second." That was Lester McDonald. As usual, he was sitting back, allowing someone else to do his bidding.

Dollar jumped right back in. "I have had many families come to me in the past few weeks to express their displeasure with the direction of our church."

James Flynn interrupted. "What do you mean that 'many' families have come to you. I'm a deacon too, and no one has come to me. How many is 'many'?"

"Let's just say it's a bunch," Dollar replied without quantifying the depth of the complaints. "They're all getting tired of the continuous harping on outreach. That's all our preacher seems to care about anymore. We have a lot of families threatening to leave, and we can't afford to lose all of them just to keep this one man on board. We all know that this is just the tip of the iceberg with all of the other issues we've dealt with in the past year."

James jumped right in to defend his pastor and friend. "John, you are either making stuff up, or you don't know what you're talking about. Were you even in the same service that I was today? We had three children who were baptized. Did you see their families here with them? None of them were even in church a few months ago. Our service was full, and our giving has gone up substantially in the past couple of months. Why are you men doing this?"

"I don't care how many people were here today. If we have a preacher who can't be trusted, and if he's not theologically balanced, then we have to be willing to make a tough decision. That's what deacons do."

"Who says we can't trust him? I'd trust him with my life. Have you even prayed about this? Do you really believe the Lord is leading us to dismiss our pastor for leading us to be more faithful to the Great Commission?" James asked.

"That's not for me to decide. I have my opinion, and I'll vote my conscience. I've got at least three other men here who will go along with me. Maybe even four if Thomas will vote right this time. I think there's going to be plenty of people here tonight that feel the same way."

"How come you haven't asked me about this?" It was Bruce Rollins.

"I didn't have to, Bruce. I know where you stand. We sure didn't want to bother you with all of this in the last couple of weeks since you've been grieving over Loretta. I hate you even have to be here tonight, but I knew you would want to be here for this vote."

"I think you may have figured wrong." Mitch and James looked at each other with surprise as Bruce made that statement.

"What are you talking about?" McDonald chimed in.

"I'm not going to vote against him. He has been there for me in the last two months. You weren't there, Lester. You weren't either, John. Mitch was the one who stayed up all night with me when we were at the hospital. He was the one there when the doctor gave us the news. He came by practically every day and called when he couldn't come by. When Loretta passed away, it was Mitch standing with me and Tonya. You men have read him totally wrong. This man is the best pastor I've ever had, and I'm not going to let you vote him out."

Lester's face turned beet red. He suddenly stood and looked down at Bruce. "You son of a…." Lester actually cursed. "You're spineless if you let him turn you like that just because he held yer hand and sang kumbaya."

Bruce's brother, Jacob, suddenly leapt to his feet, moving between where Lester stood and Bruce was sitting.

"Hey, how dare you talk to my brother like that, McDonald," he said, defending his sibling with a raised voice. Everyone suddenly came to their feet as the tension seemed to explode. Lester McDonald and John Dollar were practically squaring off against the Rollins brothers as Mitch, James Flynn, and Tim Minor tried to calm everyone down. Thomas was doing his best to get his father under control, and Mitch feared that the men were about to come to blows. Lester continued to rant and laced in some more expletives as he realized the tide had shifted, and that, at best, he now had only two votes, his and Dollar's, to go up against Mitch. He finally stormed out of the room shouting angrily, "Yor all nothing but a bunch of cowards" as he stamped down the hallway toward the exit. No one followed him. John Dollar was speechless by this point, and James Flynn took charge for the moment as Lester exited.

"Men, let's calm down. We need to stop and pray right now. We're not wrestling against flesh and blood here. Satan is trying to divide us. We've got to put our guard up and pray." Everyone was breathing a little harder from the sudden rush of adrenaline caused by the tense two or three minutes when things almost got out of hand. As James began leading everyone to pause and bow, giving time for everyone to calm down, they could hear Lester's truck motor rev loudly as he prepared to leave. He was acting like a spoiled teen that did not get his way, revving the engine and squealing the tires. Then suddenly, the sound changed. The sound of spinning tires changed subtly but distinguishably to skidding tires, and Mitch thought he heard a thud. *Did he hit someone's car?* went through his mind as they all remained with heads bowed and eyes closed.

Suddenly someone began shouting from outside. "Help! Help!" It sounded like Wyatt or maybe Dizzy. Mitch and the other men leapt to their feet. They all ran down the hallway and out to the parking lot. "Oh, no, no, no!" Mitch cried out as he absorbed what was happening Wyatt was standing in front of McDonald's truck looking down at a motionless body lying on the pavement. It was Dizzy.

Chapter Forty-One

HOMECOMING

Sunday, July 13th

"Somebody call 9-1-1," Mitch shouted as he ran and crouched over Dizzy. Thankfully, he had been wearing a helmet, but there was blood coming from somewhere. "Dizzy, are you all right?" Mitch shouted as if being loud would bring some response. Dizzy was not moving and appeared to be unconscious. It did not look good, and Mitch began to pray in his mind. He was initially hesitant to touch or move him so as not to cause any more damage. Lester had still been sitting in his truck when the men ran outside, but suddenly exited and began yelling.

"That stupid kid ran out in front of me. This wasn't my fault."

"Shut up, Lester!" James yelled. "Just sit down and shut up until the police get here."

Mitch took Dizzy's hand to see if he could feel a pulse. He couldn't tell for sure. He gently put his head on Dizzy's chest and could feel it rise ever so slightly. "He's still breathing," he said with a mixture of relief and desperation. "I think I can hear his heart beating." It was more than ten minutes before they heard the first sirens. The police arrived before the paramedics, and they immediately asked everyone to step back as they began to assess the damage to the young accident victim. Several of the men huddled to pray. Mitch tried to console Wyatt, who was in shock himself from what he had just witnessed.

"What happened, Wyatt?" Mitch asked.

"I don't know. I had just turned around, and we were about to go downhill. Dizzy was way in front me, and all of the sudden that truck came flying around the corner. I guess Dizzy couldn't get out of the way in time." Wyatt suddenly began to weep as he replayed the accident in his mind and grasped the seriousness of the situation. "The truck hit him, and he slammed the pavement real hard." Mitch put his arm around him, and suddenly it occurred to him that Dizzy's family did not know what was going on. He needed to get in contact with Dizzy's mom. The paramedics suddenly got frantic in their work and Mitch heard one shout, "He may be going into full arrest."

"What does that mean?" Wyatt asked Mitch.

Mitch ignored his question because a knot formed in his gut. He didn't know a lot of medical lingo, but he was quite aware of what full arrest meant. They might be losing him.

The paramedics worked frantically for the next few minutes. Mitch and the men prayed. The police officers had Lester in another area of the parking lot, interrogating him to figure out if he should be cited or arrested. They continued to work on Dizzy and enlisted a couple of volunteers to assist in getting him into the ambulance. James and Bruce got in a car to follow the ambulance while Thomas went to join his father. Tim Minor volunteered to stay behind to inform the congregation as they arrived for evening services about what was transpiring and to lead the people to pray. Wyatt's dad, Randall, had arrived by this point, and he said he could drive Mitch and Wyatt to the Three Branches Apartment complex where Dizzy lived to notify Mrs. Carver and to give her a ride to the hospital if needed.

They did not have a phone number for her, and then Mitch remembered: Dizzy's mom did not even have a phone. Mitch thought it was odd, and did not know if it was because she could not afford one or because she didn't want to be accessible to anyone. He prayed she would be home. They arrived within minutes, and Wyatt knew exactly which apartment unit to go to. Wyatt stayed in the car as Randall and Mitch approached the door, hoping someone would answer. A woman came to the door, and her features were similar to Dizzy's. Dressed in jeans and a T-shirt, she had a cigarette between her fingers. Her hair was clean, but not combed very neatly. She looked like someone who had aged quickly from hard living.

"Are you Dizzy's mom?" Mitch asked.

"Who?" she replied.

"Dizzy. Dizzy Carver?"

"You mean John Marc? My son Johnny Carver?"

"I'm sorry. I've always called him Dizzy. Are you his mom?"

"Yeah, is he in trouble? Who are you?"

"Mrs. Carver, I'm Mitch Walker. I'm the pastor of Stanton Community Church where Dizzy, I mean Johnny, has been attending. There's been an accident."

Her demeanor quickly transitioned from hard and aloof as her motherly instinct kicked in. "An accident? What happened? Is he OK? Where is he?"

"Mrs. Carver, he's on his way to the hospital. He was skateboarding at our church and was struck by a vehicle."

"Mom, what's going on?" A teenage girl that could not have been more than a year or two younger than Dizzy walked into the room.

Mrs. Carver ignored her daughter, pressing Mitch for more information. "Is he hurt bad? Why are they taking him to the hospital?"

"We need to take you there, Mrs. Carver. It's real serious."

Her aloof attitude quickly transitioned to concern and then panic. With the realization that something was seriously wrong, she began to weep and cry out, "Is he dead? Is he going to die?"

His sister, obviously frightened, also began to scream. "Mom, what's wrong? Is Johnny all right?"

It was pure chaos for the next several minutes as Randall and Mitch tried to help them work through the shock and pull themselves together enough to go to the car. He kept telling Mrs. Carver that they needed to get to the hospital, and she finally composed herself just enough to get out of the door. Randall drove as Mitch sat up front while Wyatt and Dizzy's mom and sister sat in the back. Randall drove as fast as he could while Mrs. Carver continued to ask questions that Mitch could not answer. He did not know if her son was alive or dead but knew that he was in serious trouble. The situation was awkward, given that they had only met a few moments earlier, and it occurred to Mitch that bringing in other family members might be of comfort to Mrs. Carver.

"Mrs. Carver, is there someone I can call? Do you have any family you would like to meet you at the hospital?"

"Oh, my Lord," she said. "It's just me and Johnny and my daughter." She paused as if she was contemplating her next steps. After almost a minute passed, she began to repeat, "I need my dad. I need my dad."

"I'll call him," Mitch replied. "Give me his number."

He was stunned at her response. "I don't know what it is."

How could you not know your own dad's phone number? Mitch thought.

She looked down continuing to wipe tears away. "I haven't seen him in a long time. We don't talk anymore. He's a preacher…like you."

"What's his name?" Mitch asked. "If you tell me his name and where he lives, I bet I can get his number."

"He lives in Rock Springs. You may have heard of him. His name is Marc Benton."

Mitch did a double take. "Did you say Marc Benton?"

"Yeah, my son was named after him back when we got along a little better. John Marc."

Mitch could not believe what he was hearing. He was in the car with his mentor's estranged daughter, the one he had been praying for over the past ten months. *Dizzy is Marc Benton's grandson.* His last name would not be Benton because that was his mother's maiden name, and she had been married at least twice, if Mitch recalled correctly. Dizzy Carver was the grandson of Marc Benton.

"I know him." Mitch said. "He's a good friend, and I have his number right here in my contact list."

"You know my dad?" she asked.

"Yeah. Real well."

"I…I…I haven't talked to him in years. I don't even know if he would want to know about this. I'm not sure if you should call him or not. I broke off contact years ago. He probably hates me now."

"He doesn't hate you. Trust me. He'll want to know what's going on."

Mitch dialed as they continued to speed toward the hospital. The conversation was quite awkward when Mitch got in touch with Pastor Benton. He told him that he needed him to bring his wife to the hospital immediately. Marc Benton was not willing to budge initially without more information, but Mitch practically begged him to trust him and to meet him there as soon as possible. He finally agreed, with understandable reservation.

Everything was chaotic when they arrived and entered the emergency room, but the first several things happened very quickly despite the emotionally charged atmosphere. They were ushered to a private waiting room and soon discovered that Dizzy was alive but in perilous condition. Pastor Benton and his wife arrived within minutes of their hearing that news, and no introductions were needed. Benton was shocked to see his daughter Emily standing with Mitch when he entered the waiting room, and the scene of the prodigal son's return was surely comparable. He did not even recognize his granddaughter, and soon discovered the serious circumstance his grandson was in.

The environment settled slowly, as everyone waited together for updates on Dizzy's condition. Mitch was able to share with Pastor Benton the miracle of his relationship with Dizzy over the past few months, including how he had trusted Jesus to be his Savior only a couple of weeks earlier. Now they prayed that God would do another miracle and spare his life so that Marc Benton could get to know his namesake.

Chapter Forty-Two

AWAKENINGS

Thursday, July 17th

The first twenty-four hours would be critical. That is what the family was told after the diagnosis was made. The helmet that Dizzy wore had likely saved his life, although he had sustained a head injury that was the greatest concern. His body had taken quite a blow, yet he had somehow absorbed it all without breaking a bone. But the trauma to his upper body is what caused his heart to stop briefly. The skilled response of the paramedics had revived him. Dizzy was badly bruised, nonetheless, and was still unconscious going into the fourth day. The swelling of his brain was a serious concern, but the prognosis the doctors were giving seemed to steer clear of worst-case scenarios. Still, many prayers were being lifted up as Dizzy's unconscious body fought to overcome the trauma of bouncing off the front of a pickup truck and being slammed onto the pavement.

Mitch was in the intensive care unit alongside Pastor Benton for the brief visit that family members were allowed every four hours. Emily Carver had finally agreed to go home with her mom to shower and rest after a 100-hour vigil, watching over her son's progress. Mitch had been present most of the time himself. Standing together beside Dizzy's bed, he and Pastor Benton compared notes and were amazed at how God had worked. When Mitch had learned early in their relationship that Pastor Benton had an estranged daughter and two grandchildren that he had not seen in over a decade, he had often felt compelled to pray for them, not knowing that as he encountered and developed a relationship with Dizzy, God was using him to answer his own prayers. How Pastor Benton had wept and embraced Mitch when he had learned that his grandson had placed his faith in Jesus as Savior and Lord only about three weeks before.

Lester McDonald had not been arrested although charges were potentially pending. Mitch had mixed emotions about that, but understood that it was not his job to make such a judgment. No one had seen Lester or his wife since the weekend, and his understanding was that they loaded up their camper and left town for parts unknown. He was not sure what he would say or do when he encountered him in the future. He was quite frankly more concerned about Dizzy at this point. It was his life that was on the line. Mitch had not seen John Dollar either since Sunday. However, all of the other deacons had been to the hospital several times. The biggest surprise was Bruce Rollins. He was there almost as much as Mitch was. Mitch could not believe the transformation in him from a couple of months earlier. In spite of the pain of losing his wife, he seemed to have a renewed spirit. God had really worked in his life.

Mitch and Pastor Benton were standing over Dizzy quietly praying as Benton ran his hand over his long-lost grandson's forehead. They were not expecting it when Dizzy first opened his eyes. He called Mitch's name first, recognizing him, but not the other man present.

"Mitch, where am I?" he asked in a childlike whisper, clearly disoriented.

"Dizzy, you're in the hospital…in Rock Springs…You were in an accident."

He paused a moment as if he were trying to interpret what he was hearing. "What happened?"

"You had an accident on your skateboard at the church." Mitch did not try to explain or give details. It was clear that Dizzy could not recollect what occurred. "Do you know who this is?" Mitch asked him, turning to Marc Benton. Dizzy appeared puzzled for a moment as he blinked his eyes.

"Is that Papa?"

"You do know who it is!" Mitch said as the weeping grandfather bent down and kissed his grandson on the forehead.

"Hey, Johnny. It's been a long time. You're all grown up."

Mitch was having a little difficulty adjusting to hearing Dizzy called Johnny and John Marc instead of Dizzy. That is the only name he had known him by since they met almost a year ago.

"It's real," Dizzy whispered as he looked up at the two men.

"Yeah, it's really him," Mitch said assuming he was referring to his grandfather.

"No, it's all real. I wasn't totally sure, but now I know. It's real."

"What's real son? What are you talking about?" Pastor Benton asked.

"I saw it. It's real just like Mitch said. I know what to do now."

A chill went down Mitch's spine. *Did he say what I thought he just said?*

Mitch and Pastor Benton looked at each another. Was he hallucinating or dreaming? What did he mean? What exactly did he see?

"I'm tired, Papa…" and just like that he was asleep. Marc Benton locked eyes with Mitch, as a tear rolled down his face.

Mitch was curious to know what Dizzy meant. "Do you think he saw something?" Mitch asked.

"I don't know what I think. Maybe he experienced something. I've heard of things like that from people but never firsthand like this. Maybe he was just dreaming."

They made their way out to the waiting area and began to tell everyone that Dizzy had woken up though ever so briefly. When Emily returned, she clung to her father and cried. Once she was composed, she walked with him back into the intensive care unit so that she could see him again. Mitch did not think it was his place to share what Dizzy said when he woke up and could not be sure exactly what it meant. But in his heart, he thanked Jesus for coming into Dizzy's life and for giving him peace instead of pain from the trauma he had experienced.

Monday, July 21st

It was two more days before Dizzy awoke again, and as the weekend progressed, his condition improved dramatically. The doctors were discussing moving him out of intensive care and into a private room within the next twenty-four hours, if all went well. Mitch sat in the waiting room, expecting Dizzy's mom and sister to return from dinner within the next hour or so. It was the first time he had been in the waiting room during the past eight days when there were not family members present. He thought of taking a nap, but that was almost impossible in the waiting room chairs. As he was flipping through a magazine, he noticed a gentlemen praying with a couple across the room. Once they finished, the couple departed, and he came and sat two seats down from Mitch. He was wearing a sport coat, had a short haircut, and carried himself like a pastor. Mitch had developed radar for spotting fellow pastors but knew he was not infallible.

"Excuse me," Mitch said to the man. "I noticed you praying with that couple. I was just curious; are you a pastor?"

"Actually, I am," the man replied. "That couple is from my church. Their daughter just got out of surgery, and happily it was a prayer of thanksgiving.

They're going to grab some coffee, and I volunteered to stay in here in case someone comes looking for them."

"Hi, I'm Mitch Walker," Mitch said as he stood and reached over to shake his hand. "I pastor Stanton Community Church over on the other side of the county."

"I've heard of that church. People are saying that your church is really catching fire and starting to grow and reach people. Oh…excuse me. I'm Donley Kent, the pastor at Trinity Fellowship Church over in Fuller County."

"Good to meet you, Donley. How long have you been there as pastor?"

"I'm in my fourth year. This is my third church where I've served as senior pastor."

"That's great. I am really glad to meet you. Our churches aren't located that far apart," Mitch replied.

"Well, maybe not distance-wise, but my church isn't exactly like yours. We're not reaching anybody where we are. I spend all my time running in circles just trying to minister to my members."

Mitch felt as if he were having a déjà vu experience. "Is that right? Do you ever feel like you have the heart for outreach but just don't have the time?"

"Apparently, you've been reading my mail."

Mitch paused for a moment looking down, and then he noticed a small stain on his left sleeve. *Where did that come from?* He covered it subtly with his right hand and looked back at Pastor Kent. A thought immediately occurred, and he asked, "Have you ever heard of the *Net Effect?*"

"I can't say that I have. What is it?"

"It's a strategy for leading your church to be intentional in evangelism."

"That sounds interesting. Where can I get it?"

"It's not something you can buy. It's something I learned from another pastor that has revitalized my church. I have an idea. I know where there's a good coffee shop in Southerland that's not too far from where you live. Would you have any interest in meeting me there sometimes so that I can walk you through it?

Chapter Forty-Three

Epilogue

Ten years later

The young pastor sat in his office with the door closed as he looked over his sermon one final time. He should have been nervous, but God had granted him a calm spirit as he prepared himself to exit the small office and make his way to the auditorium to preach his first sermon as the new pastor of Stanton Community Church. Mitch Walker had resigned after thirteen years of service to take a new church. The new, young pastor understood that he had big shoes to fill. He was actually a couple of years younger than Walker had been when he became the pastor of Stanton Community Church over a decade earlier.

Everyone expected that Mitch Walker would take a larger church at some point and he had received several tempting offers over the years, from what the new pastor understood. Stanton Community had grown quite a bit under Pastor Walker's leadership. The worship attendance was at least three times larger than it had been, but that did not reflect the whole of what had occurred under his leadership. He had led the Stanton Community Church to plant three other churches. One was located in another part of the state but the other two were within twenty miles of the current location. The closest was less than six miles away. It was much less traditional in nature than the Stanton Community Church, although the mother church's style had transitioned over the years to a more blended one.

The members were shocked at first when Pastor Walker had suggested that they release ten families as each of the two closest churches was launched. That resulted in over twenty families being sent out from the host church within a five-year span, and those sent were leaders and financial contributors. It was a sacrificial commitment, and yet to everyone's amazement the home church rebounded each time and continued to reach more people.

The newly appointed young pastor had much familiarity with the history, because he had served himself as the pastor to students at Stanton Community for the past two years. He was taken totally by surprise when the pastor search team approached him unsolicited to discuss the possibility of serving as Walker's replacement. He considered his pastor to be his mentor, and called him by his first name.

Mitch had taught him the principles of what he called the *Net Effect* (Praying for the lost, Proclamation of the Gospel, Personal Evangelism Training, Event Evangelism, Team Evangelism, and Servant Evangelism), and the new young pastor had applied them effectively to his student ministry. Mitch had actually left on his desk a framed list of these nets for evangelism. The young pastor recalled when Mitch explained how he learned the principles—from Marc Benton of the Tabernacle Church in Rock Springs. Benton was still there, though the rumor was that he would be retiring at the end of the year.

Once, Mitch had shared about his struggles during the first year of implementation of the Net Effect principles, the disappointment he had expressed when debriefing with his mentor, bemoaning how only thirteen people had been baptized in the first twelve months of application. Apparently, Benton had asked Mitch to remind him of how many were reached the year immediately preceding implementation. Mitch responded, "only one," and he said that Benton had gently rebuked him. He could almost hear Benton himself: "What do you mean you're disappointed? If every Bible-believing church in North America increased their evangelistic results by over 1000 percent as you did, we could reach the world within a decade!"

The Net Effect really worked. He recalled applying it himself in his first church as a student pastor as well as at Stanton Community when he was called to serve alongside Mitch. He had been so excited to get the chance to work on Mitch's staff and could not believe he was now called to follow him as the new senior pastor. He was truly humbled. Mitch had told him the war stories of the past decade. The church was still not perfect and had its struggles, but it was hard to conceive the battles Mitch had fought ten years earlier. Thomas McDonald was currently a key leader in the church, and the word was that his dad had wreaked havoc during Mitch's earliest years. Apparently, Thomas' father had never returned to the church after the big blow-up that Mitch had recounted in detail.

A knock came at the door, interrupting the young pastor's reflections. "Come in."

It was Wyatt Mullins, one of the younger leaders, and James Flynn, one of the revered senior leaders.

"Can we pray with you, pastor?" James asked as they entered.

How could he say no? Flynn was a spiritual giant in the church. They huddled to pray, and they all shook hands and embraced as he prepared to make his way for his first service as pastor. He slowly walked down the same hallway that Mitch had traveled on so many Sundays en route to the morning worship service. Just as Mitch had rarely made it all the way to the auditorium from his office without being intercepted, the new pastor was apparently no exception to that probability.

"Pastor, we are so glad to have you with us as our full-time senior pastor." It was Mrs. Rose, wife to another great leader in the church for many years named Danny Rose. "We've been praying for you. You did great with our young people, and you're going to be a fine pastor."

"Thank you, Mrs. Rose," the new pastor said as he shook her hand, pausing briefly to engage her personally.

"What do you want me to call you now?" she asked. "Would you rather be called reverend, preacher, or pastor, and would you prefer we use your first name or your last? What would you prefer?"

"Mrs. Rose, I really don't mind any of those. You can just call me whatever is most comfortable for you. I wouldn't mind if you just call me by my first name like all my close friends do. My friends call me Dizzy."

About the Author

Dr. Steve Parr serves as a state missionary with the Georgia Baptist Convention. He began his ministry with the convention in March of 1998 as a Sunday school consultant and served as the director of the Sunday school and evangelism teams from 2000–2012. In August of 2012 he was appointed Vice-President of Staff Coordination and Development. In thirty years of ministry he has assisted hundreds of churches in strengthening their Sunday schools by motivating and training leaders through seminars, conferences, preaching, and personal consultations. Prior to his service at the Georgia Baptist Convention, he served in two local churches. He has also led twelve churches as their Interim Pastor over the past fifteen years.

Dr. Parr was called to ministry in 1983 as he was pursuing a career in education. After four years of teaching and coaching, he left this pursuit behind to follow God's call to full-time Christian service. He has a Masters of Divinity Degree in Christian Education from New Orleans Baptist Theological Seminary and a Doctor of Ministry degree in Church Growth and Evangelism from The Southern Baptist Theological Seminary.

Dr. Parr is the author of four books on Sunday school, including a three-book series from Kregel Publications: *Sunday School That Really Works, Sunday School That Really Responds*, and *Sunday School That Really Excels* as well as one other book on evangelism entitled *Evangelistic Effectiveness: Differences in Mindsets and Methods*.

Steve is married to Carolyn and has three daughters, Leah, Lauren, and Larissa, and sons-in-law, Greg Manning and Tyler Martin.

Books by Steve R. Parr

Key Strategies for a Healthy Sunday School

Sunday School That Really Works

Sunday School That Really Responds

Evangelistic Effectiveness: Difference Makers in Mindsets and Methods

Sunday School That Really Excels

Visit: www.steveparr.net